WHISPER IF YOU NEED ME

dina silver

ONE

Julia
August 31, 2000

Every morning, my mother would remind me how easily I could die. How careful I had to be on account of germs, cars, foods, choking hazards, and cross-contamination. It was a wonder she ever let me leave the house. But she was perfectly content to care for me in this way, and she would've been highly offended if someone had questioned her neurosis.

One morning, she was sitting on the edge of my bed while I got dressed for my first day of sixth grade.

"You sure you don't want to wear the red skirt from Macy's? The one we picked out together?" she asked in her most nonchalant yet persuasive tone. It was the tone where she did her best to act like she didn't care what I wore or what I did, hoping her suggestion would trick me into changing my mind.

We'd only argued for three whole days prior to that morning about what I was going to wear. I'd chosen a denim skirt with a white tank top and a lavender hoodie.

I smiled at her. "I'm sure."

"Well"—she thrust a shoulder forward and sniffed—"at least wear your gym shoes, will you? Those UGGs are ridiculous in August." Her eyes were wide, and her arms were flailing, as always.

"Mom, please."

She pressed her lips together and squeezed her thigh, no doubt to relieve the tension in her head brought on by not getting her way. "You're eleven years old now. You can wear what you want."

Neither of us believed that she actually meant what she'd said, but I was happy to win a minuscule battle nonetheless. To say we butted heads over things like clothes and how to wear my hair and what my friends were doing that I wasn't would be an understatement, but we were as close as two fingers on the same hand—with her controlling the tendons, of course.

Naturally, most mothers were in charge of their young kids. Yet I was allowed little freedom from her. She never sent me to preschool or day camp and never signed me up for art classes or gymnastics, preferring to have my nanny, Mary, take me to the zoo or park. As for playdates, friends were always asked to come to our house where she would know I was safe. Mom would have Mary bake cookies, and we'd have a side of Diet Coke and string cheese. There wasn't much else in the fridge besides bottles of pinot grigio and diet soda, but my friends loved coming over because we could do anything we wanted—blast the TV, order pizza, slide down the stairs on my comforter. Mary never said a word about any of it, and Mom was never around.

"As long as you're under our roof, I don't have to worry," she'd say before kissing me on top of my head, grabbing her gym bag, and waving good-bye.

My father worked late every night, and Mom never ate anything, so I'd spend most meals in front of the TV with my dog, a girlfriend, or Mary by my side.

My mother was tough and strong-willed, but she was also the most captivating person I'd ever known. Quite honestly, there was no one else—friend or family member—who I'd rather spend time with. Her stories of living and working as a teenage model in New York were spellbinding. Tales of nightclubs and celebrities and parties on people's yachts would come to her with a snap of her fingers and a laugh, as if each memory was more fascinating and unbelievable—even to her—than the next. She had an explosive loud cackle that would often catch people by surprise.

"Like the horn of a car," Dad would say.

She could easily grab anyone's attention with her striking good looks, but it was her personality and exaggerated storytelling that would then hold on to that attention like a vise. And she was always moving. Her arms, her legs, her mouth, her head were constantly in motion, like she was afraid of what might happen if she stopped. Her jet-black hair was shiny and long, but she almost never wore it down. Every morning, she'd sit at her vanity and brush her hair into a tight ponytail, which she would then gel to immovable perfection. It was a purposely severe look paired with her five foot ten height. She was a force to be reckoned with, and she always got her way.

I feared nothing in her presence. She made me feel comfortable and protected. No one ever said no to her. She simply wouldn't allow it.

Except for my father…that one time.

She stood and checked her Cartier Tank watch. "Let's go then. Get downstairs, and meet me in the car. We only have ten minutes." She was always rushed.

Mom drove me to school every day even though the bus stop, littered with neighborhood kids, was in front of our house.

"Who knows what goes on during those bus rides?" she'd say. "What if the driver has been out drinking all night and falls asleep at the wheel? What if someone gives you something to eat, and you don't know what's in it?" she'd ask me, as if all answers pointed to imminent death.

But she always assured me that she would be there to protect me, so I would take her advice, and I never worried about much else.

I was a popular kid—not captain-of-the-cheerleading-team popular, but hell, I was only eleven. I had a few close girlfriends who swore they didn't talk about me behind my back. What more did a kid need? We'd hang out at the mall, walking around with little money and little else to do but look for other kids our age doing the same thing. Then, we'd talk about boys—who was hot, who was not. Then, most of my friends would have sleepovers and continue the conversation there or make prank calls to the boys we'd spent the afternoon talking about. Only, sleepovers were forbidden for me.

"Who knows what's in anyone's house?" Mom would say. "I just prefer to have you at home."

So, instead—and much to my pleasure—Mom and I would have our own sleepovers. They were rare, but they were my most treasured times. We'd drag the two twin mattresses from my bedroom downstairs to the family room and have movie night. First, she'd open her five-tiered makeup kit, similar to the kind her makeup artists would bring over to our house when she and my dad were going out to some schmancy cocktail party or charity event. She'd paint my lids with black liner and brush on mascara and sparkly eye shadow.

"She looks twice her age," Dad would growl. Then, he'd shake his head, kiss my mother, and mumble something about him having his hands full.

Mom would pour herself a glass of wine and me a glass of grape juice, and we'd watch movies until I fell asleep on her lap.

"Good luck, honey," Mom said.

I stepped out of the car with my new backpack. "Thanks, Mom. Maybe we can celebrate my first day of middle school with dinner and a movie tonight?"

She batted her eyes and then looked away. "Not tonight, honey. I have plans with a friend. Rain check?"

I nodded.

"I'll pick you up after school, okay?"

"Okay, Mom."

Later that night, after an uneventful first day, Mary called me to the kitchen for dinner. My Lab, Rainbow—Bo for short—followed me as I went to eat.

"Thanks, Mary."

"You bet," she said.

On the table, she placed a bowl filled with buttered noodles and enough grated Parmesan cheese to fill a fish tank. It was just how I liked it. I turned on the small TV and clicked the remote until I found *Friends*.

I heard Mom's heels clacking on the wood floor, and I could smell her signature scent—Dolce & Gabbana—before I saw her. Then, she appeared in the kitchen with a tight ponytail, even tighter black dress, and red lips.

I slurped my noodles and kept my eyes on the TV as she kissed my head.

"Love you, honey."

"Love you, too, Mom."

"Mary, please call my cell phone if you need me for anything. Just leave a message if I don't pick up."

"Yes, of course," Mary said.

"I'll be home late, Julia, so you go to bed when Mary tells you. No arguing. Daddy will be late, too, and I don't want him coming home and seeing you awake past your bedtime."

My mouth was full, so I nodded.

She kissed my head again and left.

If I'd known she would never kiss me again, I would've stood up from the table and held on to her for dear life.

There was never any doubt that I would listen to Mary, but Mom liked to say things like that anyway. I wasn't a troublemaker. Sometimes, I'd sneak the cordless phone into my room and talk with friends until I fell asleep, but that was the extent of my defiance. I mostly spent my free time reading or watching TV. I kept an organized, clean room. I hated when things were out of place. Even if a dresser drawer had accidentally been left open and I was across the room in my bed, I wouldn't be able to relax until I got up and made sure it was closed.

Mary was long gone when I first heard the shouting.

Dad was telling my mom, "No!"

I heard him scream as I opened my eyes. Bo and I both heard him. In fact, there was really no way not to hear him. He was yelling the word *no* so loud that I had to make sure I wasn't dreaming or imagining it. I'd never heard him so angry before. The tone in his voice alone had been enough to awaken me from a deep sleep in the middle of the night, my chest pounding with fear.

My clock read *3:30* a.m.

I ran downstairs with an equally rattled Bo trailing behind me. We both stopped on the landing and spied the scene from a safe distance.

Mom's confidence was shaken. I could tell by the way she was slumped over, sitting on the kitchen floor with her back to the cabinets and her ponytail all loose and disheveled. She would normally hate that her hair was such a mess, and I hated seeing her that way.

I was worried that she'd fallen or something. *Why else would she be sitting on the floor?*

I wanted to run to her and wrap my arms around her waist, but I was frozen. The look on my father's face made my stomach tighten. I'd never before been afraid in my own home, least of all on account of my parents.

Once my mother stood, I could see the two of them pacing around the kitchen, stalking each other like jungle cats. And they were yelling.

I looked at Bo as if she might have some answers, but she just lowered her head.

Mom was apologizing over and over.

I kept thinking, *Whatever it is, I'm sure she's sorry!*

We had a strict house rule of accepting each other's apologies.

The only time my parents ever argued was when my mom's parents would come in from Palm Beach to stay with us for two weeks each year. Dad couldn't stand Grandpa Bill and Grandma Betty. When they were in town, Dad would leave the house before sunrise, stay at work late, and make any excuse he could to be anywhere but home.

He'd told me once that, when he'd first married my mom, he hadn't had a lot of money because most of his income went to law school, and Grandma and Grandpa didn't think their daughter should be living in a studio apartment on Chicago's West Side.

"They cared more about your mom having a Neiman Marcus charge card than a roof over her head," he'd said.

He'd moved my mom and her modeling career out of New York by then, and her parents had thought she was throwing her life away.

But Mom knew Dad was special. She always told me that she had seen his potential.

"Once I'd made partner and bought this big house, all of a sudden, they wanted to come stay with us and call me son. No, thanks," he'd told me.

And up until that night on August 31, 2000, I'd never heard my parents fight about anything else.

I leaned against Bo and wiped my tears on her soft head as my eleven-year-old brain tried to comprehend what the problem could be. There was so much swearing, and I had so many confusing questions that I just closed my eyes and prayed for a resolution.

Then, I heard my name.

"Please keep your voice down, for Julia's sake," Mom said.

"Oh, now, you're so concerned with Julia? Were you concerned with her three hours ago? Well, guess what? She's my concern now! You're finished."

Mom burst into tears.

"We're through," he said. "I want you out of here, and if you don't leave now, things are going to get ugly,"

Could things get uglier?

"Let me stay the night, and we'll discuss this in the morning," she pleaded with him.

"No," he said.

"Please, Mel."

"No."

He told her no, and she never came back.

I've been looking out for myself ever since.

Two

Julia
Five Years Later

The bus fumes weren't helping me fight away my tears as I embraced my father.

"I love you, Dad," I whispered.

As soon as he pulled away, my stepmom, Sharlene, came forward, dressed head to toe in Lululemon with her Starbucks triple-shot iced latte in one French-manicured hand and her BlackBerry in the other. Sunglasses covered her puffy eyes after too much wine and sushi during her girls' night out the night before where she and her gaggle of friends had predictably complained about how their husbands and kids didn't appreciate everything they did for them in between yoga classes and brunch. I'd appreciate it if she just went to the grocery store once a month. God forbid if I ever found a half-pound of lunchmeat and a fresh loaf of bread in the house.

About six months after my mom had left—or had been forced to leave—I had a breakdown. I refused to go to school because I knew Mom wouldn't want me to ride the bus, and my dad didn't have the time to drive me. He'd arrange carpools for me, but he'd leave for work at the crack of dawn, and I simply wouldn't answer the door when my ride showed up. The school would then call him at the office, and he'd be furious with me. Eventually, I'd begun riding the bus, but that had led to panic attacks, which had led to kids making fun of me. What kid could refuse mocking someone who was hugging herself like a mental patient? Eventually, the mocking had led to me refusing to go back to school.

Needless to say, I hated busses.

Sharlene placed her hands on my shoulders and kissed the top of my head. I heard her say how much she loved me and how much I would benefit from going to camp, but her contrived words had been carefully chosen. She was the last person I wanted talking to me that day—and most other days for that matter.

Dread pooled inside my stomach as a few camp personnel made some announcements and then instructed us to board the busses as quickly as possible. If I burst into tears in front of all the other teenagers enthusiastically streaming onto the bus in giggly pairs behind me, things would only get worse.

Prior to that day, I'd spent three weeks begging not to go to camp, promising to stay out of Sharlene's hair. I'd offered to get a full-time summer job, to babysit my stepsiblings so that Sharlene would be free to get pedicures and bikini waxes at her leisure, to do whatever it would take, but she'd said no. She'd said camp would be good for me, and Dad had agreed.

Sharlene lowered her head to try to make eye contact with me. "I said, I love you." She blinked.

I nodded and looked for my father. He was always off shaking hands and talking to someone. He was an attorney, but he'd consistently lie about his job when he met someone new. It amused him to no end.

I walked toward him and heard him introducing himself to one of the camp staff who was checking people off on a clipboard.

"I'm Mel Pearl, editor in chief of *Jewish Cigar* magazine," he said, shaking the man's hand.

I rolled my eyes but couldn't contain my smile. To be part of his family was to be his improvisational sidekick, and he would feel gravely betrayed if I did not play along with his charades.

"The number one rule of improv—'Yes, and…'" he'd told me. "I say something, and you say, 'Yes, and…' Then, you add to whatever story I started."

No one made me laugh like my father. His knack for sarcasm and desire to make fun of people without them knowing was a true gift. I loved my father, and it had taken me a long time to forgive him for keeping my mother at bay.

"You might not have the capacity to understand, but you have the capacity to forgive," a therapist had once told me.

She'd also told me I should look at my poop, so there was that.

When Mom had left, my father had given me very little information. He'd simply told me, "She needs help, and that's all there is to say."

Even if I'd wanted to hate my father, it wasn't an option. He was all I had.

"I see," the staff member answered, confused, trying to place the nonexistent magazine.

Dad noticed me and extended his hand to my shoulder. "This here is my daughter, Julia. Don't let those dimples on her cheeks fool you. She's a tough cookie, and she's always wanted to go to overnight camp," he said with a wink. "Begged us for weeks."

"No, I didn't." I crossed my arms.

"Sure you did! One time, when she was little, she 'camped' out in the yard." He used air quotes when he said *camped*. "Took the police three hours to find her tent."

"I ran away," I told the man.

Dad tousled my hair. "Quite the little explorer, this one."

My father and I both grinned when we saw the expression on the guy's face, but my smile faded as Sharlene approached. She and my father had been married for three years, and she believed in the power of a *family unit*, meaning that there was never any reason I should spend time alone with my father when I could be spending it with Sharlene and her two kids, Liam and Lulu.

I was grounded for two weeks one time after screaming, "Fuck the family unit!" at one of Liam's soccer games.

"I love you, Dad," I said again before Sharlene was near us, and then I threw myself into his chest.

"Love you, too, Julibean."

I dropped my backpack, and we hugged. My dad was a large man. He was tall with broad shoulders and professor-type longish gray hair, and he always smelled like his pipe. I inhaled the hint of sweet tobacco on his golf shirt and relaxed for a moment.

He released me. "You go and have fun, okay? This little adventure of yours is costing me thousands. Thousands, I tell you!"

"I'm happy to stay home and save you the money."

"What do I need with your pouty face all over the couch this summer? Go on. Get on that bus, and live a little. And don't come back until you've learned something, like waterskiing or basket-weaving or—forget that. Learn something employable, for God's sake."

I shook my head.

"Can I have a hug, too?" Sharlene asked.

I stood still as she hugged me. It was our typical routine. She'd ask for a hug, and I would stand frozen with my arms at my sides for a second.

"Don't be a little shit," Dad said, smacking the back of my head. "Give Shar a hug. She had to give up eight weeks of private Pilates sessions and six chemical peels for me to be able to afford this," he joked.

I lifted my backpack off the ground just as my dad walked away, and I watched as he extended his hand and introduced himself to the bus driver.

"I'm a deli owner from North Miami—kosher meats only," and, "Of course we franchise," were the last things I heard him say.

Sharlene folded her hands in front of herself. "Try to have fun, Julia."

"Like you care," I said for no other reason than to be obnoxious.

Her lips crumpled up like they always did when she hated the things that had come out of my mouth. "You know I care about you."

She was right. I knew she cared about me—as much as someone could care about another person's kid—but I still abused her to no end. And she'd take it.

Most times—in fact, all the time—I felt badly about my behavior toward her, but I never stopped, no matter how guilt-ridden I was. She was my punching bag, and without Sharlene, I would undoubtedly channel my anger and rejection into some other socially unacceptable manner, like huffing or cursing at small children.

I stared at her and wanted to nod in agreement. She was a nice enough person. Hell, if she could put up with my father and his antics for the rest of eternity, the least I could do was give her a hug. But I couldn't bring myself to do it that day.

Instead, I thrust my chin toward my right shoulder, spun around, and stomped onto the bus without a word. I could live with the guilt. I'd done it thousands of times before.

I kept my eyes on the black rubber floor mat that led the way to the rear of the bus and tucked my oversized backpack and myself into the last seat. Despite the stifling air inside, I pulled the hood of my sweatshirt over my head, placed my sunglasses over my eyes, turned up my headphones, and observed my surroundings.

The first people I noticed were blonde twins standing in the aisle, swinging matching ponytails behind them like pom-poms. One was lifting her arms up so that her crop top exposed her stomach to some guys who were Counselors-in-Training—or CITs. It was an all-girls camp, but there were a few male CITs and some sports counselors who were a part of the staff. Her attempt to look as though her flirting had been accidental, in fact, reeked of desperation. I hated her almost immediately, and then I hated myself for being so judgmental. Maybe she and her golden-haired sister would turn out to be my best friends. Maybe we'd paint each other's toenails and brush each other's hair. Maybe she'd pull a tick out of my ass one day.

Not surprisingly, one of the boys stood and yanked the rubber band out of Twin Number One's hair, causing her to react as though she'd won the lottery or seen a snake. I rolled my eyes as she shrieked, achieving her goal of getting the attention of everyone within two miles. She bent over the seat in front of her and flashed her butt crack to the back of the bus.

Who can't feel a breeze wafting their anus? Seriously, pull those low-riders up.

"All right, all right, all right." A man stepped onto the bus. "Take a seat, Brittany."

Her name was as unsurprising as her lack of modesty.

"We're going to be heading out in about five minutes. This bus is senior villagers and CITs only, so make sure you're on the right bus." He paused. "Anyone here think they're in the wrong place?"

I do.

He waited for a moment. "Okay then. As you know, no cell phones are allowed, so if you've made the unfortunate decision to try to smuggle one on this bus and into camp, I advise you relinquish it now. Anyone?"

A few random people shook their heads.

"Good. For those of you who don't know me, I'm James Keating. I'll be your bus driver today and your chef for the next eight weeks."

Applause broke out, and James quieted everyone down with a wave of his hands.

"I see a lot of familiar faces, but if there are any new campers, please come introduce yourself, if you'd like," he said, craning his neck. "Or cower in your seat and bite your nails. Either is fine with me."

I sank lower into the seat and pulled my hood forward. *Please just drive. And cook. And whatever the hell else you do. Anything but make me stand up.*

Thankfully, he turned around, and everyone took their seats.

I sat up a little to open my window to let some fresh air in. It was mid-June, and the truly hot, humid summer had yet to arrive in Chicago, so there was still a nice cool breeze outside. I could see Sharlene and my dad standing on the curb with all the other parents. She was staring dutifully at the bus through her Tom Ford sunglasses, waving, and Dad was deep in conversation with some stranger while reeling in an imaginary fish. His voice was so loud that I could almost hear him over the roar of the crowd as they all waved and cheered from the bus while it pulled out.

Three hours later, there was a tap on my shoulder, and I awoke with a start.

"Hey there," a guy said to me, motioning for me to take out my headphones. He was crouched next to my seat, wearing a baseball cap turned backward, as he stared at me with a pair of alarmingly green eyes.

Our faces were mere inches apart as I yanked the earbuds out.

"I thought maybe you were dead," he joked, backing off a little.

"I'm a heavy sleeper."

"I guess so." He paused. "Well, we're here at camp. Hopefully, that's where you intended to end up." He lifted a brow and smiled, revealing an orthodontist's job well done. "Anyway, the bus has arrived, and you're the only one left on it. Can I persuade you to get off?" He looked at me with his brows raised.

He had a face that could sell a thousand pairs of jeans. I bet he thought he was hot shit and that every teenage camper wanted to drop her Juicy sweatpants to snuggle up next to him after rubbing roasted marshmallows all over herself for him to lick off. He probably hadn't read a book in ten years, and he most likely checked himself out in any reflective surface he came near. I knew his type—cocky and crass and got everything he wanted with a wink and a smile. If I leaned forward and he smelled like Axe, then I'd know I was right.

Instead, I nodded, sat up straight, and removed my hood.

"I'm Jack," he said, extending his hand. "Jack Dempsey. I'm the assistant waterfront director. I also run the Voyagers program, and I'm in charge of collecting sleepy campers from each of the buses. You're my last victim today." He pointed to my iPod. "What are you listening to?"

"Coldplay," I answered.

Then, I turned away from him and glanced out the window at the throng of kids hugging and squealing. Their familiarity with one another made my heart ache.

I looked at a few of the buildings near where the bus had pulled up. It looked as though they'd fallen out of the sky, *Wizard of Oz* style, and landed safely in the epicenter of some dirt paths and birch trees. It was somewhat of a time warp, as the camp was over fifty years old and hadn't been updated since its inception. Rusted metal signs were nailed onto the sides of trees, and a large wooden post had directional arrows, as if an arrow was all one would ever need to find their way around in life.

Which way to eternal happiness? Thataway!

"Coldplay's cool," Jack said. "I like Fall Out Boy, too, but lately, I've been more into the old stuff—Stones, The Who…hell, even Talking Heads. I'm kind of all over the board."

I spun back around. "I'm Julia."

"Nice to meet you, Julia. Is this your first time at Hollow Creek?"

I nodded.

"What group are you in?"

I didn't have an answer, so I shrugged.

"How old are you? That will tell me where you belong."

"I'm sixteen. I'll be a junior in the fall."

He gave me a nod. "Are you happy to be here?"

His question caught me off guard, and I tilted my head and looked at him. I'd expected something more along the lines of, *Are you ready to get off the bus now?*, or, *Were you put on this planet to waste my time?*

"Are you trying to get me to open up or something?" I asked.

"Just making idle bus conversation. Literally, the bus is idle. Get it?"

I nodded and tried not to smile.

He stood and leaned on the back of the seat in front of mine. "You know what I'm not happy about?" he asked.

"That you're stuck trying to get me off this bus?" I put my iPod in my backpack, zipped it up, and then sat back. "By the way, I had no intention of staying on here. I just fell asleep."

He waved me off and stuck a pen behind his ear. "No. I'm pissed that they did a remake of *Willy Wonka and the Chocolate Factory*. Have you heard about this? Comes out next month with Johnny friggin' Depp as Willy Wonka." He pursed his lips and made a face that said, *What a shame.*

I couldn't hold back my smile that time. "Not a Johnny Depp fan I gather?"

He feigned a gasp. "It's a classic! You don't remake a classic. These people ruin everything. What are they going to do next? Turn Harry Potter into a theme park?" He shook his head. "*Charlie and the Chocolate Factory* is my all-time favorite story. Have you ever read the book?"

"I haven't."

"You should," he said.

"I've seen the movie."

"Everyone's seen the movie. Quite honestly, if you hadn't seen the movie, then our friendship would have ended here."

I rolled my eyes.

"I see we have ourselves an eye-roller. You'll fit right in. The camp's full of them." He patted the seat. "So, now that you're awake and properly annoyed with me, let's continue this string of productivity by getting you outside, okay?"

He stood straight and took a step backward so that I could exit past him.

Jack was, by every giggling teenage girl's definition, a great-looking guy. He was tall and fit with a strong jawline to protect his flawless teeth. He had thick brown hair and limes for eyes. He and Brittany would be a match made in Abercrombie & Fitch heaven. I wanted to hate him, but he was too cute.

You know those people. They have you charmed before they even open their mouths. What they say wouldn't matter because they'd already won you over with their power of attraction.

Jack was one of those people…and so was my mother.

Jack could have awoken me and said he'd accidentally run over my dog with his Vespa, backed up to see what he'd hit, and then ran over her a second time, and I would have forgiven him.

Also, he was funny and nice to me, so there was that.

Despite my current body language and snide comments, there was a time when I'd really liked meeting new people. I'd never been timid about starting a new school year and never shied away from going to parties where I wouldn't know anyone, and I'd always loved spending time with my friends.

But that was all before my mom had left.

Jack gestured with his hand for me to walk in front of him down the aisle that would lead to eight weeks of hell.

As soon as we stepped off the bus, I drew in the scent of smoldering embers in the distance. It was about eighty degrees outside, and only a few delicate clouds floated above in the mid-afternoon sky. My hoodie would need to go.

Jack produced a clipboard. "What's your last name, Julia?"

"It's Pearl."

"Julia Pearl. Here you are. You're in cabin twelve. Do you know where that is?"

I shifted my weight to one hip. "You just asked me if this was my first time at Hollow Creek, to which I said yes, so how would I know where cabin twelve is?"

He lowered his clipboard and crossed his arms, and then his perfectly preppy lips curled into more of a menacing grin. "Well, well, well, we have an eye-rolling smart-ass on our hands. Lucky for you, I like smart-asses." He winked at me and then shouted over my head, "Yo, Liz! Can you take the gracious Miss Julia Pearl here over to twelve?" Then, he looked back at me but kept shouting to Liz, "Looks like she's your problem now."

Liz absentmindedly raised a finger and nodded.

"Sorry," I mumbled. I was annoyed by how whiny and immature I'd acted. I hadn't meant to be rude to the first person who was nice to me.

"No sweat, Pearl. I can spar with the best of them. That's why I'm in charge of all reconnaissance missions."

"Re—what?"

"Reconnaissance. It's where they send me in to assess the opposition—the squatters, the protesters, the bus dwellers."

He smiled again and made me blush.

"Liz is one of the head counselors here, like me. She'll show you to your cabin." He rested his right hand on my shoulder. "Okay?"

I nodded. "I was sleeping. I wasn't protesting."

He squeezed my shoulder and bent down toward me. "Don't worry about a thing. You're going to have a great time here. I promise."

I looked up into his eyes. They were honest and kind, and they might have put me at ease if he hadn't been talking to me like I was a lost child.

"Thanks," I mumbled in the same bratty tone I'd apologized in.

He gave my shoulder one last squeeze before letting go as Liz approached us with her arms held out wide. I stepped backward, but she managed to hug me anyway, causing me to drop my backpack on her foot. She was unfazed by all of it.

"Hi, Julia. I'm Liz!"

Please lower your voice. People are staring at me. Or maybe they're staring at Jack? Liz certainly is.

Jack spoke up so that I wouldn't have to, "Julia here is a first-timer, and lucky for her, there isn't anyone better equipped to show her the ropes than you."

Liz threw herself at Jack and wrapped her arms around him like he was a soldier returning from war. "You're the best, Jack," she said mid-squeeze as he placed a hand on her back. "I missed your face," she added.

"You, too, Liz."

"Are we going to go for *gelato* again soon?" She accentuated the word *gelato* as though there were some torrid tale of cold, creamy misbehavior hidden within her inquiry.

I looked up at him with wide eyes and a grin of my own, hoping he'd answer with more details.

Instead, he smiled politely and said, "We'll see."

She pulled back from him but remained bouncing on the balls of her feet. She then threaded her arm through mine and winked at Jack. "I'll see *you* later," she said to him.

She pulled me forward.

I turned around as Liz was dragging me, and made eye contact with Jack again. He nodded as if everything would be okay, and after meeting him, I believed for a second that it would be.

I followed Liz and four other girls down a long-ass dirt path to cabin twelve. The whole place smelled like a wet leaf, like I'd stuck my face in the center of a leafy berry bush after a rainstorm and inhaled. As soon as we walked into our cabin, there were screeches and squeals that would do a flock of seagulls proud as everyone got reacquainted after a long winter. Then, there was me, standing under the doorframe, quiet and idle—like the bus—wishing for no one to look at me or talk to me, but desperately yearning for someone to tell me what to do. Thankfully, I saw no sign of Brittany and her doppelgänger.

Liz ushered me in with a wave. The cabin walls looked like the inside of an old soda crate. Large wooden planks were covered with years of carvings and signatures in multicolored markers. There were two sets of windows, one next to the only entrance—a screen door with no springs that slammed anytime someone opened it—and one set on the opposite wall. Six pairs of bunk beds with mattresses thinner than deli meat were lined up along the perimeter. Yet, despite my foreign surroundings, I found something familiar about the cabin. It took me a minute to place it, but I realized it was the smell.

In a storage room in the back of the basement of our home, Dad kept some old albums and file boxes with tax returns and other crap. The walls were lined with that pink insulation that looked like cotton candy, and the floor had a drain in the center. I never had any reason to go in there. It looked like the ideal place for someone to commit a crime and hide the body. The room had flooded one year when our sump pump malfunctioned, ruining most of the papers along with about half the records and some boxes of my old baby clothes. Dad had hired some guy with a wet vac to get the standing water out, but the room was never quite the same. It always smelled like a wet pair of gym shoes.

And that was exactly what the cabin reminded me of—the icky room in our basement.

Some girls had already claimed their bunks and were jockeying for positions near each other. I felt as though I'd walked into a room of twelve sisters, and I was the stepchild, a role I was very familiar with.

The intruder. The new kid.

I knew all too well that it was hard to fit in somewhere you didn't want to be.

I turned my head to the left and noticed a tiny room to the side where I assumed the two counselors would sleep. A girl walked out as I was about to stick my head in and take a peek.

She clapped her hands in an attempt to silence the chatter. "Listen up, please!" She glanced at me and then turned back to the group. "I know you're all excited to see one another, so just let me get through a few announcements, and then you can have your fun. I'm Maggie, and this is Liz. We'll be your counselors for the summer, and we're really excited to have you here. Some of you have been here before." She paused for the applause. "And it looks like there are a couple of new faces."

Oh God, please don't ask me to introduce myself.

"I'd like to take a moment to ask the new girls to introduce themselves."

Seriously? Why do I bother hoping for anything?

All of a sudden, everyone's energy and chitchat subsided for a moment as they looked around to see who was new. All eyes landed on me. It was like the flock of squawking seagulls had just spotted a small child standing at the edge of the ocean, holding a foot-long submarine sandwich.

I swallowed.

"Would you like to introduce yourself to the group?" Maggie asked me.

Not especially.

Liz chimed in, "This is Julia Pearl. Let's all give her a Hollow Creek hello!"

"Holloooooooow!"

I'm in hell.

THREE

JACK

"What the hell are you doing?" my uncle said to me under his breath.

I was sitting on the steps of the main lodge, petting the camp dogs. Plankton and Squidward were a pair of Alaskan huskies who were required to spend their summers in the Wisconsin heat.

I stood up quickly. "I was waiting on the busses."

"They're here!" He threw his arms up, exasperated, and then let them dangle from his slumped shoulders. "Seriously, Jack, pay attention to what is going on for once."

Aunt Sally walked out as he was berating me, and the dogs ran to her. "For heaven's sake, Bob, they pulled up two seconds ago," she said. "And would you change your shirt?" She stopped to look back at her husband. "You've had mustard on the lapel for three days."

I looked at my uncle as he scanned his shirt for the mustard stain, which was right next to the maple syrup one from yesterday's breakfast. "Go on now!" he yelled at me.

I saluted him and then grabbed my clipboard.

"Damn it! I hate when you do that!" he shouted, wiping sweat off his brow with a Hollow Creek bandana he'd pulled from the front pocket of his droopy shorts. "Don't salute me like that in front of the staff or the campers. It makes it look like I'm some sort of dictator."

I laughed as inconspicuously as possible and walked off.

I'd already been at the camp for two weeks, cleaning the cabins and the boats, training new personnel, scrubbing the kitchen floors, and hanging out at night with the rest of the staff and counselors as we prepped for arrival day. It was the day the campers had been eagerly waiting for all winter long—most of them anyway.

Seven buses total would arrive between noon and three p.m. Each time a bus pulled in, the entire staff would line up to cheer and applaud, as if we were fans greeting a tour bus carrying our favorite rock stars. It was actually a pretty fun time with high energy, lots of smiles, and good positive vibes all around. Even Bob would get into it. Once everyone began to emerge from the buses, it was my job to make sure they were all clear, and no one was left quivering under any seats.

After I checked the one from Indianapolis, another bus pulled up from Chicago. The doors flew open, and my man James was the first to topple out. He wiped his forehead and let out a long breath. Then, he gave me a hug, slapping my back.

"What's up, man?" I said to him. "Good to see you again."

"You, too, Jack. College treating you all right?"

"All but the food." I patted my stomach. "Couldn't wait to get back here and meet up with your blueberry pancakes again."

He smacked me on the shoulder. "You look good, kid. Eat as much as you want. I can't wait until you turn forty, and it all catches up with you," he grumbled, starting to walk off.

"Only twenty-one more years, my good man!" I shouted after him.

Once all the passengers had come off, I hopped onto the bus and quickly scanned the aisles. I was about to turn around when I saw her. She was asleep and curled up like a puppy under her sweatshirt. I looked around. She must not have known anyone on the bus. Otherwise, someone would have woken her up.

"Time to get up," I said. Then, I waited for a response. "Hey there"—I leaned in—"you're at camp."

Nothing.

I spun my baseball cap around and then crouched down beside her. I tapped her on the shoulder and got closer. "Hey there," I repeated softly.

She finally opened her eyes.

"I thought maybe you were dead," I joked.

When she looked alarmed, I backed off. A moment later, she composed herself, and I was grateful to see that she didn't seem too pissed or offended that I'd said she looked like death, which, now that her eyes were open, was far from the truth. I never knew when I would find someone who didn't want to get off the bus because he or she hadn't wanted to get on in the first place.

"I'm a heavy sleeper," she said, focusing her gaze on me.

Her blue eyes were almost the same color as Plankton's. I kept that to myself, assuming she wouldn't appreciate being compared to a dog, mere seconds after being compared to a corpse.

I smiled, and she removed her hood, revealing long dark hair and headphones. She had an interesting face with a little too much space between her eyes and a high forehead, but somehow, it all came together in a rather exotic way. Although she had yet to crack a smile, she hadn't slapped me either, which was encouraging. Either she was numb to my charms, or she didn't want to be here. I watched her look out the window at the other campers with no real incentive to join them.

After a few minutes of conversation and me turning up the charisma, she was easily persuaded to exit the bus, and when I asked if she knew where to go, she even dared to give me shit. Of course, I appreciated it.

Once I determined where she should be, I handed her off to Liz—that was another story—but I made a mental note to keep my eye on Miss Julia Pearl.

"Jacko!"

I heard someone shout my name, so I spun around. It was Will Davies, one of my water sports staff and the better half of my esteemed camp musical duo, Two Guys and a Guitar. He sang while I played acoustic alongside him. He was running slowly toward me, dragging his feet, with his head down.

"What's up?" I said.

"Not much. I just ate." Will slammed his fist on his chest and burped.

Will was my favorite person on the planet. We'd only met last summer, but he had become like a brother to me in eight weeks' time. This was his second summer at Hollow Creek. He was from London, and he'd flown over with a group of other college kids from England on an exchange program that had set them up to work at various summer camps throughout the States. He was twenty-one, two years older than me and able to buy beer, another great thing about him.

Will was a rock star in the making, and you'd know it as soon as you saw him. He was tall and lanky with Beatles lyrics tattooed up and down his arms. When he didn't have to be in swim trunks, he would wear tight black jeans and ribbed tank tops that only made him look even thinner than he was. His hair was long and greasy because he liked it that way. The summer before, he'd washed it with shampoo only twice.

"What's the point? I'm in the lake every day, mate," he'd said, pulling it back in a rubber band.

Most of the girls loved him because…well, what young girl didn't love a budding rock star? And when you threw in the British accent, forget about it.

Truth was, the hardest part of our jobs was keeping the girls at bay. When you had a girl to guy ratio of fifty to one, there was bound to be estrogen-fueled drama, even when they were well aware of the rules. That included no fraternizing with the campers, or you'd lose your job and your college credit. You'd think that rule would be pretty easy to follow, but you'd be wrong. The girls ranged anywhere from nine years old to sixteen, and not one of them cared about the rules—least of all the older ones who were only a few years younger than us.

In fact, I hadn't been so sure Will was going to be allowed back this summer because it was rumored that he and one of the girls from the senior village, Miranda, had gotten caught getting it on by the docks one night last year. Now, Will had admitted to me that it had indeed happened, but since no one could prove it and the girl never filed a complaint, the camp director—Uncle Bob—had dropped it. It was a miracle, too, because Bob was always looking to bust us for something—me especially.

"Where are you headed?" Will asked.

"Nowhere, dude. Just got finished cleaning up the squatters. You want to go practice for tonight?"

He folded his arms and drew his head back. "I don't need to practice, mate. You know that. Let's hit up the nurses' station. I need Tabitha to tend to my boo-boos."

He winked, and I slapped his arm.

Tabitha was my cousin, Bob and Sally's daughter, but she was really more of a sister to me. She worked in the camp infirmary with Alice Darwinkle, the resident nurse, every summer. Tabby and Will had had a *thing* last summer—until she'd found out about the rumors with Miranda. It was hard to keep up with Will's women, but he was in love with my cousin, and according to him, he'd only gotten it on with Miranda because he felt bad for her.

"You understand," he'd said to me. "She's mad about me, mate. She would've been crushed if I didn't let her get with me."

Something told me that Tabitha had had everything to do with Will coming back to camp—and with Miranda's absence this summer.

"Sure. Let's head over there," I said.

We started walking toward the medical building, but my uncle caught up to us just as we reached the steps.

"Bobby, ole man!" Will said enthusiastically. He raised his arms for a hug but got a scowl instead.

Bob hiked up his shorts. "We need some more wood for the bonfire. You two get down there and help the others, will you?"

"Right, Bob. We're on it. We're your guys for the job, Bob! But first, my hand is bleeding, and I need to get it looked at," Will said as seriously as he could.

Bob shook him off. "Jack, get your ass down there while princess here gets his hand kissed."

"I'll just wait for him—"

My uncle threw his hands up. "Just get on it, Jack. For once, can I not have to ask twice?"

He stormed off, and Will and I rolled our eyes.

"See you down there," I said.

Will drew in a breath. "Yeah, not so sure I should be lifting logs, what with this paper cut and all." He ran inside.

I shook my head as I turned around with my gaze on the ground and bumped smack into someone. "I'm so sorry." I stopped. "Oh. Hey, Brittany. Good to see you again."

Brittany Bingham and her twin sister, Brianna, were Hollow Creek *lifers*, as we called them. They'd been coming to camp since they were nine years old, and they were now senior villagers, the oldest camping group. Next summer, their only choices would be to become CITs or to vacation in the Mediterranean with their parents.

Brittany spread her arms and batted her eyes, waiting for a hug, so I gave her one.

27

"So amazing to see you, Jack. I missed you."

"Thanks," I said. "Hi, Brianna."

"Hi, Jack."

Brianna was sweet and quiet and tolerable for the most part, but Brittany was another story. She was flat-out trouble with a capital T and had been my biggest hurdle last summer—in that, much like today, every time I turned around, she would be right there.

To call her a flirt would be putting it mildly. She'd touch my arm when she talked. She'd come up behind me and jump on my back without notice. She'd put her hands over my eyes and whisper, "Guess who?"

The trick to girls like these at camp was to find a way to be polite but clear in my rejection. After two years as the assistant waterfront director, I'd had plenty of practice. Don't even get me started on what some of them behaved like when they had their bikinis on.

"Good to see you two again," I said. "Did you have a nice winter?"

Brittany locked elbows with me, and I gently slid mine out.

"Don't be so formal. Of course we had a nice winter. Who cares? We're just happy to be back here. Are you and Will playing tonight at the opening ceremony?"

"We sure are. Can't keep Two Guys and a Guitar down forever."

"We can't wait," she said, twirling the ends of her hair and chomping her gum.

Don't get me wrong. Brittany was hot. She was tall with nice boobs and a tiny waist. Think Barbie's second cousin with brown eyes and wavy blonde hair, and she'd been boy crazy ever since I'd known her. I'd be lying if I said I wasn't flattered.

"It was fun emailing with you," she teased.

At the end of last summer, she'd asked for my email, and I'd given it to her. Going off to college, I'd figured there was no harm in keeping in touch, but it'd only added to the flirting fire that was Brittany Bingham.

"Yeah, I got pretty busy toward the end of the year. Sorry I wasn't more responsive."

She slipped her arm through mine again, but I let it stay that time.

"No sweat. Nice to know you can get busy."

Brianna giggled.

"Well, great catching up, but I have to get some wood for the bonfire tonight."

"We'll help you." Brittany perked up.

"No, thanks. We're all set, but I'll see you there later," I said.

I whipped my arm back as Bob walked up. He had different personalities for different people—jerk for me, partial jerk or sometimes pal for most of the other staff, and all-around Good Guy of the Year for the campers. He could turn it on and off like a light switch.

"My two favorite girls!" he bellowed as he pushed his comb-over out of his face.

Brittany sighed. "Hi, Bob," she said, her energy deflating by his presence.

He walked up and hugged them. "I take it you both had a great year?"

They nodded.

"And I see you've managed to intercept this guy, which couldn't have been too hard."

"I was just on my way down," I said.

"Bob"—Brittany turned on the charm—"do you really need Jack's help right now?"

He looked at me, and I looked at Brittany.

"Because our duffels are ridiculously heavy, and we came to see if Jack could help get them to our cabin for us. There aren't too many guys around who can lift something so heavy."

She reached for my bicep, but I ran my hand through my hair before she could make contact.

Bob was confused and annoyed, but only I could tell.

"Your bags should have been brought to your cabin by now," he said.

She crossed her arms and shrugged. "Well, they haven't been."

I exchanged looks with Bob before he spoke, "Well, I suppose he can help. Then, head straight over to the logs, Jack. I'll be waiting for you."

He shot me a dirty look, so I saluted him.

FOUR

Julia

"Lunch is in ten," Liz announced. "We'll go through the job chart afterward, so Maggie and I will be the table setters for this meal. Everyone meet back here after lunch, please."

After unpacking my things, I left the cabin in search of something to eat. Since I was a senior villager, it meant that I didn't have to do every activity with the group. Certain things, like meal times, were scheduled, but mostly, we were given our freedom to sign up for whatever activities we wanted, whenever we wanted.

Once at the mess hall, I pushed my way through a small crowd standing in front of the double doors, and I was the first in line for lunch. Sharlene had forgotten to pack me any snacks for the bus ride, and I was starving.

Could I have packed snacks for myself? Yes, I could have.

Only, she'd insisted on packing something special for me, and then she'd forgotten. At least I would have something to write about in my first letter home.

I grabbed a tray and made my way past the mac and cheese, pizza slices, and chicken fingers. I stopped at the salad bar and filled my plate. Next to the dessert table was a small kiosk where kids like me could find foods that met special dietary needs, but I was hoping to avoid it at all costs.

I rolled my eyes at the huge *Kids with Food Allergies* sign posted above the counter.

How about making the general public feel like an outcast for once instead of singling us out?

As the rest of the camp began to filter in, I took my tray outside and sat under a large birch tree behind the building. Two gorgeous Alaskan huskies slept soundly on the porch of a building marked *Camp Office.* Next to that was the infirmary and then the canteen, a shedlike shop where kids with money in their accounts could purchase stuff like candy and stamps and Hollow Creek spirit wear.

Just as I stood to return my tray, I heard over the loudspeaker, "Could the following campers please report to the infirmary: Michelle Reardon, Alexis Carter, Emma Marquardt, Julia Pearl, and Samantha Bruce?"

I tossed my tray through the tray return window and walked slowly to where I was supposed to be.

"Take a seat," a woman in her mid-fifties instructed me.

Then, she repeated it as the rest of the summoned few arrived.

She had wiry dark hair with two white skunk stripes in the front. Somehow, the front of her head forgot to tell the back of her head that it was time to go gray. Reading glasses hung around her neck on a beaded chain, and her shorts went just below her knees. She fumbled with some papers until the last person arrived, and then she smiled at each of us with her hands on her lap, like a grandmother would as her grandchild came bounding through the front door. I would have no problem coming to this woman if I got sick.

"Hi, everyone. I'm Miss Alice, the camp nurse. I promise not to make this too long, but I just want to be sure I have everyone's medications in order." She turned her attention to the clipboard on her desk and put her glasses on. "Okay, so we have one egg, two shellfish, and two nuts!"

She snorted with amusement, but only one girl in the group so much as cracked a smile.

"Tough crowd," she mumbled.

Then, I felt bad for not laughing.

"I have all your medications and EpiPens. Your counselors have EpiPens as well. As you might have seen, there is a wonderful designated area in the cafeteria where you can be sure the foods are uncontaminated. It's the first time we've ever done anything like this, and it was all the chef's idea, so be sure and eat from there.

Now, anytime you and your cabinmates venture outside of campgrounds for, say, a field trip or overnight or something, there will always be appropriately healthy snacks for everyone. We don't want you to feel out of place."

Too late.

"Does anyone have any questions?"

The girl who'd given the courtesy laugh raised her hand and introduced herself to Miss Alice as Emma.

She was not in my cabin, but she was a senior villager like me. When I'd first boarded the bus, I'd noticed her sitting alone with similar trepidation.

"Do we have to eat from the designated area only? I was told the salad bar and baked potato bar were also nut-free."

Miss Alice smiled, revealing a set of clear adult braces. "That's a great question, and you're correct. Both those stations are maintained under the same allergy standards. However, I would encourage you to stick to what's best for you." She looked at each one of us and smiled. "I don't want to keep you any longer than I have to, so that will be all. You know where I am now, so please don't hesitate to come to me for any reason."

"Thank you, Miss Alice," a couple of the other kids mumbled in unison.

I hurried out of there with nowhere to go, so I walked the long dirt path back to my cabin. Apparently, the older you were, the farther your cabin was from civilization.

Sitting on the edge of my bed, I quietly flipped through *People Magazine* as the other girls loudly filtered in after finishing their lunches.

"Hollow!" Liz walked in, clapping.

She stopped in the center of the room with Maggie right behind her.

"We want to quickly go through the job chart, okay?" Maggie started. "We've posted it here on the back of the door, and we'll rotate names each morning. Some days, you won't have anything to do but always make sure to check."

Liz walked over to the door. "The tasks are sweeping the floors, turning off lights, emptying the garbage cans, distributing the mail during breakfast, and making sure no clothes have been left on the clothesline." She waved her arms and shushed the few girls who were chatting. "This last one is really important because they can get moldy, and then slugs will live on them."

Mental note: Never hang anything on the clothesline.

There was a collective, "Ew."

She continued, "Last are the setter and the runner jobs. Every meal, two people are in charge of the table. Someone from the kitchen staff rings a setter bell as an advance warning because the setter must arrive at the mess hall ten minutes before mealtime. Basically, the setter makes sure there are enough plates, napkins, and silverware for the cabin. And the runner is in charge of picking up the platters of food and bringing them to the table. We all eat family-style unless you want a salad from the salad bar, which is what I usually eat."

"Everyone clear?" Maggie asked the group and we all nodded.

A few hours later, we ate our second meal of the day with a girl named Amber as our trusty setter and Monica as our runner. Then, we all made the trek back to our cabin to change for the evening program.

It was an event I realized I was highly unprepared for as I watched the girls getting dressed to the nines. Along with glitter body spray, feather boas, and sequined tops, there were pink tutus, camouflage tutus, and glitter tutus. Just the mere fact that I hadn't packed a tutu put me at a huge disadvantage. It was a situation I couldn't have predicted had I tried. Nowhere on the Hollow Creek Packing List that had been sent home could I recall seeing mention of a tutu. And I was certain Sharlene would've been all too happy to buy me one. Thankfully, a couple of other holdouts like myself opted not to paint their faces, wear wigs, or shimmy into tutus.

"Don't look so horrified. It's not required attire," Amber said to me as she was changing out of her denim shorts and into a terry cloth Juicy Couture tube dress.

"I feel like I packed all the wrong clothes, like shirts and pants and shorts," I said.

She laughed. "Getting dressed up for the evening program every night is kind of a tradition. But since my four-year-old sister makes me wear tutus around the house while reciting lyrics from *Beauty and the Beast* with her, I refuse to wear one here or anywhere else."

"Gotcha." I watched Liz paint some of the girls' faces while Maggie sprayed their hair with glitter.

For a moment, I wanted to join in and let loose, but I couldn't force myself to do it. As I just sat and stared, I wished they would call me over and insist on making me look ridiculous, but they left me alone.

"Want to head over to the bonfire with me?" Amber asked.

"Yeah, that'd be great."

I walked with her down the trail, passing a cluster of cabins, to a large open area behind the main lodge called The Cove, which was a section of graveled pavement in between the beach and the grass. Rows and rows of logs circled a huge campfire area, and many of the other campers had already taken their seats. The younger girls sat in groups with their cabinmates.

"Gum?" Amber offered.

"No, thanks."

Amber was taller than me, but so were most people. She was slim with no chest, no butt, and no curves, yet she was really pretty. She had a long neck and big eyes, and she wore her dark hair in a pixie cut. If she had makeup on, she would be stunning.

"I just went to the canteen and grabbed some snacks. You should check it out when you have a chance."

"I'm not sure my dad put any money in my account for me."

She crossed her long legs at her ankles. "I'm sure he did. The camp requires that all parents put money in each camper's account. Trust me, you'll spend it all and write home for more in no time. Just don't blow all your money at the canteen because the Franteen has better snacks. The Franteen is a smaller canteen with mostly candy and crap. It's named after by Fran Weisberg, the sister of one of Hollow Creek's original founders. Twizzler?"

"Sure." I took the licorice from her, and we waited for everyone to take their seats.

Just then, the twins from the bus—Brittany and her sister—came over to where we were sitting and said, "Hello," to Amber.

She stood and hugged them, and then she introduced me. I hadn't known them for five seconds before I felt myself recoiling. They smiled at me and seemed nice enough, but there was something inexplicable in the air between us, like an animal instinct that made me want to foam at the mouth.

"Hi, I'm Julia," I said with a forced smile and a wave.

Brittany looked me over from head to toe. "I love your sandals," she said in a way that made me think she hated them.

I looked down at my very plain, very faded yellow rubber flip-flops. "Thanks."

"Brianna, don't you love those?" She nudged her sister. "You love yellow."

Brianna looked at my sandals with the same unimpressed expression Brittany had. "Cute," she said.

The microphone let out some ear-piercing feedback when the camp director stepped up and tapped it. "Hollow!" he cheered.

The crowd echoed his greeting and then applauded.

"As most of you know, I'm your fearless leader, Bob Hanson! That is, except when it comes to spiders and snapping turtles."

The crowd laughed, and Amber leaned in. "Bob the Slob Hanson. He's notorious for being a complete mess—hence, the nickname. He never wears deodorant, and he hardly showers. He brings, like, four outfits for eight weeks of camp and *never* combs his hair."

"Ew," I added.

"He's an old hippie at heart—at least, that's what my mom says."

I nodded. "I think your mom's right. Did they not have deodorant in the sixties?"

She shrugged.

Bob made some announcements, and thanks to their brevity, they pleased the crowd. Once he was done, I was excited to see a familiar face. Jack Dempsey, from the bus, and one of the other male counselors took their places in the middle of the circle, next to the mic. There was a collective swoon among the audience members as Jack swung a guitar strap over his chest. He was wearing a tutu.

"That's Jack and Will," Amber informed me. "All the girls are hot for them every summer. Even if they were trolls, we'd probably be hot for them anyway, but it doesn't suck that they're easy on the eyes, if you know what I mean. Is this your first time at overnight camp?"

"Is it that obvious?"

She smiled. "You'll learn pretty quickly that, despite the tons of activities they have for us here, all the girls want to talk about are the male staff members. For real."

"Will is the singer?" I pretended not to know.

"Yeah, and Jack is the Slob's nephew. He's worked here every summer since his parents died when he was little."

My eyes widened. "Seriously?"

"Seriously. I don't know the story, but I guess they were in a nasty car accident or something, and afterward, Jack was sent to live with the Slob and his wife, Sally."

Jack started playing, and Will began to sing. It was a beautiful thing. Will's voice was low and scratchy and the perfect accompaniment to Jack's music. I allowed my eyes to wander to the sky while my ears enjoyed the serenade, which profoundly affected me, echoing inside my head and putting a smile on my face.

I craned my neck to stare over the group at Jack. His eyes were closed, and he had a peaceful grin as he strummed the guitar with ease, nodding his head to the beat. There was nothing in that moment that would've indicated he'd suffered through what Amber had told me.

My smile faded. "Does he have any brothers or sisters? Do the Slob and Sally have kids of their own?"

"Ole Sloborino does have a daughter who works at the camp, too. Her name is Tabitha. She's, like, pretty vanilla, if you ask me." She yawned. "Jack's the shit."

"Poor guy." I looked over at him.

"Who? Jack? I think he's over it. He was, like, five or something. He couldn't be nicer. Wants to be, like, a social worker or motivational speaker or some shit. Maybe because of what he's been through."

Over it? I thought to myself.

Whether you'd lost a parent to death or disappearance, there was no getting over it.

The conversation about Jack made me think of my mom and one of the last times we'd spoken. It was in my father's office shortly after I'd developed my aversion to school bus fumes, and I'd had an epic hair-pulling freak-out over attending school.

My therapist, Joyce, had said she wasn't surprised that I'd finally lost my shit, and she'd insisted that my father allow me to contact my mom, something he'd refused to do prior to that day.

So, six months and eight days after seeing my mother cowering on our kitchen floor, I had sat in my father's office, waiting to talk to her, with Joyce by my side.

My dad's assistant brought in a tray with Snapple.

"Thank you." Joyce grabbed a peach tea.

Sitting in a chair, my shoulders slumped, and feeling aggravated because a phone call wasn't good enough for me. I needed to see my mother, to smell her, to have her wrap her slender long arms around me and tell me she'd protect me like always. I wanted to bury my face beneath her hair and feel my heart beat at a normal pace again. I wanted to hear the click-clack of her heels on our wood floors and watch her frantically scurry around the house, looking for her keys. I did not want to call her on the phone with a therapist staring at me over her reading glasses, nodding as if I were participating in a spelling bee.

Dad handed me the receiver and left the room.

"Please hold," a voice said.

I scooted to the edge of my seat, and Joyce smiled at me. I wanted to smack her.

"Hello?"

The sound of my mother's voice made my throat tighten. Tears came fast and furious, and I was sobbing before I could even get a word out.

"Oh, honey," Mom whispered. "Shh…it's okay, Julia. Please don't cry."

It took me a couple of minutes before I could speak. "I want to see you. I need to," I choked out.

Mom sniffed. "I'm far away, in California, getting help. As soon as I'm better, I'll come for you."

"I'll come see you then! I'll come to California. Please, Mom!"

Joyce pursed her lips, and I fumed.

"How are you, sweetheart? I miss you so much," Mom said.

"I'm terrible! I hate it here. I need you! Dad won't tell me what's going on. Please, Mom. I'll do anything to be with you. Please come back and get help here. I can help you with anything you need." I glared at Joyce. "I can't even have a phone call without some idiot staring at me."

Joyce was unfazed by my insult.

"Please, Mom." I sank back into the chair.

"I've made some mistakes, my sweet girl, and I can't see you until I'm better. That's all I can say. I love you more than anything in the world, but I need help, and I need you to be a big girl for me and understand."

"I can't."

"Yes, you can."

She was trying to hold back her tears, but I could hear soft whimpers through the phone. I hated to think of her as anything other than Wonder Woman, so I composed myself and promised to be a big girl. Then, I placed the receiver in Joyce's outstretched hand and watched as she hung up the phone.

What other choice did I have?

The sun had just set behind the camp, and the fire was casting a glorious radiance on the evening sky. Once it was dark, it was like we were the only people on earth. It was as if there was nothing beyond the glow of the flames but darkness for miles.

Jack sat on a stool and continued to play while Will led the camp in a sing-along. I had a hard time taking my eyes off of Jack. Most of the campers did. He was bobbing his head to the music while staring at his guitar's strings. Periodically, he'd look up at the crowd and nod and smile, encouraging the group. He acted like there was nowhere else he'd rather be, and I envied him for that.

They played for about thirty minutes, and then the campers were dismissed by groups, the younger campers leaving first. The remaining senior villagers were invited to stay for as long as we wanted. Once most of the camp had dispersed, we moved to the front of The Cove. There were about three cabins of senior villagers, around thirty-six of us in all.

After a while, some girls left to go to bed, and others went down to the lake for a night swim, leaving only half of the senior villagers at the bonfire. We were eager for Jack and Will to continue.

Will was nice-looking, too. He was different than Jack, much more rock-'n'-roll wannabe. Clearly, in order to be a male staffer at Hollow Creek, you had to have a solid muscular physique, friendly smile, killer tan, and enough self-confidence to spend twenty-four hours a day trying to guide hormonal teenage girls clad in bathing suits through a variety of sports and other activities.

The male counselors were not cabin counselors. They all slept in staff housing and were in charge of things that required a little extra muscle, like water sports, land sports, climbing, or waterskiing.

"Gather 'round. Come closer," Will said into the mic to the eighteen or so of us left.

We all moved a few logs forward.

The thing about early summer in the Midwest was that once the sun had set, it was cold. Needless to say, I'd forgotten to bring a sweatshirt with me, so I was shivering and hugging myself with my arms.

"Why don't you run up and get a jacket?" Amber asked.

I shook my head. "I'm fine, really. I don't think I'll stay very long anyway. I'm kind of tired."

She leaned over, and with her bare hands, she rubbed my arms up and down. It was a sweet gesture, but it didn't do much to warm me up.

"Pearl!" someone shouted.

It was Jack, and all the other girls looked over at me, so I cautiously waved at him.

"Come down here," he said.

I hesitated, and my body stilled with uncertainty. *There's no way he'd ask me to sing along or play the tambourine, would he? Too bad I left my kazoo at home with my tutu.*

"I certainly wouldn't make him ask twice," Brittany said in a low voice from behind me.

I stood and stepped over a few rows of logs before walking over to him.

"Here," he said, untying a gray hooded sweatshirt from around his waist. "Put this on." He shook it at me. "Go ahead. You're shivering."

"Thanks." I took the sweatshirt from him and put it on as I walked back to my spot next to Amber.

Brittany looked as though she wanted to kill me—and steal my ugly flip-flops for her sister and Jack's sweatshirt for herself.

"Do you know him?" Amber whispered.

"I met him today when he got me off the bus. I'd fallen asleep on the ride up."

She made a sound. "Hmm..."

"What does that mean?" I asked quietly.

She popped a ninth piece of gum into her mouth. "I'm just wondering why he did that."

I pulled my knees in close and tugged the cuffs of the sleeves over my hands. "Is *just to be nice* out of the question?"

She continued talking, "You know, *all* the girls, even the little ones, are gaga for him. There were rumors of him sneaking other female counselors into his room last summer, but I have no idea if they're true or not."

"Couldn't he get kicked out for that?"

"Hell yes! In fact, one counselor got kicked out because she wouldn't leave him alone. He was as polite as he could be up until she showed up on the dock one evening, wearing only a raincoat and nothing else, when he was cleaning out the boats."

"No way!" I whispered loudly.

"Way. She just stood there and opened her coat, and he dragged her naked ass straight to Bob."

I shook my head and sniffed. "How embarrassing."

Amber just smiled. "This camp thrives on gossip, so we were all thrilled to death when the story made its rounds. The poor girl was gone before sunrise the next day. Could you imagine having to explain that one to your parents?"

I zipped Jack's sweatshirt. "Maybe her mad flasher routine had worked in the past, and she thought Jack wouldn't be able to resist."

"The worst part was, the Slob pulled him from his post for the rest of the summer, so we all had to suffer for her mistake."

"I think you mean, her indiscretion."

She laughed and then nudged me with her shoulder. "I've never seen him give anyone his sweatshirt before."

"Oh, please. He probably saw you rubbing my arms, and he was doing his Good Samaritan duty. Just keeping campers happy and warm at all times!"

Someone kicked the log we were sitting on.

"Do you two mind? Some of us are trying to listen to the music. Show some respect," Brittany reprimanded us.

But I had the sweatshirt.

Afterward, Brittany, Brianna, and some other girls ran down to Jack and Will.

Amber and I hung back.

"I'm going to turn in," I said to her.

"Okay. See you in the morning."

I started to walk off, but then I stopped halfway up the hill, trying to decide if I should drop Jack's sweatshirt off right then and there at the camp office, which was always open, or return it in the morning.

"Julia," Jack called my name, strolling toward me with the ease of a cat. "What did you think of the opening night ceremony?"

I sank my hands into the front pockets of his sweatshirt. "It was great. Really, you and Will are mesmerizing," I said.

He made a face.

I rambled on, "You know, captivating, engaging—"

"I know what the word means."

Behind him, a gaggle of five senior villagers were starting to gather, so I began to unzip his sweatshirt.

He raised a hand to stop me. "Keep it until tomorrow."

"I'll be fine."

He took a step closer and swung his guitar behind his back. "It's no big deal. Return it tomorrow. Either bring it down to the docks before breakfast, or bring it to me during activity selection."

"Okay. Thanks. I was getting pretty chilly."

"You'll learn." He pulled at his long sleeve. "I wear these every night until mid-July." He took a step closer. "I was thinking about you today. I'm really glad you're enjoying yourself." Jack smiled, and then he turned and walked away.

I watched him saunter off toward Will, another staffer named Tommy, and the remaining senior villagers.

Once he was out of sight, I pulled the zipper all the way up to my chin. His sweatshirt was soft and warm and smelled like smoke from the bonfire.

I wrapped my arms around myself and walked back to my cabin, alone and snuggled in his sweatshirt, as a chorus of crickets serenaded me. I couldn't wait to return it to him in the morning.

FIVE

JACK

"A few of the girls want to head down to the water," Will said as I rejoined him.

I nodded, but Will gave me a pleading look, like he was ready to turn in.

"Uh, I think we'd better wrap things up. Will and I have an early morning," I said to them.

"Aw," Amber said. "Tommy and Liz said they'd get the inner tubes out."

"My boy Jack is right. We've got ourselves an early morning, girls," Will said.

Brittany pushed forward. "You sure you're not just cold, Jack, since you handed out the shirt off your back?"

I smiled at her. "Good night, everyone! Awesome opening ceremony." I hugged a few of them, including Brittany. "Get some rest, and be sure to sign up for our activities tomorrow."

"Right!" Will waved. "See you in the morning, ladies."

Will and I walked off together. It was close to eleven o'clock, and we were worn out. We'd been loading and unloading equipment, logs, and luggage all day, and I couldn't wait to hit my pillow.

"Dude, I'm exhausted. Thanks for not making me stay out," I said.

"I'm beat, too, mate."

Bob was standing in the lobby of the staff housing, finishing up a conversation on his handheld radio, when we walked in, intending to breeze right past him.

"He's right here," he said. "Jack!"

"Shit," I mumbled. "Yeah?" I said over my shoulder.

"Alice needs you to pick up a prescription at Walgreens. One of the kids in cabin eight has pinkeye already. Pinkeye on day one! Can you believe it?"

"Why can't Tabitha do it?"

He dropped his arms and tilted his head so far to one side that I thought it might snap off.

Then, he blew out his lungs in exasperation. "Because I asked you. Now, go."

Will gave me a look. "I'll go with you, mate."

I shook my head. "Get some rest."

He slapped my shoulder. "Far be it from me to argue with you there, brother. Working the boy hard today, eh, Bob?"

Bob pulled up his sagging Bermuda shorts with both hands and grumbled, "Just bring it over to Alice as soon as you're back. She's waiting up for you."

I went to the office to grab the keys to the Jeep and saw Tabitha and Sally crouched in front of the computer.

"I'm heading to Walgreens," I told them.

Sally looked up. "Thank you, Jack."

She was my father's younger sister, and she'd had gray hair ever since she was thirty years old. The good news about that was now, at age forty-eight, she didn't look a day over thirty—at least to me. Aunt Sally was quiet and kind, and she'd worked as a librarian before she met and married Bob. Tabitha was born soon after. In fact, Aunt Sally liked to tell everyone that she was barefoot and pregnant the day she married my uncle on the beach in Milwaukee.

I took the Jeep to Walgreens, and then I was back with the medication in about twenty minutes. As I was walking toward the infirmary, I saw Julia Pearl walking out. It was just past midnight, and she was still wearing my sweatshirt.

"Hey you," I said.

She looked startled and pleased at the same time. "Hey, Jack."

I gestured to the building. "You feeling okay? Don't tell me you're the one with pinkeye?" I held up the bag.

She wrapped her arms around her middle. The sweatshirt was so long on her that it looked like she had nothing on underneath it. "Oh, no. I forgot to take my medicine earlier." She shook her head as if she'd just spaced out. "I guess I'm a little off my normal schedule."

I nodded but didn't feel it was my place to ask her what medication she was taking and why. "Let me run this up there, and I'll walk you back to your cabin," I offered.

She blinked and smiled. "That would be great."

SIX

Julia

I awoke with a jolt and searched for Jack's sweatshirt next to my pillow. I felt reassured by its presence. I leaned over and took a whiff of the scent of smoldering embers lingering on the cotton threads, my head still reeling from our midnight stroll. Thankfully, no one had noticed me sniffing his clothes, so I tucked it under my blanket, grabbed my shower caddy, and went to get washed up.

Unfortunately for me, the twins and I were on the same schedule that morning.

"Oh, hey you. Julia, right?"

"Yes. Good morning, Brittany, Brianna."

"Brianna and I were just talking about how much fun we had last night. How did you like your first opening ceremony?"

"It was really nice. Such a great group of people here. I really feel like it's like one big family," I said quickly, needing to pee.

"It is!" Her eyes went wide as if I'd answered a game show question correctly. "We missed you afterward though."

The thing about girls like Brittany was that they tried so hard not to be fake that they would end up being grossly obvious and predictable. I didn't know if they were simply clueless, passive-aggressive, or plain stupid. I had an idea about which one Brittany was, but I'd promised myself that I wouldn't be judgmental—this morning anyway.

Since I had to pee and she was desperate for me to ask her why they'd missed me, I decided to walk away. "I'll catch you both later. I really need to use the—"

She stepped in front of me and blocked my exit. "After you left, Jack and Will took Brianna and me down to the docks, and we sat there while they played music until the sun came up."

"It wasn't that long," Brianna chimed in, her eyes all shifty.

I knew Brittany was lying, but I chose not to call her out on it. Instead, I gave her a look that said, *Is that all?*

"I'm sure we'll do it again though, so no worries. You can join us another time."

"Great," I said.

Brianna was picking dirt out of her nails, equally bored with the conversation as I was.

"Excuse me," I said.

But Brittany didn't budge. "So, where are you from?"

I crossed my legs and inhaled. "I'm from Chicago."

"We are, too—sort of. We live north of the city in Highland Park." She paused. "What does your dad do?"

"My dad?" I thought about him and the care package that had been waiting for me when I arrived. He'd sent it so that I would have some mail on the first day. Inside was a roll of three-ply toilet paper, a whoopee cushion, and a Chia Pet. "He's a lion tamer with Ringling Brothers Barnum and Bailey circus."

"Bullshit," she said.

"No one ever believes me when I first tell them, but it's true. You're the one who asked me. It's not like I was bragging about it."

She let out a laugh and crossed her arms, looking over at her sister. "Not sure it's anything to brag about."

"It is." I curled my lips. "I really need to pee."

Brittany moved aside and thrust her chest out like an angry baboon. "Sure thing."

Once I was dressed, I grabbed Jack's sweatshirt from my bunk and threw it in my backpack. After my encounter with the twins, I didn't feel like prancing down to the docks before breakfast, so I decided to deliver it during activity selection.

As I made my way down the dirt path from the senior village to the main lodge, all I could think about was how Jack had said he was the assistant waterfront director and how there would be water sports in my future. I spotted Emma, my allergy pal, as I was walking.

"Hey," she said, waving at me.

Emma was a little taller than me at about five foot five, and she was slightly overweight—not where she might get teased too often for being fat, but just a little extra plumpness in places like her stomach and thighs and arms. I could tell she was self-conscious about it because she was always tugging at her shirt and hiking her shorts up over her waist. She was really cute though with strawberry-blonde curls and a bright smile. I'd liked her immediately.

"Emma," she said, reminding me of her name. "Nut Number Two!"

I laughed. "I remember. I'm Julia."

"Want to pick some activities together?"

"Sure. Why not? Is this your first time at camp?"

"It's my first time at Hollow Creek. I've been to summer camp before, but the one I went to for three years refused to accommodate my new peanut allergy. I was just diagnosed last year."

"That's a bummer."

Every kid with any sort of food allergy had their own tale of woe. Their first reaction to whatever edible weaponry would haunt them for the rest of their lives. Mine had begun at the age of two.

"I found out at a pretty young age. I was licking some peanut butter off a spoon and broke out in hives around my mouth. The doctor told my mom I might have a peanut allergy and that I'd probably outgrow it but not to give me peanuts again until I was five. Then, at age three, my nanny disregarded my mom's instructions and gave me a Reese's Peanut Butter Cup. Almost immediately, I began coughing and throwing up, but my mom just thought I was sick. When she told the doctor what had happened, he said I was lucky, and I could've easily died. After that, Mom never left my side—until my dad kicked her out."

Emma stuck out her bottom lip. "I'm so sorry. Where is she? Your mom?"

"I'll tell you some other time. I really don't feel like talking about it right now." I swallowed the lump in my throat that always accompanied thoughts of my mother. For so long, life without her had not seemed worth living. I wasn't in the mood to uproot that darkness. "How did you find out about your allergy?"

"It's so mortifying. I can't even talk about it." Emma slapped her hand to her forehead and cringed.

"Oh, come on."

"If you laugh, I will pummel you."

"I won't. I promise." I crossed my heart. "Unless it's just too hilarious."

"It is." She stopped walking to face me and then lowered her voice as she said, "Okay, I was sleeping over at my best friend, Andrea's, house. Her parents were out of town and thought she was sleeping over at my house."

"Nice."

"Anyway, we invited these two guys over, Jared and Mason. Jared and Andrea were going out, and I had a huge crush on Mason. He'd never given me the time of day before then, but Andrea bribed them both by promising access to her parents' liquor cabinet. So, the four of us were hanging out in her basement, sipping from a bottle of gin and eating whatever processed crap we had found in their pantry—Oreos, Nutter Butters, Doritos, Fritos, and Cheez Balls by the fistfuls. You get the idea."

I nodded.

"After we sufficiently drained the bottle and then filled it back up with water"—she rolled her eyes at the sheer stupidity of it— "we decided to 'watch a movie.'" Emma made air quotes, indicating they'd all had something else on their minds. "Andrea and Jared were molesting each other behind the couch before the opening credits had even finished rolling while Mason and I sat, drunk and awkward, next to each other." She looked behind her as if he might be standing there.

Then, she laughed and shook her head. "I was buzzed. I had never really drunk alcohol before. But Mason was wasted. He kept laying his head on me and petting my hair and tickling me. To be honest, as goobery as it sounds, I was in heaven. I'd been crushing on him all semester. He was on the varsity basketball team, and I couldn't have cared less that he would never have paid me any attention had he not been drunk." She lifted her arms. "What did I care? Mason Drunk-Ass Daniels was hitting on me! I had to pinch my love handles just to prove I wasn't dreaming."

I laughed. "Would you get to the point?"

"Chill, little woman. This is an epic story—unlike your yawnfest at the pediatrician's office." She placed a hand on her chest. "Personally, I don't like Nutter Butters, so I'd devoured most of the Oreos and Cheez Balls." She pointed a finger in the air. "But guess who loved and had devoured two sleeves of Nutter Butters?"

"Mason?" I stated the obvious.

"Right you are. And guess who—after all my internal wishing and pleading—gifted me with an epic French kiss?"

My hand went to my mouth in a lame effort to suppress my gasp.

"Yep!" she said. "Not three minutes into my first real French kiss did I start feeling like it was the most uncomfortable act of intimacy on the planet. My lips felt numb and puffy, and I was trying my best to relax, but just as I was wondering how people managed to enjoy this, Mason pulled away, looked at me, and screamed, 'Holy shit!'"

"No," I whispered, my eyes wide.

She nodded. "Oh, yes. Yes, yes, yes. My lips went from a size extra small to a triple XL in seconds. I brought my hand to them, and it felt like someone had placed a water balloon under my nose." She paused. "A water balloon covered with blisters, I might add. And as if that wasn't pretty enough, as mayhem ensued and lights were being turned on, hives began to crop up everywhere on my chest and back and circled my ears, eyes, and mouth."

"Oh my God!" I screamed. I laughed, jumping in place. "Emma, no!"

She crossed her arms again and shrugged proudly. "Oh, hell yes."

"What happened next?"

"By the grace of God—some other God than the one who had allowed Mason Daniels to see me that way—Andrea's baby sister had a milk allergy, so her family had an EpiPen in the house. My girl Andrea just immediately recognized the signs she had been told to look for in her little sister, so even in a gin-induced haze, she was able to think on her feet and inject me with the EpiPen like a sick horse."

My mouth was as wide as my eyes.

51

"Then, they called nine-one-one, and we all got our asses kicked and grounded—for many reasons. So, that's how I discovered my peanut allergy."

At that point, all I could do was applaud, and Emma curtsied.

"Bravo, Nut Number Two. Bravo."

She locked her arm with mine, and we began to walk.

"It is what it is."

"I couldn't agree more," I added. "Ever hear from Mason again?"

"Hell no."

We entered the lodge through the large swinging double doors and paused to check out the many offerings. Tables lined the perimeter of the room with the activity heads standing behind them, talking to campers about what they had to offer.

I spotted Jack within seconds and took a deep breath. He was at the water sports table with two other guys beside him. He had a baseball cap on, set backward, and was sitting in a chair, writing something in the three-ring binder in front of him. A long line of girls stood before him, each one waiting her turn. I guessed I wasn't the only one with a sudden interest in tubing.

Emma caught me staring. "He's hot," she said, leaning in.

"He really is."

"You have any interest in water sports?"

"I didn't two days ago, but I do now."

"Gotcha." She stared him down, too. "I know his name is Jack Dempsey, and some people call him J.D. I heard two of the female unit heads dated him. Last year, they got into a massive catfight over him. I guess one of them got fired halfway through the summer." She grinned and rubbed her hands together. "Nothing passes the time better than some good gossip. Got any?"

I shook my head and then turned to face her. "I'd feel silly, standing in that long line for him."

"It wouldn't be for him. It's for waterskiing. Let's go." She grabbed my elbow. "Besides, you're a little hottie. He might actually go for you. I've got my eyes on one of the kitchen staff. Anyone who looks good wearing a mesh shower cap is my type of guy."

"Staff-camper relations are a no-no, you know?" I waved a finger in her face.

"Puh-lease." She rolled her eyes. "Clearly, you've never been to camp before."

Truth be told, relations between campers and staff was so forbidden that it was treated like the most unspeakable of human crimes even though we were all essentially the same age.

I didn't know that I would ever refer to myself as a hottie as Emma had. *I mean, what kind of a douche refers to herself as a hottie?*

But I was attractive, and I knew that mostly because I looked somewhat like my mother, who was gorgeous. We both had long dark hair, light-blue eyes, and high cheekbones. My dad always told me how much we looked alike, and then he'd close his eyes and shake his head, like he did when he smoked his pipe.

The thought made me miss him terribly. I couldn't wait to write home and tell him he was a lion tamer.

Emma and I headed over to the arts-and-crafts table in hopes of letting the water sports line die down a bit. Brittany and Brianna—of crop-top, ponytail-flop fame—were standing there, waiting their turn, as we walked up. They scrutinized us with their eyes once we'd stopped and stood behind them.

"You like what you see?" Emma said.

"What?" Brittany responded.

"Do you like what you see? I mean, that was quite a body scan you gave me. You girls batting for the other team?"

I smiled.

Then, they looked at each other and began to snicker as if Emma and I were so ridiculous in our attempt to converse with them that there was nothing to do but mock us. That, and there was no way in hell these two could muster up a clever comeback, so they reverted to rolling their eyes and laughing. It was a sure sign that someone was an idiot.

"We're literally standing here to say hello to someone—not to sign up for craft hour, like you two. But good luck with baking pottery or whatever."

That was followed by more snickers.

"Literally?" Emma added.

"Did you return Jack's *sweatshirt?*" Brittany asked me, moving on and drawing out the word *sweatshirt.*

I tightened my grip on my backpack. "It's not really your concern."

She touched her heart. "No need to get defensive. I was just asking."

Emma blinked and was about to add something to the riveting conversation, but someone squealed Brittany's name from behind, and she and her sister strolled away without giving us a second thought.

Emma looked at me and shook her head.

"Hi, girls," a voice beckoned from behind the table. It was Liz, my cabin counselor. "What can I get you ladies signed up for? We've got lanyard bracelets, pottery, painting, table-making, and papier-mâché."

I rubbed my chin. "What do you think, Em?"

"Do we get to take our table home if we make one?"

"No. We donate them to the local old folks' home," Liz said.

"Lanyards seem very campish. Don't you think?" Emma asked me.

"I do. Lanyards it is."

Once we were destined to have our wrists covered in braided poly-nylon, we headed to the water sports table, and only three other girls were ahead of us. As we waited, Emma stood, facing me, with her back to Jack so that I could ogle him while pretending that I was talking to her. It was Emma's idea, and it was genius.

"Next!"

We stepped up to the table.

"Hello, Pearl."

"Hi, Jack." I raised the fingers on my hand that was gripping my backpack strap.

"I'm Emma." She leaned forward and shook Jack's hand. "Emma Marquardt."

Jack leafed through a list of camper names in front of him before looking back up at the two of us. "Well, girls, what's it going to be?" He slid a list of water sports toward us on the table. "Decisions, decisions, decisions."

"Which sports are you in charge of?" Emma asked.

"I sort of oversee all of them, but I personally handle waterskiing and Voyagers."

"Then, waterskiing and Voyagers it is!" she announced.

Jack let out a small laugh. He looked up and caught my eyes on him, causing me to glance over my shoulder as if someone had called my name. No one had.

"Have either of you skied before?" he wondered aloud.

We both nodded, and he wrote something down next to our names.

"And you both want to join Voyagers?"

Emma and I looked at each other and then back at him.

"Could you tell us a little about it?" I asked.

He set his clipboard down. "It's sort of a *Survivor*-like adventure challenge course for campers who are looking for a little more camp in their summer experience. It's a ten-day program in which you have to pass some basic survival skills."

He placed a sheet of paper on the table in front of us, and we read it.

1. PORTAGE A CANOE.

2. BUILD A FIRE.

3. BOIL WATER.

4. PERFORM BASIC FIRST AID.

5. CANOE A CERTAIN DISTANCE ALONE.

6. COOK A FULL MEAL OVER AN OPEN FIRE.

7. SPEND A NIGHT OUTDOORS ON YOUR OWN.

There wasn't one skill on there I ever intended on needing.

He continued, "This list is in no particular order, except for the final challenge. It's a test of endurance where you each sleep alone in the woods, overnight, with only the bare necessities. It concludes the program."

We both looked up at him.

"Which are?" Emma asked.

"Let's just say, it's bare. You'll have to sign up to find out for yourselves."

Emma turned to me. "What do you think?"

"I'm out," I said without hesitation.

The program sounded interesting, and the skills would certainly impress my father—who thought I only knew how to use an iPod, a TV remote, and a carryout menu—but as soon as the words *alone in the woods* had come out of Jack's mouth, I panicked.

Emma shrugged. "She's out, I'm out."

Jack put his pen behind his ear and leaned back in his chair, crossing his arms over his chest. "That's too bad," he said. "Take this pamphlet, and think about it. It does fill up quickly, so don't take too much time. I wouldn't want you two to miss out."

He held on to the pamphlet, tug-of-war style, as I tried to take it from him.

"Especially you, Pearl. Something tells me that it might be good for you," he said before letting it go.

I reached into my bag, pulled out his sweatshirt, and handed it to him. "Thanks again for this."

He placed it at the end of the table. "Anytime."

Emma raised her brows.

I wanted to ask him what he'd meant by "it might be good for you," but I was tongue-tied. As I searched for a witty retort, Tweedledum and TweedleBrianna waltzed up to the table.

"Let's get out of here," Emma whispered. "Thanks, J.D.!" she said to him. "See you at the campfire later. And we'll think about taking your voyage, okay?"

The twins laughed at her, but Jack winked at us.

He has to know we're way more awesome than those braless freaks, right?

When we walked outside, the sun hurt my eyes. "Damn, I left my sunglasses in the cabin."

"You have to do Voyagers. I'll do it with you," Emma said as we crossed the dirt path to the mess hall.

"Honestly, I don't consider myself any sort of diva or anything, but it's just not my thing. It's enough for me to endure a pre-Civil War bunk bed in a room with twelve other girls and no running water."

"He wants you to do it," she said, poking my shoulder, as we walked.

"He wants you to do it, too."

"He only wants me to do it because he thinks you'll do it if I do it."

"You're insane."

"I'm telling you, he wants to take a voyage with you. He wants to be your voyager. He wants to park his camper in your camp."

"Oh my God!"

We both cracked up.

"I'll think about it," I said.

SEVEN

Julia

A fter lunch, I left Emma and went back to my cabin to grab my sunglasses. Then, I walked alone to the edge of the lake and sat down.

There was an all-camp assembly on healthy eating that I was trying to avoid because it made me think of Mom. She had been my food champion at one time, my everything champion, and I hated thinking about her.

I closed my eyes, but that only made things worse. My thoughts of her were now accompanied by images—her dressed up and gorgeous as she'd bent down to air-kiss my cheek so that she wouldn't mess up her lipstick, her waving to me from her car and getting off the phone as I'd opened the door and slid into the backseat after school, and the last time I'd seen her in a heap of tears and despair and humiliation while she was crumpled on the kitchen floor with her hair and makeup destroyed.

I opened my eyes and wiped my tears. She never would have allowed me to go to camp.

Twenty minutes later, I heard a speedboat and saw it coming around the bend. I knew immediately that Jack was in the driver's seat. He had one hand resting loosely on the wheel and one leg propped up on the console. The boat slowly floated up to the dock, and he leaped off onto the wooden planks before securing it with a rope. He wore nothing but his swim trunks, showing off a golden tan on his trim physique. His trunks sat low on his hips, and

I could clearly see his tan line about an inch or two below his belly button. What little chest hair he had, had been bleached by the sun, and was glistening on account of his sunscreen. He ran one hand through his hair and wiped his forehead before hopping back into the boat to kill the engine.

I felt like a creeper, spying on him in broad daylight, but at least no one else was around. I managed to tone down the goofy smile on my face. He paused when he noticed me, and then he pushed his sunglasses up onto his head.

I waved, and he grinned as he pulled on a T-shirt. Then, he rolled up some of the lines from waterskiing and threw them over his shoulder before walking toward me.

"Hey you," he said.

"Hey."

He took a seat on the ground, facing me, and let the ropes drop off his shoulder. "You out here looking for me?"

"No. Just took a walk."

"During the assembly?"

"Obviously."

"And right when I'm doing my lake run?" He cocked his head.

"Looks that way."

He smirked.

"Would it be so outrageous for me to want to leave a stupid assembly about eating healthy when nothing they're covering applies to me whatsoever?" I asked.

He pulled in his knees and rested his elbows on top of them. "Why wouldn't it apply to you?"

"It just doesn't."

"Fair enough. Something tells me you had no intention of sitting there, regardless of the topic. I mean, why should you do what you're told?" He shrugged, challenging me with his grin. "You were looking for me, weren't you?" He reached out and nudged me.

Maybe I was.

"What's the matter?" he asked. "You look a little down."

"I'm not. I'm fine."

"You don't seem fine. You look...depressed."

"Well, I'm not," I snapped, tossing a rock into the lake. "Just because I don't like assembly halls filled with adolescent BO and sweaty-ass vinyl-covered chairs doesn't mean I'm some moody, suicidal bitch."

"Who said anything about suicidal, drama queen?" He lowered his chin. "Have you thought about killing yourself?"

I laughed aloud. "Wow! That's a bold question," I blurted out, meeting his eyes. "I can't believe you just asked me that." I shook my head. "Who asks someone that?"

"I just did."

"You're insane."

"You're the one who brought it up," he noted.

"I was trying to make the point that just because I prefer my own company to almost anyone else's and loathe large cultlike groups of people singing camp songs around a fire pit, it doesn't make me emotionally unstable. In fact"—I pointed a finger at him, and he mockingly raised his hands in surrender—"I'm probably one of the most stable people here."

He lowered his hands. "Clearly," he said. "So, have you thought about killing yourself or not?" he asked matter-of-factly.

I didn't answer. If I had been hoping to run into him, I was now regretting it.

"Because, statistically, more people have considered it once in their lives than those who haven't," he continued. It was his turn to point a finger at me. "That means, there's actually something wrong with you if you've never even considered it."

"No, I haven't, but it wouldn't be that hard if I wanted to."

"It wouldn't?"

"No. All I'd have to do is eat a spoonful of peanut butter."

He nodded with understanding. "Ah, so you have given it some thought."

I wanted to smack him. "No, I haven't thought of offing myself, but I have thought about dying. I've thought about it for as long as I can remember. Ever since I was little, I've been forced to think about dying. Every cake at a birthday party, every playdate snack, every amusement park vendor is a potential death trap. My whole life, my mother would tell me that I was one bite away from death. There's a difference between thinking about suicide and thinking about dying, neither of which I'm interested in at this point in my life—despite what my mood is telling you." My stomach clenched, so I paused.

"I'm sure your mom was just trying to help," he said.

My heart stilled.

I shook my head. "She doesn't give a shit about me."

Jack leaned back on his hands and stretched his legs out in front of him. "Why do you think that?"

I looked out at the water, regretting that I'd said anything about my mother—especially to Jack. "Forget it."

"I don't want to forget it."

"Please drop it. I don't feel like talking about it."

He met my moist eyes. "I promise I'm not prying, but sometimes, it's better to chat it out, you know? You were thinking about her just now, enough to mention her, and that's your subconscious telling you that you need to put it out there, get something off your chest."

I raised an eyebrow.

"I'm studying child psychology in college," he added.

"Are you shitting me?"

"I shit you not." He smiled. "So, let's have it. What's the dirt on you and your mom?"

I picked up another rock and rolled it between my fingers. I had no intention of unearthing my most personal struggles to Jack or anyone else. My father had tried for years to get me to talk to a therapist, but after two months of me sitting in Dr. Joyce's office for each appointment—at a hundred twenty-five dollars an hour—and not saying anything, he'd finally relented. Everyone was always insisting that I needed to talk to someone when all I ever wanted was to talk to my mom.

I shrugged and looked around at the trees, water, dirt, and rocks. The only thing intimidating about my surroundings was Jack, yet as nerve-racking as his presence was, it was also quite liberating. I wanted to open up to him because I wanted his attention. I wanted his eyes on me, his thoughts to be about me, his brows to bend with concern for me.

"She left when I was eleven."

"Why?"

I scratched the back of my neck and waited for a moment. "She was addicted to drugs and sleeping with some dude," I said dismissively, trying to make light of it, as if her actions hadn't unplugged me from the wall of life.

"Bummer," he said. Then, he let out a small laugh. "Bummer is a technical child-psych term, in case you didn't know."

It was hard not to smile at him, regardless of the topic. "I didn't know that. College has been good to you."

"Yes, psychologists have been known to use it instead of, 'Wow, that blows,' or, 'You certainly have been through some hardships.'"

"You're an ass."

"I am. I'm sorry." He leaned forward. "How often do you see her?"

"Never."

"Never?"

His eyes were on me, but I looked away.

"You haven't seen her since she left?"

I shook my head.

"Have you talked to her?"

"Once," I said. I shook my head again.

The conversation was getting embarrassing, and I quickly remembered why I never wanted to discuss her with anyone.

But Jack kept on talking, "I really am sorry, Julia. I was making light of it, and I shouldn't have. I didn't mean to pry. I lost my mom when I was five, and I know what it's like to live with that void."

"Can I ask what happened?"

"Of course." He crossed his legs and plucked a few lonely strands of grass in front of him. "My parents were killed in a car accident on their way to the hospital. My mom was in labor with my little brother, and they'd left me at home with my grandmother. It was the middle of the night and raining really hard. From what I was told, a deer ran out in front of them, and their car swerved straight into an oncoming semi. I don't remember much about it, other than bits and pieces from the chaos that ensued afterward."

I brought my hand to my mouth. "Oh my God. I'm so sorry."

"Yeah."

"Did the baby die, too?"

"Yeah." He pursed his lips and gave a tiny nod.

My chest was heavy as I studied his face—handsome and regal yet rough around the edges—and his deflated posture. The sun filtered through his hair and rested on his wide shoulders, as if even Mother Nature couldn't resist shining a spotlight on him.

"Do you remember them? Your mom and dad?"

He glanced up at the sky and narrowed his eyes. "Um, sort of and not really. I have vague memories of things we used to do together, like riding a tricycle with my dad and reading books with my mom before bedtime. She loved to read. But most of my memories are from pictures…or on account of pictures."

I completely got what he meant by that. The strongest memories of my mother and events we'd shared together were the ones that I had photographs of, like my seventh birthday party at the Lincoln Park Zoo or when my friend Amanda had peed her pants and wouldn't come out of the ape house until her mother came to pick her up. And on Halloween, when I was nine years old, Mom and I had both dressed like Disney princesses. She had been a midriff-baring Jasmine, and I had gotten to be Belle. Then, there was the day my dad had bought her a new car, a cherry-red Lexus, and she and I had both sat atop the hood, barefoot, while my dad took a photo of us.

"Do you remember what books she read to you?" I asked.

"*Charlie and the Chocolate Factory* mostly."

He smiled, and so did I.

"Who raised you?"

He put his hands behind his neck and stretched. "My grandparents did for a while, and then I was sent up here to live with Bob and Sally and Tabby. Tabitha and I are about the same age. We grew up together. She means everything to me."

"You guys lived here at the camp?"

"No, about twenty miles from here in a town called Lake Delton. Water Park Capital of the World!"

I laughed. "For real?"

"For real." He lifted both brows and checked his Swiss Army watch. "I moved out of Bob and Sally's house as soon as I went off to college. Once I turned eighteen, I was allowed access to my parents' life insurance—some of which had been set aside in a college fund and some of which I was allowed to use to live and be free of whoever had been squashing my dreams my entire youth. I get the rest when I turn twenty-one, and I'd much rather be on my own than under Bob's thumb for the rest of my life. I work here every summer because of Tabitha and Sally and now because I get course credits. Truthfully though, I love this place." He looked me squarely in the eye. "So, you see, we've all got our own shit. You're going to be all right, Pearl. Just like me."

He spread his arms in a simple gesture, and I wanted to leap forward and hug him.

My heart ached for him and me and everyone who had their own shit to deal with.

Why did that stupid deer have to run into the middle of the road at the very second Jack's parents were driving past it? Who could have known that little boy would need someone to read Charlie and the Chocolate Factory *to him every night? Who could have guessed someone as vibrant and full of life like my mother was a cocaine addict?*

I straightened my spine. "Don't give me that poor-you look. I'm really not a miserable person. I promise," I said with as much conviction as I could muster.

"I never thought you were."

Every time he looked into my eyes, I would feel a rush of emotions coursing through me like a speeding train about to burst through a tunnel.

"Can I suggest something?" he asked.

"Sure." I wished the two of us could sit here, talking, for days.

"Why don't you write your mom a letter?"

"I've written her letters in the past but never got a response." I heard the rejection and heartache in my own voice, and it bugged the crap out of me.

"How do you know she got them?"

"Why wouldn't she have?"

He mockingly threw his arms up. "Um, hello? Haven't you seen *The Notebook*?"

I laughed so hard that I snorted. "I'll think about it."

I'd stopped trying to contact my mother right around the time my dad remarried. He'd seemed overly anxious and bothered at the very mention of me writing to her, and I'd hated upsetting him, so I'd stopped mentioning it. Before that, I'd written letter after letter because I hadn't been given any other option, but I never received one response. It was as dumbfounding as it sounded, like she'd disappeared off the face of the earth. Only, she hadn't. I'd known my father knew where she was and how to get ahold of her, but he'd said she was sick and unfit to speak with me.

What else could I have done but taken him at his word?

I loved him, and I wasn't about to alienate my dad, too.

"Hey, I never liked peanut butter anyway," Jack said with a shrug. Then, he stood and brushed off his shorts. "You're not missing anything—except maybe Reese's Peanut Butter Cups, Reese's Pieces, Nutter Butters, Fluffernutters, PB and Js. You get the idea."

"You're an ass."

"Gotta go, kid. See you around."

I got up, too. "Jack?"

He turned and looked back at me. "Yeah?"

"Don't call me kid."

He tilted his head. "I'll call you what I want, Pearl." He smirked. "What's wrong with kid?"

"Because I'm not a kid. I'm sixteen, and you're nineteen. I don't want you to think of me as a kid."

His lips went from a smirk to something more serious as he looked me over and landed on my eyes. "I apologize. You're anything but a kid. I wasn't thinking. I throw the term around to people all the time. I don't mean anything by it." He put his hands in his pockets. "How do you know I'm nineteen?"

"Everyone knows everything about you."

He snapped his fingers and pointed at me. "Ah, that is true." He took a step forward and opened his arms. "Friends again? Let's hug it out. Quick, so I don't get canned."

The hug I had been desperate for was mine for the taking, but I was frozen. When I didn't move, he wiggled his fingers on his right hand, motioning me into his embrace. I took a few steps forward, and Jack wrapped his muscular lean arms around me like a cocoon. I'd never felt safer in my whole life—at least not in the past five years. If he'd smelled like a pipe, I would have melted into him. Instead, his shirt smelled like a campfire, smoky and earthy and hot.

I just closed my eyes when he released me, and he placed his hands on my shoulders, causing me to gaze up at him.

He shook some loose hairs out of his eyes before speaking, "You good?"

I nodded, and he removed his hands.

"Hey, I'm glad you bumped into me on purpose because I was thinking about you and hoping you'd consider signing up for the Voyagers program. There are only a couple of spots left, and it starts next week."

"Thanks, but no thanks," I said.

"Hmm." He crossed his arms. "Pretty little rich girl doesn't think she can handle it, or she doesn't ever picture herself outside of a one-mile radius of a J.Crew or a Jamba Juice?"

He amused me, but I wasn't about to let it show. "Why do you think I'm rich?"

"This camp costs one thousand two hundred fifty dollars a week. Every kid here is rich."

"So, as far as you're concerned, for one thousand six hundred fifty dollars, I should at least learn how to boil water?"

He nodded. "I'm concerned with helping people face their fears and accomplish something other than lanyards and lunchtime. If you don't sign up, I'll just assume you're weak." He lifted a brow to challenge me.

He was teasing me, and I knew it, but something came over me like a black storm cloud.

I took a step backward. "Assume what you want. Assume I mope around, feeling sorry for myself, while listening to Green Day. Assume I have no friends. Assume I've thought about killing myself or running away or carving my name into my arm. But I haven't! So, also assume that you know nothing about me!" The tone of my voice surprised both of us.

Jack's eyes went from playful to regretful in a second. Then, he hugged me again, and I burst into tears.

EIGHT

Julia

I signed up for Voyagers the next day, and I made Emma and Amber sign up with me. I didn't do it because Jack thought I was weak but because Jack was in charge. If he were in charge of me, I knew that I could achieve anything. Also, it wasn't such a bad idea for me to learn how to survive on my own.

Who knew how long J.Crew would be around to clothe me or how long Jamba Juice could provide sustenance?

And, bottom line, I wanted to be around Jack as much as I could. There. I'd said it.

I had, in only a few days' time, turned into one of those girls who obsessed over a guy and whose world revolved around seeing that guy, talking to that guy, and getting that guy's attention. The problem was, so had many other girls.

If the camp were smart and really committed to enriching young girls with an experience focused on the outdoors and living outside the box, then they wouldn't have staffed the place with good-looking young college boys. As far as I was concerned, it was the camp's fault that we were all in heat…in the Wisconsin heat.

For the most part, we'd all survived the first week of camp.

The following Monday, Jack held the first Voyagers meeting under a tented seating area with benches behind the mess hall. Much to my displeasure, Brittany and Brianna were there.

"You've got to be kidding me," I whispered to Emma.

"She's doing it for the same reason you are, Julia," Emma said without moving her lips.

"Great."

All the girls sat a little straighter when Jack walked up with his backpack on one shoulder.

"Good morning, ladies. I'm happy to have you all here, and I'm really looking forward to working with this group. I think you'll all benefit from the things you'll learn from me over the next ten days. And if not, hey, you'll at least know how to boil water."

His comment could hardly pass as funny, but Brittany cracked the hell up, laughing hysterically, like she was in the front row at a Jerry Seinfeld stand-up show. It made me want to smack somebody.

He continued, "I know there are only six of you, but I'm going to do a quick roll call to make sure I know everyone's names, and so you all know each other. Here we go. Emma Marquardt, Julia Pearl, Amber Sykes, Rebecca Newman, Brittany Bingham, and Brianna Bingham." He looked up and smiled.

"It's Bree-*ah*-na," the least offensive of the twins corrected Jack.

"Oh my God. Who seriously cares?" I mumbled under my breath.

Emma snickered.

"What did you say?" Brianna asked me loud enough so that the entire group could hear, including Jack.

He turned to look at us.

I lifted my chin. "I said, I'm sorry that you think anyone cares about how to pronounce your name."

She gasped, and Jack glared at me. I sank into my chair. I hadn't meant for her to hear that, but I wasn't going to lie.

"Come on, guys. That's enough. This is a special program, and if you all can't be nice to each other, then you shouldn't be here," Jack chimed in, visibly annoyed. He took a breath and shook off the immaturity started by yours truly this time. "I actually do care how to pronounce your name, Brianna. I apologize. It was my mistake. I would not want people calling me Jacques or Jake or something other than my name." He looked at me. "And let me be clear about one thing. We are all going to get along. Is that understood?" He did not move his eyes from mine.

I stared back at him and nodded.

"Julia, is there something you'd like to say to Brianna?" he asked.

I shook my head so slightly that it appeared to be locked in place between my shoulders, but he got the message.

"I think you should apologize."

Emma looked at me to gauge what my reaction might be. In fact, all the girls were staring at me with the same look.

I sat up in my seat and apologized, pronouncing Brianna's name incorrectly. Naturally.

After the meeting, Jack pulled me aside. "Julia, can I talk to you for a sec?"

"Sure," I said.

Emma and Amber went back to my cabin.

"Sit down."

I did, and he sat across from me at the picnic table.

"What was that all about?" he asked.

I didn't answer.

"With that behavior, you're no better than them."

It was hard for me to look him in the eyes because I knew I'd lose all sense of rational thought if I did. Instead, I stared at the table and picked at the chipping paint. "I know. I didn't mean for her to hear."

"That was obvious, but if you're trying your best to show off to Emma by putting someone else down, then you're more like Brittany and Brianna than you think." He lowered his head to try to meet my gaze. "And I know that's not the case."

"You do?"

"Yes. You're better than that."

"How do you know?" I asked.

"Well, you tell me. Are you better than them or not?"

I smiled. "Does this pep talk come with a survival badge? Like, Self-Awareness one-oh-one or Finding Your Inner Bitch?"

"No, but I'll take that into consideration for next summer."

I sighed and slapped my forehead. "I really am sorry." I meant it—not so much for annoying her, but for behaving that way in front of him.

Those twins brought out the worst in me for some reason, but that was no excuse. It was petty and stupid. There was nothing guys hated worse than a girl who behaved that way—at least, according to my father.

He'd always tell me, "A real man wants a lady, not a bitch."

Jack nodded and pursed his lips. "I haven't had a chance to talk with you much this week. How are you adjusting to everything else?"

"Pretty good. Emma and Amber are awesome. In fact, I might have a massive girl crush on Emma. She totally gets me, and she's an absolute riot. Oh, and she's allergic to nuts, too!"

"Awesome. I have a couple of nuts on my Voyagers crew this year."

"If my memory serves me right, you were the one who talked me into this adventure. I'm expecting great things."

He lifted his arm and tousled my hair like one would do to a puppy. "As am I, Pearl. As am I. Will I see you at the Rock 'n' Roll bonfire tonight?" He stood.

I nodded and gave a thumbs-up.

Jack walked away from me, backward, facing me. "Great things are coming your way. I promise."

He then turned and disappeared around the side of the building, taking my breath with him.

NINE

JACK

It was almost midnight by the time I put out the bonfire and cleaned up the trash between all the logs. The Rock-'n'-Roll–themed evening program had seemed to produce more glitter and confetti than any actual concert I'd ever been to. Pretty much everyone was asleep, except for the night guard, Theo, who walked the campgrounds every evening.

Theo was a senior at Michigan State. He'd played football his first two years there, and then he'd gotten an injury that sidelined his career. He was a big dude, about six feet six, with wide shoulders and no neck. He'd been working at the camp, doing odd jobs and security, for a couple of years.

We'd never had a security guard on the campgrounds until after 9/11 because Bob, in his infinite wisdom, assumed the Taliban would strike somewhere near the Water Park Capital of the World next.

The littlest girls loved Theo the most. He'd carry four to five of them at a time on his back, like a grizzly bear carrying its cubs, and then he'd teach them how to play football and tackle one another.

I saw his expansive shadowy figure as I was walking up from The Cove.

"Good night, Theo."

"Night, Jack."

"You need anything, man? I'm going to grab a bowl of cereal before I turn in. I can get you something from the kitchen."

"Thanks for thinking of me, but Midge let me snag some Chewy SweeTarts from the Franteen before she locked up." He patted the overstuffed pockets on his raincoat. "So, I'm good."

"Midge knows how to take care of her people."

"Yes, she does. She knows I'll protect that Laffy Taffy cabinet with my life."

I laughed and patted him on his concrete shoulder as I passed. Only a few senior staff members had keys to every building, including the kitchen, and I was one of them.

In the back, near the large pantry, were cereal dispensers that would be rolled out every morning for the campers, so I let myself in to satisfy my growling stomach with a bowl of Lucky Charms before bed. But before I could get a spoon out of the drawer, I heard a noise in the pantry. When I moved to go check it out, I accidentally knocked the bowl to the floor, and it shattered loudly, causing the noise in the pantry to go still as the bowl spun itself into silence next to my foot.

"Hello?" I shouted over some nonthreatening whispers.

A moment later, Tabitha came out of the pantry, staring at me sheepishly. She, too, had a master set of keys.

"You okay?" I took a step forward.

She tucked her hair behind her ears. "Yeah. What are you doing here?"

"Breaking a bowl of cereal. What are you doing here?" I looked over her shoulder at the pantry door. "Who's in there?"

She glared at me. "Please just go."

"Tabitha, what the hell is going on? Are you with some—"

"Jack, please. This is mortifying."

I'd always taken care of Tabitha. She was my little sister by default, but I never saw it that way. She and I had been close our whole childhood, and we were always protective of each other.

It was no secret that Bob was hard on me, even as a little kid—acting as if I'd asked to be dumped in his lap, as if I'd chosen to lose my parents and be force-fed a heaping pile of guilt stew every day for the rest of my life, as if I'd ever dreamed of spending my entire youth at Hollow Creek. Tabitha was the one child they wanted and could afford. I was an uninvited houseguest who ate all their food and refused to leave. Circumstances had led me there, and obligation and lack of options kept me there.

But Tabitha had my back, no matter what, especially where her father was concerned. We'd been through a lot together, but this was the first time I'd busted her in a compromising position, and it didn't sit well with me, especially on an empty stomach.

"Please tell me, you and some of the girls are giving each other midnight pedicures in there."

She looked up at me and crossed her arms. "I'll clean up your mess. Just go to bed."

"Who's going to clean up yours?"

She sighed. "Good night, Jack."

I stared at her and the door behind her for a good long minute and then did what she'd asked of me.

When I got back to my room, Will's bed was empty.

He walked in about two hours later and tripped over the stack of books I'd deliberately placed just inside the door.

"Bloody hell!" he spewed under his breath.

"What the fuck is going on with you and Tabitha?"

"What's with the pop-up library, mate? Nearly severed my kneecap on the bedpost."

"Wanted to make sure I heard you when you came in."

I turned on the table lamp as he sat on the edge of his bed, rubbing his leg.

I lowered my voice. "Seriously, dude, what are you thinking? You can't be messing around, especially with my sister, or you'll get your *arse* kicked out of here. Then, who will I find to sing off tune with me?"

"Only bloody everyone." He lowered his head to his hands. "Shite, she asked me to meet her after the bonfire, and I should have said no, but I could never say no. I like her, Jackie Boy. I really do. Did she tell ya we talked all winter?"

I shook my head. "No, she didn't."

Will lay down on his bed and closed his eyes. "She wants to tell her mum. She wants Bob and Sally to know we're dating."

I swung my feet off the bed and leaned forward. "Are you?"

"Not really. I mean, you know, it's a camp thing, like you and Liz."

I huffed and nearly spit when he'd said that. "Me and Liz? There's no me and Liz. Why in the hell would you say that? Don't try to drag me down with you, brother."

"I'm not. She told Tabby you were keen on her."

The night before the campers had arrived, a few of the staff and counselors had driven into town. There hadn't been much to do around here, except mail a letter, see a movie that had come out months ago, and grab a brat and a beer. Some of the group had gone to dinner, and some had gone to a local dive bar that hadn't asked any patron for an ID since prohibition.

Liz and I had chosen the bar over dinner. One tequila shot had led to another, and before I'd known it, we had been the only ones from our group left. Liz had been drunk—a happy drunk, I'd give her that, but a handful. We'd danced a little to Guns N' Roses and The Who on the jukebox. When I'd suggested we get out of there, she'd latched on to me like a leech—sucking behind my ears, licking my face, trying to kiss me in between the slobbering. I had done my best to keep her at bay, but my resistance was low.

We'd ended up ferociously making out in an alley behind the bar for a few minutes until I'd convinced her that we should head back. When we had gotten back to camp, I'd walked her to her cabin, and she had given me one last kiss and a pat on the ass. We'd agreed to tell everyone we'd gone for gelato in case they asked what had happened to us.

I was not one to place blame. I didn't kiss and tell, and neither had the countless other staffers I'd swapped spit with over the years. The fact that Liz had been blabbing to Tabitha was a problem.

"Ah, shit." I fell back onto the bed and turned off the lamp. "Things are getting off to a great start. I don't care what you and Tabitha do. Honest. Just leave me out of it."

He tossed a book at me. "Keep a stash of midnight snacks under your bed then, and we won't have a problem."

Ten

Julia

It was two a.m., and one of my cabinmates had a nasty cough, so I was lying awake, thinking about Jack, my life, my lack of mail, my nasty stupid behavior toward Brianna, and the ease of how I'd stooped to her sister's level of ridicule. I guessed some girls never could escape who they were and how they behaved, no matter how far into the woods their parents had sent them. I rolled over and put the pillow over my head.

The next day, after breakfast, was our first official Voyagers outing, and the six of us followed Jack into the woods. Like baby ducklings following their mother, we were trusting, naive, and a little wobbly.

I made sure to say hello to Brianna, and I pronounced her name correctly. Thankfully, everyone was civil to each other.

Jack didn't seem like his chatty self, so we all quietly trailed behind him. He stopped near the edge of a small pond and told us to put on some bug spray. I turned and lifted my hair, so Emma could spray my neck and the back of my arms.

"Skeeters and ticks. Nothing creeps me out more than skeeters and ticks," she said. "A wild black bear could walk up and tap me on the shoulder, and I'd be less scared of him than I am of those bugs."

"Just spray yourself until you gag."

Jack swung his duffel bag off his shoulder and onto the ground. "Welcome to day one. As promised, the Voyagers program

is a test of endurance and survival skills, consisting of seven levels."
He pulled out the sheet he'd shown Emma and me during activity
selection and read aloud, "You'll be learning how to portage a
canoe, build a fire, boil water, perform basic first aid, canoe a
certain distance alone, and cook a meal over an open fire. Finally,
the program will conclude with a solo overnighter where you'll
each spend twenty-four hours in the woods."

Emma and I exchanged a dreadful glance.

"So, today, my privileged little ladies of luxury, we're going to
begin with steps two and four—building your own fire and
performing basic first aid. Come with me."

Jack walked a few steps away from the pond, toward the trees,
and sat down, so we all copied him.

"Everyone, sit about two feet apart from each other, and clear
away a space in front of you, like this." He took his hand and
began brushing away at the ground, clearing a small area of rocks
and twigs and dirt, until all that remained was a clean spot that
looked as though he'd swept it with a broom. "You want a nice
unpolluted space for the base of your fire, so nothing will get in
its way."

We each did as we had been told. Emma wiped her hands on
her white T-shirt when she was through.

"Okay. Next, we're going to go to the pond and find
some rocks. Now, you might not always be in an environment
where rocks and stones are at your disposal—"

"Or in an environment where I'll need to build a friggin' fire
on a dirt patch," Emma said.

Jack raised an eyebrow and continued, "But we're going to use
them today because it's ideal to give your fire some boundaries."

Once we'd returned with our rocks, we each made a circle in
our little clearing. Brittany made hers into a heart shape, and I did
not make one snide comment about it.

"Good job, everyone, but don't get too comfortable. Now, we
need to go into the woods and get our kindling and sticks. Look
for some dry small twigs, leaves, and also some larger sticks. Don't
get anything that will stick outside the boundaries you've created
for your fire though," Jack cautioned us.

"Can you help us?" Brittany asked.

"I could, but I want you girls to do everything on your own,
okay?"

She pursed her lips. Again, I kept my mouth shut. There should be a survival badge for biting my tongue every time Brittany said something annoying.

I went in the opposite direction as her and her sister and walked deep into the woods but not far from the pack. Like Emma had noted, I couldn't imagine a scenario where I'd be alone in the woods—besides our impending solo overnight—without my cell phone. I'd never feel the need to light a fire before help arrived—unless, of course, there was no cell service, and I'd been kidnapped by an angry client of my father's. In which case, the kidnappers would undoubtedly want money, and they'd need to place a ransom call, so there would have to be cell service—unless they'd locked me up in a cabin and called my father from the landline, which would mean I'd be inside said cabin and have no use or means to build a fire even if I had been left to fend for myself.

I gathered what looked like dried twigs and leaves and some stuff that resembled the clumps of hair I'd pull out of my hairbrush once a week. I thought Jack would be particularly proud of that find, and he was.

"Okay, ladies"—he craned his neck and assessed each of our assembled piles—"looks pretty good to me. Now comes the hard part. We're going to start a fire."

"How hard could it be with matches?" Emma looked at him. "You do have matches, right?"

He grinned and shook his head. "No, ma'am. We're hunters and gatherers now, and we're going to start our fires the old-fashioned way—by rubbing two sticks together."

We all stared at him with our mouths agape.

"What? Are you girls always looking for the easy way out?"

I was noticing a pattern. He reveled in pointing out our entitlements. I wondered what his child-psych professor would say about that.

"Keep your kindling in the center of your rocks, and find one of the strongest sticks in your collection. I'm not going to leave you completely high and dry." He pulled six boards out of his duffel. "These are fireboards, and you're going to use your stick as a spindle, creating friction in this notch here at the bottom. Then, it should light your kindling on fire first. From there, you will add fuel to your fires."

Jack handed out small planks of wood. Each one had a circular indentation carved out near one of the edges. Determined not to complain and be without heat, I reluctantly took my stick and placed it in the notch of the fireboard. I began to roll it between my hands. It immediately came out of the hole, so I repeated my steps eight more times until I was able to balance it and roll it as fast as I could while keeping it in place. We all tried and had to stop to catch our breaths.

After about twenty minutes, we were all sweating and staring at our sore palms in defeat. Not one of us had so much as a puff of smoke.

Jack smiled proudly and repressed his laughter. "All right. Hold up, ladies. I just remembered I have a book of matches for each of you."

If evil eyes could kill, Jack would have died six times over.

"Are you serious?" Brianna asked. "I barely have any skin left on my right hand."

"Me, too," Amber said, throwing her stick at him.

He paced the space between us and pulled something out of his duffel. "Precisely why we're almost ready to move on to lesson number two—performing basic first aid."

When we returned to our cabins with our hands covered in Vaseline and gauze, Emma came with me and plopped down on my bunk.

"Well, that was fun," she said.

I lay next to her, and our legs dangled over the side.

"I think Jack had the time of his life, trying to torture us," I said.

"And draw blood."

It was a kick, seeing him in his element, and despite whatever satisfaction he got out of dragging prima donnas into the woods, he had been extremely patient and attentive with each of us.

I looked over at Emma, whose eyes were closed, and I was about to gush about Jack when I noticed something behind her ear. It looked like a bubble or a blister, but when I got closer, I could tell it was a tick. It was dark brown with a flat head and a U-shape on its back. After watching it fill with blood, my eyes went wide, and I gasped as I sat up. It took every ounce of my self-control not to scream.

"Emma," I said calmly, hands shaking, "please don't freak out."

"About what?"

"Just promise me that you won't freak out."

She sat up and angrily looked at me. "What?" she screamed.

I lifted a nervous finger. "I think you have a tick behind your ear." I pointed.

"Ha-ha-ha. Very fucking funny. I know you're screwing with me," she said, assuming I was teasing her.

Who could blame her?

Then, she must have registered the reaction on my face, coupled with my wobbly finger. She slowly reached behind her ear, and as feared, she freaked the shit out. She shook her head from side to side, and her piercing panicked screams sounded like she was being abducted. But, if she were, she would now know how to build a fire in the event her abductors abandoned her in the woods, assuming they'd left behind one of those craptastic fireboard planks or a book of matches.

"Help! Get it off me! Get it off me!" Emma ran around the cabin.

Everything I knew about ticks and tick removal, I'd learned in the past week. Lesson one: Ticks could not simply be brushed off as they'd buried their heads into your skin, so if you only removed the body, you would be left with a bloodsucking tick head inside of you, and you would be no better off than you had been moments before. Lesson two: They needed to be removed with tweezers or a needle of some sort to extract the entire thing. Lesson three: There were only two ways to kill a tick—chop it in half or burn it.

Maybe lighting Emma on fire wasn't the worst idea.

Emma's screaming incited my screaming, and we both had a full-on freak-out before I managed to calm her down. She stared at me with tear-filled crazy eyes until I put my hands up and pleaded with her to run to the nurse with me. She agreed, but before doing so, she couldn't resist reaching back and touching it again, which sent her into a full-out sobbing meltdown of a mess.

I dragged her behind me—like pulling a baby carriage with no wheels, which was also on fire—down the longest dirt path known to man. We barged into Miss Alice's office like hysterical mutant ninja teenagers, one of which had emerged from the fiery baby carriage.

"Oh my God! Ow! Help me!" Emma screamed.

Miss Alice dropped her coffee mug, and three office staff ran in from another building to assess the commotion.

"Oh my God! Please get it off me! I can feel it growing!"

Miss Alice waved her hands, trying to get ahold of Emma's arms.

"She has a tick behind her ear!" I yelled.

"Okay, sweetheart, calm down. Emma, honey, the sooner you relax, the sooner we can get that little bugger out of there. Please have a seat, and place your hands on your lap."

I helped Emma to a chair and held her hand as she rocked back and forth like a mental patient.

"Take a deep breath," I said. "Miss Alice is going to get him off, and then we'll murder the sucker."

She closed her eyes. Her body was shaking as she began to mumble, "It's sucking blood from my brain. I can feel the blood being sucked from my brain, and my brain is losing oxygen. I'm going to pass out soon, and blood will be everywhere. Brain blood!"

I knelt beside her chair.

"Julia, can you hold both of Emma's hands for me?" Miss Alice asked. "I'm going to have Tabitha here pull back your hair, Emma. Don't be alarmed, and don't worry. This won't hurt."

"He's extracting brain mass!" Emma howled.

Miss Alice shot me a look that said everything would be all right, but I sensed she would have preferred to roll her eyes instead.

"He...or she is nowhere near your brain. I've done this a hundred times, but I do need you to try to relax if I'm going to get it on my first try."

Emma took a couple of deep breaths and nodded at me. Tabitha held Emma's hair to the side. Her eyes and teeth were clenched. Miss Alice gently bent Emma's ear with one hand and snatched the tick with tweezers in the other. The contrast between the drama Emma had caused and the ease of the procedure was pretty funny.

"Ta-da! The tick is out!" Miss Alice said, holding it in between the pointy blades of the tweezers for Emma to see.

Emma went pale. "He's still moving."

"I think Emma should do the honors of killing him," I said.

Miss Alice looked more disgusted than she had when she was behind Emma's ear. "Well, all right. Take it outside then."

I grabbed the tweezers and a pen, and Emma followed behind me, sniffling and wiping her tears, but not before she'd tackled Miss Alice in a bear hug.

I put the tick on the ground. "Stick it through him," I said, handing her the pen as if she were Attila the Hun.

"Seriously?"

"Seriously."

Emma narrowed her eyes, bent over the ground, and stabbed the tick with the pen. "Die, motherfucker bloodsucker!" she screamed.

I laughed so hard that I peed.

The next twenty minutes were like the aftermath of a hurricane. It was like walking outside, after you'd been huddled, frightened and trembling and screaming for what seemed like an eternity, to a warm and peaceful calm in the air, shielding your eyes from the bright sun.

Emma was a mess. She'd popped a couple of blood vessels in her eyelids, snot was running out of her nose, and blood was slowly caking up behind her ear at the scene of the crime. She sat, slumped over, on the ground, next to a set of wooden stairs that led to the mess hall. When she finally looked up at me, there was a hint of a smile, and then she laughed. We both did.

"J.D. is going to die for this," she whispered.

"It's not Jack's fault."

"Oh, and I'm done. If you think I'm going back into those woods without a hazmat suit, then you are delusional."

"You can't quit on me! You talked me into this damn thing," I said.

She rolled over and lay facedown in the sandy earth with her arms and legs splayed to the sides.

I sniffed out a laugh. "Oh my God, Emma. What are you doing?"

"I need a moment to rest. That asshole tick got me. He won. And I know it was a *he* because he went all sneaky and romantic behind my ear."

I shook my head and tugged at her right arm. "Would you get up? Let's hit the Franteen. I think this whole ordeal calls for some Fun Dip."

She sat up and brushed herself off. "I think you're right. Hey, thanks for being there for me. That was some pretty fierce shit."

I loved that she wasn't embarrassed one bit by her behavior.

Thankfully, ticks weren't rampant, but we'd seen some other girls having them removed at the bonfire or outside their cabins. Even the little eight-year-olds hadn't caused a commotion like Emma's. But she never commented on her conduct, only on how many Fun Dips it would take to suppress her anxiety.

Eleven

JACK

Before meeting up with my Voyagers group, I wanted to talk to Liz and see where her head was, so I had her paged to the office, and I met her in front of the building.

She had a big smile on her face when she saw me. "Hi, Jack! Fancy meeting you here. I was just paged." She hugged me.

"I know. I had them call you. Do you have a sec?"

"I always do for you," she said as we separated.

Liz was the same age as me, and we'd known each other for about five years, back since she was a camper, but it wasn't until last year when we'd started to become friends. She went to Southern Illinois University, and we'd emailed each other a few times throughout the school year. We'd actually tried to arrange for her to come visit me one weekend, but as the date had approached, I'd decided to cancel.

We walked up the driveway that led in and out of the campgrounds—one of the only paved roads on the premises—to a short hiking trail near the main road.

"Off the beaten path today?" she commented.

I stopped when we got a few steps into the trail and put my hands in my pockets. "Hey, I just wanted to talk to you—"

"I'm so glad." Liz stepped closer.

She slid her hands inside the crook of my elbows and embraced me. Then, she stood on her toes and pressed her lips to mine. We kissed, and then I took my hands out of my pockets and removed hers from around my waist.

She giggled, and it annoyed the shit out of me for some reason. I looked behind me and then back at her.

She went in for the kill a second time, but I stopped her.

"What?" she said, all pouty.

I rolled my neck. "Liz, look, I want to talk to you because I need to make sure things are cool between us. I mean, before camp started was kind of weird. After the night we went out drinking, I felt bad about things the next day."

She shrugged. "There's nothing to feel bad about, Jack, only good." She launched herself at me again.

"Liz—" I put my hands up to stop her, and they landed on her breasts, so I immediately dropped them. "Sorry."

"It's fine," she quipped.

"I just want to make sure we're both on the same page here. I can't get involved with you while we're at camp. You know that. Bob would kill me, and I'd risk losing my college credits."

She smiled coyly and batted her lashes. "He's your uncle. He'd never do that to *you*."

"Ever since I was five, he's been looking for a reason to rid himself of me."

She reached out and grabbed my hand, and I let her.

"Jack, you are too cute. Just know that we can sneak off like this anytime you want. In fact, I will talk to Maggie, and you and I can have *gelato*"—she winked, and I cringed at the word—"in my bunk while the girls are all at dinner one night."

What is it with women?

They'd say they wanted you to be honest and up front with them.

Just tell me the truth, they'd say.

Just don't bullshit me and lead me on, they'd plead.

But when I tried to be polite and get to the point by being kind and conversational, rather than confrontational, they wouldn't get the point.

If I flat-out said, *I'm not interested in you. Please stop massaging my bicep and blinking at me like you have cat hair stuck in your eye, so we can both move on and ignore each other*, then I'd be an asshole.

But when I tried to be courteous and precise, all women would ever do was ignore what I'd said because they assumed it wasn't rude enough for me to actually mean it.

"That's not going to happen," I said.

"Don't worry. I've already talked to her about it, and—"

I took a step backward and ran my hands through my hair. "Liz, don't fucking talk to anyone about me at all. Do you understand?"

My choice words caught her off guard.

As soon as I'm a dick, girls take notice. Mr. Nice Guy never gets the same attention. Women have no clue what they want.

I shook my head. "I'm sorry," I said. "What happened between us that night was fun, but it can't go beyond that, and I can't have you talking to people around camp about us."

She cocked her head to one side and crossed her arms. That was never a good sign.

"Fun?" she repeated.

I knew better than to respond.

"What happened was *fun*?" she said.

"Liz, I'm sorry if I misled you. That was not my intention."

She uncrossed her arms and pointed a finger in my face. "This is about Brittany Bingham, isn't it?"

"What?" I nearly lost my footing.

"I hear her talking about the two of you all the time, but I assumed she was delusional. You're dumping me for some sixteen-year-old sleazebag? Have a nice time in prison, Jack."

I was now blinking faster than her. "I seriously have no clue what you are talking about. There is nothing going on between Brittany and me. Nothing. I barely talk to her. I don't know what she's been saying, but it's not true. I promise you."

"She's been saying that you two sneak off to the docks at night, that you've fooled around together more than once. All the counselors assumed she was lying. But now that you're dumping me, I'm thinking that maybe she's not."

Maybe once I've been a practicing child psychologist for a couple of decades, I will have a better understanding of the female brain. Until then, I'm screwed.

I took a deep breath and met her eyes. I kept my voice low and in control as I said, "First of all, I am not dumping you." I felt compelled to implore her ego and put it at ease. "I mean, we were not officially dating, so there's no way you could be getting dumped, right? Second, you've known me for a long time, and I think you know—I hope you know—that I'm not a bullshitter."

She nodded.

"Thank you. So, please believe me when I tell you that there is nothing, nada, going on between Brittany Bingham and me, and there's no chance of it happening."

She nodded again, and I let out a sigh of relief.

"Well, you might want to tell her that," Liz said, crossing her arms again.

"I will handle that on my own. Just leave it be, please. You know as well as I do how these girls like to make up stories."

"That's for sure."

"So, are we good? You're one of my favorite people here, and I'm sorry this conversation went south. I never wanted to make you upset or mad at me, and I definitely don't want to lose our friendship over some stupid *gelato*."

She giggled. "We're all good, J.D." Then, she leaped forward and stuck her tongue down my throat. "Just wanted one more lick." She winked and walked away.

I checked my watch and realized I was fifteen minutes late to the Voyagers meeting, so I sprinted from the front of the campgrounds to the back where the girls were all waiting by the docks.

I had to catch my breath before I spoke, "Sorry to keep you all waiting."

Brittany smiled at me. The smart half of my brain knew I shouldn't say anything to her. Girls were always gossiping and creating stories, simply for the sake of doing so. The stupid part of my brain wanted to take her to the boathouse and bitch her out for being an obnoxious brat. Hopefully, the smart part would eventually explain that time alone with me in the boathouse was precisely what she would want.

I looked at all the girls, and only Julia was looking everywhere else but at me.

"All right, today, we're going to tackle steps one and five—portaging a canoe and canoeing a certain distance on your own. Portage means to carry, in case anyone was unclear about that. Has anyone ever been in a canoe before?"

All but Emma and Julia raised their hands.

"Okay. Emma and Julia, I will ride with each of you for your first time out."

Brittany raised her hand. "My mistake. I haven't canoed before either."

"Very funny, Brittany. I know you've canoed many times before," I said.

She shot Julia a dirty look.

"Will is already down by the water with the canoes, so let's head over there, and he'll get you situated."

Emma raised her hand. "How much do they weigh?"

"About forty-five pounds. It's not so much the weight as it is the size. Concentrate on the balancing act, and you should be fine."

"Oh, yes, because I'm so graceful," she said.

"And strong," I told her.

We all walked to the water's edge.

"Let's go, everyone. Pick your canoe. Will here is going to help make sure none of you drop a canoe on your head or your foot…or on someone else's. Will, can you demonstrate for us?"

Will nodded. "Sure thing. Watch, and do as I do. First, stand your canoe on its side, like this."

The girls looked at each other, stretching and yawning, before doing as he'd asked.

"Now that your canoes are on their sides, you're going to grab the yoke—the bar in the middle—on each end with opposite hands, like this." Will expertly flipped the canoe in the air and above his head.

Almost all the girls' canoes fell over with a loud bang as they attempted to follow suit, except for Julia's.

"Pick 'em up, ladies!" Will shouted.

They did, much like reluctant children being forced to clean up their toys.

"Let's try this again. Next, lift the canoe—please do not drop it—up to your waist and then over your head as you pivot your body forward. Watch me first." Will whipped the boat over his head.

The girls laughed as if they'd never be able to match what they'd just seen.

Emma raised her hand again. "I'm going to need a helmet."

"You'll be fine," Will told her. "Let me demonstrate one more time. Once it's in the air, it's really more about finding a balance and keeping your arms tight."

He flipped the canoe over his head once again, and Julia did it along with him at the same time.

"Hey, good job, Pearl," I said. Then, I saw her arms beginning to shake, so I ran over to help her. "I got it."

"I'm fine," she said.

"You sure?" I asked with my hand still on the front end.

"You're messing up my balance." Her lips were tightly pursed, and sweat was pooling on her forehead.

I smiled and removed my hand, which caused the canoe to slam on the ground.

Once the girls had each achieved a modicum of success with their portage skill, we tackled the water. Will assisted the four girls who'd had some experience before while I helped Julia and Emma.

"She can go first," Emma said as she lay flat on the sand, soaking up the sun. "I need a nap."

Julia looked at me.

"You ready, Pearl?" I asked her.

"Ready as I'll ever be."

"You never know, my friend. You just never know."

We both stood there, staring at the boat.

"Portage your canoe to the water, sailor," I told her.

"Aye, aye, captain." She saluted me.

"What? No eye roll with that?"

She laughed but kept her eyes level. She definitely struggled to lift the canoe over her petite self, and then she disappeared beneath it. Watching her carry it to the water was like watching an ant carry a raisin. Once at the water's edge, her arms shook as she carefully lowered the canoe into the lake and held it in place with her foot.

"Good job, kid. I mean, Pearl." I paused to look at her expression. "And there's my eye roll. Okay, get your life vest zipped, and step in. I will give us a push off and then join you."

I removed my shirt and put on my sunglasses that had been hanging around my neck. The boat tilted to one side when I got in, and there was about two inches of water sloshing around the bottom. Once I sat down and we were stable, I maneuvered us away from the shore, and then I handed her the paddle.

The lake was flat, and the sun was bright. A couple of dragonflies buzzed by as she was getting her bearings.

"Did you bring any sunglasses?" I asked.

She shook her head. The blues of her eyes were iridescent.

"Take mine." I lifted the glasses and the rope over my head.

"Thanks," she said with a tiny grin and put them on.

There was something about this girl's smile that made me sit straighter. I felt strong and accomplished if I was able to make her happy and bring her personality to light.

We were facing each other, and I saw her struggling to stay confident, so I leaned forward and adjusted her grip on the paddle. "Let me help you. So, you're going to take a few strokes on either side until you find your rhythm. The trick is to move the boat and not the paddle. What I mean by that is, you want to pull the boat, rather than splash the paddle around in the water."

She looked at me, listening.

"You want to keep the paddle shaft vertical to the boat and then pull back. Don't lean your body over the side to paddle, or we'll both be going swimming."

"Gotcha," she said.

"You'll get the hang of it. Just play around with the paddle at first to find which side you're most comfortable on, and you'll be able to tell how to maneuver the boat. If you want to turn the boat, you will keep the paddle on one side until you've spun it around."

She nodded, and I sat back and let her take over.

"You really need to keep your hands in position—one at the top and one at the bottom of the shaft, like this." I took her hands and slid them into place.

She seemed nervous.

"You okay?"

She nodded.

"You're kind of quiet today."

Julia laid the paddle across the boat, and we drifted toward the other side of the lake.

"I did what you told me," she said.

"Uh, no. I told you to keep your hands on the paddle."

She gave me a smirk. "I wrote my mom a letter."

I let my arms fall in my lap. "When?"

"Yesterday." She looked out at the water.

Julia intrigued me. In the few weeks I'd known her, there were times when I'd come close to reaching out to her—wanting to find her after dinner to see if she wanted to talk, to try to get her to open up to me again so that I could comfort her. But it would be hard to care for her without letting my own curiosities get in the way. I'd thought it would be better to pull back, but every time we were together, I could feel myself being drawn back in.

"Did you mail it?"

She shook her head.

"Why not?"

She thought for a moment as she adjusted the rubber band in her hair. "I don't have an address for her. Anytime I've written a letter to her, I've handed it to my dad to mail."

We both looked at each other, thinking the same thing.

"Do you think he's kept your letters and never mailed them? That would be a dick move."

She sat up straight and glared at me. "My dad's not a dick."

"That doesn't answer the question," I said.

The corners of her mouth turned down.

"Hey, I'm sorry. I'm sure he's a great guy."

"He is." Her voice cracked.

I leaned forward and gently removed my sunglasses from her face. Her eyes were filled with tears.

"Don't get upset. Please. I'm much happier when you're smiling."

She wiped beneath her eyes. "I'm fine."

"Why don't you just ask your dad if you can have her address to send the letter directly?"

She nodded, her expression shy and sweet. Then, she picked up the paddle and began to move the boat back toward the camp, but we were only going in circles.

"You need to place your hands in position and then anchor the paddle in the water before pulling. Here, let me show you. Can you turn around so that your back is to me? I'm afraid if I stand up, we're going to capsize."

Julia stayed low and scooted her body around, and I moved forward, so she was nestled between my legs. I'd instructed hundreds of campers the same way over the years, but this time felt intimate. We held the paddle together and made uniform strokes in the water, my chin brushing the side of her face, just above her temple.

"Can I ask what you said in your letter? Or is it private?"

"It's private, but it was nothing too exciting. Just that I'm at camp, that I miss her, and that I've met some really great people."

She leaned back and pressed her shoulder into the base of my neck, and I had to fight the urge to embrace her.

"Your turn."

I let go of the paddle, and she steered us to shore.

I lowered my head. "I'm proud of you, Julia," I whispered into her ear.

"Thanks."

TWELVE

Julia

After her canoe lesson, Emma literally emerged from the lake, soaking wet. She and Jack had capsized four times as the rest of us looked on.

She peeled her T-shirt away from her skin as she walked onto shore, and it bubbled up before settling about two inches above her belly. "I did it!" she hollered, raising her arms.

We all laughed and clapped for her.

Jack, still shirtless and glistening in the afternoon sun, dragged her boat up the sand. "Okay, Voyagers, great job today. You should all be really proud of yourselves."

"Some more than others," Brittany said under her breath, chiding Emma.

But Emma didn't hear. She was too busy high-fiving Will and congratulating herself. I wasn't about to let Brittany spoil it for her.

"I'll see you all tomorrow at the same time, but we'll meet near The Cove," Jack said.

Then, he and Will went about putting the boats and paddles in the boathouse.

Emma wrapped a towel around her shoulders and grabbed her beach bag, and then we started to walk back to our cabins to shower and change for dinner.

"Well, that was fun. Not," she said. "Looked to me like you and J.D. were getting cozy out there. Don't tell me you didn't die when he took off his shirt."

"Oh my God, totally."

"Now, correct me if I'm wrong, but were you sitting on his lap out there, or what? It looked like you were sitting on his…" She elbowed me in the chest. "Lap."

I stopped walking and lifted my brows. "I sort of was."

"I knew it!" she whisper-shouted. "Why, you little slut. You gave him a lap dance and sat on his canoe!"

We both snorted with laughter.

I threw my hand over her mouth. "Would you shut it?"

Okay, so maybe I hadn't actually been sitting on his lap, but I was in between his legs with the warmth of his chest pressing against my bare skin.

Thank you, Tommy Hilfiger bikini! I am never washing you!

My head had never spun so out of control as it had in that canoe with his arms hovering over mine as I tried to slide my hands into position on the paddle. Then, his hands had rested on my wrists, staying there and guiding me long after I'd gotten into the groove of paddling on my own.

I was imagining him kissing my neck and brushing my hair and being my boyfriend, my everything. He would call me each night before bed, and we'd talk on the phone until I'd have to hang up. He'd beg me to come visit him at college where I'd stay in his room and watch TV while he was at class. His roommate would for sure think I was awesome and introduce me to his girlfriend. She and I would do our nails together and hang out until our boyfriends came back, and we'd all go to dinner. Buffalo Wild Wings maybe? And I'd drink, like, two liters of Coke while they flashed fake IDs and drank beer. Then, we'd go back to Jack's dorm room, and we'd give each other back massages. He'd be drunk and handsy, and I'd be in heaven.

I'd only ever kissed two people before. One was like a saliva volcano erupting in my mouth, and the other was everything I'd hoped it would be—until the blue-raspberry slushy had happened.

The first was Doug Dillard. He was two years older than me, and it was a dare. We had all been hanging out in my friend's basement, and he and I had gone into a brightly lit spare room where neither of us could find a light switch, so we'd kissed under fluorescent lighting, like two criminals under interrogation. I'd watched him close his eyes and open his mouth at the same time, and then he'd put his hands on my shoulders and pressed his lips to mine before licking me like a Popsicle.

The other time was with a boy named Jimmy Scarpino. He was Italian, and I'd loved him. He was my age, and he'd grown up down the street from me. His father owned about forty Blockbusters in Illinois, and Jimmy used to give me free rental coupons. They had a lot of money, and every summer, they'd host an annual neighborhood block party—which Mr. Scarpino naturally called the Annual Blockbuster Block Party—with bouncy houses and catered food and a local band.

Jimmy and I had been dating—which at thirteen years old had pretty much meant just saying that we were dating—for about two months when he kissed me on the night of the party. He'd taken my hand and pulled me behind our neighbors, The Hanleys', house, and we climbed into their hammock. Lying on his side, Jimmy had leaned over me, and a second after we'd locked eyes under the moonlight, he'd kissed me, soft and warm and careful. It was like nothing I'd ever felt before. My heart had started beating faster as his body pressed into me, and his hands had reached for mine. He had been gentle and loving—nothing like drooly Doug Dillard—as he pressed his lips to mine, softly and with the utmost expertise. My hands had flown around his neck, and I had felt like I was flying, floating, flailing as we kissed each other all over.

I would have stayed in that hammock for all eternity if something freezing cold and wet hadn't hit my head and begun dripping down the sides of my face. I screamed, and so did Jimmy, and we were both thrown off the ropes onto the grass. Apparently, he'd been expertly locking lips with the Hanleys' daughter, too. She'd chosen to let me know by dumping a blue raspberry slushie on my head.

Idiot.

Emma was searching my face for more details of my time alone with Jack. "You love him," she said matter-of-factly.

"Shut up."

"You love him, and you want to be his personal sun lotion puter-on-er, so you can rub greasy oil over his biceps and his canoe." She laughed at herself.

I looked over my shoulder and then back at her. "He's really nice, too."

Emma's comments were frivolous, but my feelings for Jack weren't.

She made an expression that said, *So what?*

"I mean, he's easy to talk to. He's sort of helped me with a few things with my mom."

She now looked confused.

"I haven't really told you anything about my parents," I said.

"Are they divorced?"

"Yeah."

"Mine, too. No biggie." She shrugged.

As we walked, she kept tugging at her shirt, so it'd dry faster.

"It's just that I haven't seen her since I was eleven. My dad kicked her out, and that was it."

"Why did he kick her out?"

My stomach tightened as it normally did when I talked about my mom. I looked up at the warmth in Emma's face. Her question was honest and curious and not judgmental, as often was the case.

"I didn't know it at the time, but she was doing drugs and sleeping with some guy behind my dad's back. I think she might have had one too many DUIs also."

It always sounded so scandalous because it was. Even after all these years, I still couldn't say it aloud without shaking my head in disbelief. My mother was a drug addict. *Seriously?*

"Whoa. That blows." Emma whacked a couple of trees with a stick she'd picked up along the way. "Have you tried to find her?"

"She was in rehab for a while. I have written to her. For a long time, my dad made it seem like I wasn't allowed to ask about her, and then he remarried and acted like the first eleven years of my life had never happened." I paused and shook it off.

"Do you get along with your dad?"

"It took me a while, but yes, we're close now. He's all I have, and even if he did something extreme, I know that it would be because he loves me."

She smirked. "How many years of therapy did you have before you could say that with a straight face?"

"Two and a half." I laughed. "Anyway, Jack was really great when I told him about everything."

Emma tossed her stick and dug a pack of gum out of her bag. She handed me a piece before unwrapping her own. "I've got stepparents, too. You want to know the secret to getting along with your stepmom?"

I chewed my gum and nodded. "Sure, but I think it's too late though."

"It's never too late. Does she have kids of her own?"

"Two. Both younger than me."

She stopped walking, and so did I.

"Perfect. When you get home, you become their best pal. You buy them shit, you play with them, you invite them to sleep in your bed with you...and then you turn them against her."

I burst out laughing. "Sounds like a lot of work for something that's never going to happen."

Emma stretched her arms over her head. Then, she bent forward at her waist and hung there. "My muscles are sore." Her shirt dropped down to her shoulders. "As soon as my stepsister, Kaley, thought I was the bomb, she started getting mad at her mom anytime her mom would reprimand me for anything. It was awesome! Her mom hates when Kaley is upset about anything, even the goddamn weather, so she immediately backs off my ass."

"I'll have to give that a try. So far, avoidance and bitterness have been my weapons of choice," I said. "Anyway, Jack suggested I write my mom a letter. It's weird because you'd think I would've come up with that all on my own. Sometimes though, she's so off my radar, but other times, I think of nothing else but her."

Emma rolled herself up, red-faced after letting the blood rush to her head, and she shook her shoulders. "So, did you write her?"

"Yeah, but I haven't mailed it yet."

"That's cool. Can I read it?"

"Why?"

"Why not?"

I glanced at the ground and then back at her. "Maybe. Let me think about it."

Just then, the twins, in matching crop tops and running shorts, walked past us in a bit of a hurry.

"You two sloths haven't showered yet?" Brittany said, halting her pace.

"My pits are just getting ripe," Emma added. "Where are you off to? Dinner's not for an hour."

"We're assisting in the kitchen tonight as part of our cooking class."

"Thank God we have our own food section," Emma said.

"Oh, wow, you're hilarious. Well, too bad you'll miss out. Hope you enjoy your salad or whatever it is you're allowed to eat." Brittany turned to walk away but then spun back around and raised a finger at me. "Oh, and don't get too chummy with J.D. I saw you two on the canoe today."

Emma and I looked at each other and then back at the twins. Brianna just stared at her sister as if she were standing there, reading a menu.

"She'll do what she wants." Emma took a step forward, so I put my hand on her arm. "And on what planet do you think he'd be interested in a Anna Nicole Smith wannabe?" She paused. "She is your idol, right?"

Brittany lowered her lids and released a manufactured laugh, and then she slapped her sister's shoulder, causing her to almost fall over. "Look who's got a bodyguard?"

The twins walked away, and Emma took my hand.

"I'd rather eat tick poo than anything those bitches cooked for me," she said.

Emma and I showered, and then she came to my cabin where she sat and read *InStyle* magazine on my bunk while I swept the floors. She was wearing a Hollow Creek sweatshirt with shorts, long running socks pulled up to her knees, and her shower sandals.

"Let's talk more about lover boy," she said.

"Let's not. Brittany is no more delusional than I am."

She threw the magazine down. "I seriously think he likes you." She bounced like she was testing a new mattress. "Do you or do you not want to lick his face?"

I laughed.

"Well?" she asked.

I finished sweeping and put the broom away before joining her on the bed. "There was something between us today." I balled my hands into fists. "Like when he was behind me in the canoe. But it's probably all in my head."

"Did he press his paddle against you?"

I smacked her, but I couldn't get my mind off of him. I thought of the warmth of his skin, his tenderness and patience with me, his chest brushing against my spine. Recalling his legs wrapped around me sent chills down my arms.

She continued, "He's totally into you. He gave you his sweatshirt. He begged you to be in Voyagers. He asked about your mom and your family. He takes all these little moments to be alone with you. You love each other. It's as simple as that." She put her mouth next to my ear. "Would you have sex with him?"

Her question made me picture him naked—naked and kissing me in a rainstorm. No, a thunderstorm. Then, I fidgeted and shook away the imagery.

"Have you had sex before?" she asked.

I shook my head. "I want to, but I haven't. How about you?"

"Twice. With a guy named Tig."

I wasn't surprised that Emma wasn't a virgin. It was just one more interesting thing about her as far as I was concerned. "Tig?"

"His last name was Tiggerson."

I nodded. "Was it fun?"

She stuck her bottom lip out and pondered. "It was kind of fun. We were walking home together from the library, and he asked me if I wanted to hang out at his house. His parents weren't home, so we went to his bedroom, and it just kind of happened. Before I knew it, I had been devirginized, and I was downstairs on his couch, watching *Wheel of Fortune* and eating carrot sticks and hummus."

I snickered. "I think I love you."

"Oh, I know you do." She shoved my shoulder with hers. "So, how many times have you thought about getting sweaty with our fearless, hairless leader?"

"Who are you guys talking about?" a voice trailed in from behind us like a poisonous gas leak.

We both spun around and saw Liz standing there with her hands on her hips, and her head was cocked to the side.

"No one," I said quickly.

She came closer. "No, seriously. Who are you talking about? Not anyone here I hope. You know it's strictly forbidden to *fraternize* with any of the male staff. You'll get kicked out of camp, and your parents won't get their money back. And if any of the male staff is coming on to you, you'd better come clean right now because that is an offense that will get him fired."

I'd never seen Liz so intense. If she had wanted us to be honest and confide in her, she'd taken the wrong approach.

Emma stood. "Oh, Lizzard, of course we're not talking about anyone here. We're talking about Julia's boyfriend back home. He's a studmuffin, naturally, and she's missing him."

Liz looked at me, wanting to believe Emma. "Aw, what's his name?" Vapid Liz had come back in a snap.

I froze. "His name...it's, uh...Jimmy. Jimmy Scarpino. And he hasn't written yet, so I feel like he's totally blowing me off now that I'm away all summer. Probably hooking up with this sleazebag neighbor chick who lives on the same block as us. He promised to be faithful and not to even text another girl, even as friends, but you know..."

Emma drew her finger horizontally across her neck, so I shut up.

Liz curled her lips in sympathy. "I thought you were maybe talking about Jack."

I swallowed.

"Jack who?" Emma asked, batting her eyes.

"Jack, J.D., your Voyagers leader." She didn't say, *Duh*, but her tone did.

Emma burst out laughing. "As if!" she said. "He sure is hot though."

Liz plopped down on the bunk across from us, kicked off her flip-flops, and sat cross-legged. "Yes, he is." She paused. "He and I are dating, so that's why I might have sounded a bit defensive."

Emma and I exchanged wide-eyed glances as Liz gazed down at her hands.

I managed to respond, "No way."

She nodded and then threw her head back, stretching her neck. "We kinda started liking each other last summer, and then we finally hooked up this year before all you guys arrived."

Her words *we finally hooked up* hung in the air like a fart.

Emma leaned forward and propped her head up with her elbows on her knees. "Do tell," she said.

Liz scanned the cabin and then gave a small shrug. "We're trying to keep it under wraps."

Obviously not.

She uncrossed her legs and stood. Then, she slid her feet back into her shoes. "You two coming to dinner?"

"Wouldn't miss it," Emma said.

Liz left, grabbing a clipboard on the way out.

"Weird," Emma said to me once she was gone.

I got up and went to my shelves where I found a hooded sweatshirt, slipped my arms in the sleeves, and zipped it up. "Weird how?"

Emma followed me, and we exited the cabin. "Weird that she would confide in us and weird that he would be interested in her. Something's up, Julia."

"The first day I got here, she jumped him like he was a mechanical bull, and then she whispered something about the two of them having ice cream."

"Ew," she said.

We both giggled, but I was deflated.

My head was screwed on just as loose as Brittany's. I had been convincing myself that Jack had singled me out—that I was someone special, that he'd chosen me to befriend, to care about, and to dote on—when, in fact, it was his fucking job. He was paid to attend to the campers and make sure they felt loved and safe and protected while away from their families.

I shook my head as we walked, and I felt as stupid as I'd ever felt. I couldn't believe I'd told him about the letter to my mom. *Like he cares.*

We were almost to the mess hall when Brittany jogged past us.

"Where to, Martha Stewart?" Emma shouted after her.

"Liz and Maggie asked me to get the box of bandanas from the cabin. It's *ho*edown night," she said, emphasizing the *ho*. "Unless you want to get in a little extra workout and run back there for me?"

"I'm the picture of good health," Emma said, slapping her thighs.

Brittany turned and went on her way.

Once inside the mess hall, we made sure to hit the Kids with Food Allergies buffet just to spite the twins and make sure we wouldn't eat their food.

After dinner, the whole camp gathered at The Cove for a barn dance–themed bonfire. Two Guys and a Guitar played some country music, and we all were given Hollow Creek bandanas as a gift.

Once the music was over and the little kids had gone back to their cabins, Emma, Amber, and I, and two girls from Emma's cabin hung out on the logs, talking in the dark and drinking warm apple cider, when Brittany came up behind me and started talking—or rather, reading.

"I wish I knew what to say. I don't know why you haven't come to see me or called me or answered any of my letters. Daddy tells me you're fine, but—"

My ears went hot. "Give that to me!" I stood and almost fell over the log, trying to grab the paper out of her hand.

"I miss you so much that it hurts when I talk about you—"

My teeth were clenched, and my body temperature matched the dissipating flames behind us. "You went through my things?" I screamed.

Brittany kept reading.

"Give it to me!" I hollered.

Just then, Emma came up behind Brittany and put her in a choke hold, causing Brittany to drop the letter I'd written to my mom.

When Emma released her, Brittany rubbed her neck and laughed. "It was Bree-*ah*-na's genius idea. Maybe you'll remember how to pronounce her name next time."

THIRTEEN

Julia

"Jesus!" Emma chased after me as I ran. "Julia! I can't keep up. I
had, like, fourteen Southern-style s'mores!"

But I didn't stop. I ran up the hill, past the office building and
the mess hall, behind the staff quarters, and up the paved road that
led to the main road. Emma eventually caught up to me and bent
over, her hands on her knees, as she tried to catch her breath.

"She's just jealous of you," Emma managed to say.

I wasn't crying. I was enraged, infuriated, violated. Even
though Brittany had only entertained the group with a portion of
the letter, I knew she and her sister and God knew who else had
read the whole thing. And it had been buried under my bed with
my personal things!

"Jealous of what?" I screamed, spinning around to face her.

Emma lifted a hand like she needed a minute, and then she
took a deep breath and let it out. "You're gorgeous and smart. You
have Jack's attention, and she doesn't. I don't give a shit what Liz
told us. Maybe he's a total man-whore, but he's into you, and it's as
obvious to Brittany as it is to me. She's as jealous of you as I am
out of shape."

I couldn't see or think straight. I wanted to tell Emma she
wasn't out of shape and that I loved her more than anything for
choking Brittany, but I couldn't speak, so I spit. I spit on the
ground. Then, I tore up the letter, tossed it on the ground, and spit
on it, too. And then, the tears came.

Emma hugged me and let me wipe my eyes on her bandana. "She'll get what's coming to her. I promise you. My mama swears that Karma's a bitch, and my mama don't lie. Maybe Karma will take a dump in Brittany's pillowcase. Who knows?"

I choked out a laugh and wiped my eyes and nose. "Thanks for stepping in."

"Of course."

"Why did you have to let go of her neck?"

Emma shrugged. "If Brittany is dead…well, where's the fun in that?"

I met her eyes. "I don't want anyone else knowing what happened—obviously besides whoever was standing there."

She zipped her lips with an imaginary zipper. "What about your mom's letter?" She pointed at the paper shreds.

I stared at the torn pieces, mortified. "She probably wouldn't have gotten it anyway."

Emma and I walked back down the hill to the campgrounds, and Liz was standing outside the office building with one of Brittany's counselors, Elaine. Elaine was short with stubby legs and huge calf muscles. She had naturally curly hair that she'd force into an unkempt bun each day and little hands, one of which was disappearing into a bag of Skittles at a furious rate.

"Oh my God, Julia. What happened back there? Some of the girls told me Brittany said something to make you cry. Are you okay? What did she say?" Elaine proceeded to chew, crunch, chew, crunch, and then she put her hand in the bag to repeat the cycle.

Emma looked at me, and I looked at Liz.

"Is this about *Jack*?" Liz said.

"Jack?" Elaine squealed. "As in, J.D.?"

I clutched the pieces of torn paper in my hand and then slid my hand into my pocket. "No!" I snapped at Liz. "Why would this be about Jack? Why would you even say that? Seriously, you need to stop asking that." My eyes went wide as I stared her down.

Is there no one with any sort of tact around here?

But the truth was, it was about Jack. I was falling for him, and Brittany knew it. *Why else would she have been hell-bent on shaming me?*

Elaine shook her unruly bun, as if she felt out of the loop. And she was, but I wasn't about to rat on Brittany because then I would have to tell everyone standing there my business, exposing my deepest, darkest, most personal shame. And I was guessing Brittany knew I wouldn't want to make a big spectacle because she didn't seem too concerned when she, her sister, and another girl from their cabin sauntered by without a care in the world.

"Brit!" Elaine screamed to her.

Brittany stopped walking but didn't come over to us. "What?" she answered, annoyed.

"Come over here," Elaine said.

"I'm on my way back to the cabin. I'll talk to you there." Brittany turned and walked away.

Thank God.

Emma shoved her open palm in front of Elaine, and Elaine poured about five Skittles into her hand.

"Thanks. We're going to head back, too. It's all good," Emma said.

"You sure?" Liz said to me.

I rolled my eyes. "I never said anything was wrong."

"Okay." She put her hands up in defense and exchanged a look with Elaine that said, *Whatever.*

Somehow, I made it through the night without sneaking into Brittany's cabin and dumping sugar packets all over her bunk bed in hopes that she'd get swarmed by a colony of angry red fire ants. I would act as her Karma, if need be, but it wasn't going to be tonight.

A few welcome uneventful days later, Jack asked all the Voyagers to skip lunch in the mess hall and announced that we'd be tackling steps three and six of our survival skills—boiling water and cooking a meal over an open fire. We met him behind the staff housing and walked off into the woods until we found a small clearing. Emma wore a baseball hat, a long-sleeved shirt, jeans, socks, and gym shoes.

All six of us dropped our bags where Jack stopped, and we listened as he recited the menu.

"This is the fun stuff. We're going to start by lighting our fires again, but I'm not going to have each of you do your own. Instead, I'm going to split you into two groups. Can you ladies manage to make two groups of three on your own, or do I need to assign you?"

Emma grabbed Amber and me. "We're all good over here, Coach!"

"Okay, good. First, we're going to boil water just for practice. Then, we're going to dump the water and make some grub. Brianna, your group is going to make campfire nachos. Emma, your group is going to make campfire sausages and breakfast potatoes. Even though it's lunchtime, it'll still be delicious." He reached into the cooler he'd dragged with him and pulled out a five-pound bag of shredded cheddar. "And we can melt cheese on everything if you'd all like. I know I would." He left the lid open. "All the ingredients and recipes are inside, so come and get what you need." He took a step back. "Julia, can I talk to you for a second?"

Before answering him, I looked over at Brittany. "Of course!" I said with the enthusiasm of a caffeinated preschool teacher.

Jack loosely placed his arm around my shoulder and led me a few steps away but in full view of the group.

"What's up?" I asked.

He shifted his weight to one hip, put his hands in his pockets, lowered his chin, and looked me square in the eyes. "I heard something went down with you and Brittany the other day."

I shrugged. "You heard wrong." I remained as cheerful and upbeat as ever.

Brittany would get no satisfaction out of embarrassing me in front of Jack.

He cocked his head to the side and narrowed his eyes. It was hard to keep my cool with him staring at me. He'd captivated me from the moment we met, and I knew that my fascination with him read like a flashing digital sign running across my face.

I THINK YOU'RE HOT. PLEASE TAKE YOUR LIME-GREEN EYES WITH THEIR CUPID'S ARROW LASER BEAMS AND POINT THEM ELSEWHERE BEFORE I PASS OUT LIKE SOME ROOKIE FAN AT A BACKSTREET BOYS CONCERT. PLEASE DON'T THINK I'M LIKE EVERY LOVE-STRUCK HORMONAL FEMALE CAMPER WHO HAS

DREAMED OF MARRYING YOU. I'M DIFFERENT.
I'M REAL. I'M NOT LIKE EVERYONE ELSE.

Or am I?

He cleared his throat. "I want you to tell me if she or anyone else is bothering you."

I crossed my arms but kept my smile. "I'm fine, really. There's nothing she can do to bother me because I don't care about her." I looked away for a second and then back at him.

My dad always told me not to let people get a rise out of me. "If someone is bothering you, you just pretend you don't care," he'd say. "Once they know you care, it's all over. But if they think you don't give a shit about what they're doing, then there's no fun in it for them." He'd usually finish with, "Or we could just sue them."

Jack smiled at me with his lips together and replied with a singular nod.

I uncrossed my arms. "Better help with those campfire taters." I walked off. I could feel his eyes on my back as I deliberately passed Brittany on the way to my trio, and I gave her the happiest look I could muster.

Maybe, despite holding my chin high and not telling the counselors what Brittany had done, I did care that she'd invaded my privacy and mocked my weaknesses, and maybe she knew it. And maybe my mother would've gotten the letter if I had been able to find her address rather than rely on my father to send it. And someday, just maybe, Jack would look at me like a woman and not like a young camper covered in mosquito bites with dirt under her nails.

Emma tore open the bag of diced potatoes so hard that about half of them fell to the dirt. That led to a quick game of flicking the frozen potatoes at the other group, which was quickly squashed by Jack.

After our meals were complete, we all sat in a circle and enjoyed the feast. Thanks to me, there was no tension between Brittany and me because I wasn't going to give her the satisfaction. If she was head over heels for Jack, so was I. If she was delusional enough to think he'd risk everything to be with her, so was I. She and I had more in common than she realized.

Jack sat in the circle between Emma and Amber, and I couldn't help but wonder what it was like to be him. He was a smart, good-looking guy, who had to know that all the girls lusted after him. It was quite the responsibility for a young man—to be burdened with being one of a handful of men in charge of so many horny girls.

Jesus, do all the girls think about him the same way I do? Does he talk with each of them on a one-on-one basis where he looks into their eyes and studies their souls like he has with me? Does he pretend to care about their broken families like he has with mine? Is the entire charade for college credit?

I took a deep breath and caught Brittany smiling at him, and he smiled back.

"All right," he began, "tomorrow night is the big solo overnight. Who's excited?"

A couple of girls mumbled, and others raised their hands.

"I thought we could maybe have a conversation about it, and this would be a good time to answer any questions you might have."

Crickets.

"No one has a question? Emma, I know you must have a question about something. Ticks? Flesh-eating spiders? Anything?" He laughed.

"Very funny," she said. "What if we have to take a shit?"

Most everyone in the circled laughed. Brittany rolled her eyes, but Jack took the inquiry in stride.

"That's actually a very good question. You take one wherever you can. I would suggest a few feet away from wherever you plan on sleeping."

Emma nodded. "Got it."

"Anyone else?" He looked around. "Don't be shy."

Amber lifted her hand. "What if something goes wrong, and we need help?"

"What could go wrong?" Brianna added.

Jack looked at them. "Chances are, other than extreme boredom setting in, nothing bad will happen to any of you, but there are a number of reasons you might feel you need help. In the past, one of the girls got her hair stuck in the zipper of her sleeping bag, so we don't do sleeping bags anymore, just blankets. Another time, we had a camper get her period unexpectedly." He paused to make an uncomfortable grunt of a noise. "So, now, I just ask that you be prepared. I want you all to bring as little as possible. Obviously, if you have any medications or might need feminine stuff, please bring it along. However, if you wear contacts, I'd prefer you to leave those behind and bring your glasses."

"I'm going to bring a box of maxi pads and build my own survival pillow," Emma declared.

Jack smiled and moved on. "Any other questions?" He looked around the circle. "No? Job well done tonight, ladies. Oh, wait. I forgot dessert. The lovely and talented cooking class—or as I like to call it, James Keating's Good Eating—prepared some cupcakes for us. Nut-free, of course."

"Of course," Brittany repeated as if she and her cooking class had been put out by the request.

Jack handed out the treats, and we all snarfed them down as we cleaned up our mess and threw everything back in the cooler.

"A camping rule of thumb is to make it look like you were never here. No trash or debris left behind. No burning flames left unattended. Always leave your spot as close to as it was when you arrived."

Like thieves in the night, we exited the woods without a trace and headed back to camp. The sun had set, and the lampposts had flickered on, lighting the dirt paths that ran in various directions all over the campgrounds.

Theo, the security guard, walked by and gave Jack a high five.

"Good night, everyone," Jack said to us.

"Good night," we answered in unison.

We all began going our separate ways.

Just then, Bob came out of nowhere and grabbed Jack by the elbow. I was too far away to hear what he was saying, but it didn't look too complimentary.

Fourteen

JACK

"Come with me, Jack." Bob pulled at my arm but I yanked it away.

"What's up?" I asked him. "Is this about leaving the coffee maker on? Because that wasn't me."

He rubbed his overgrown eyebrows. "Meet me in the office, and bring Will. Five minutes."

"I haven't seen Will since this morning. I don't know where he is. Have you checked with Tabitha?" I immediately regretted asking.

Bob, who'd been clumsily walking away, took a few hurried steps back to me. "What would Tabby know of his whereabouts? Are you being smart with me?"

I shook my head. "I'm always being smart, Bob. You taught me that." I smacked him on the shoulder like a basketball coach would slap his players as they came off the court. Then, I snapped my fingers. "Have you paged him?"

Bob dropped his hands to his sides and looked at me like I was a moron. I'd seen that look so many times before that it actually brought me a sense of comfort. I smiled.

"My office. Five minutes," he demanded before walking away.

"I'll be there in four and a half! Just need to change my shirt and wash my hands," I shouted after him and headed for the staff quarters.

Once I pushed through the front doors and walked inside, I grabbed a walkie-talkie out of my duffel and pressed the button on the side. "Will, it's Jack. Come in."

I tried again, but there was no answer. Will was notorious for never carrying his walkie, and since I didn't consider myself his babysitter, I tossed mine back into my bag. Bob could find Will himself.

I took two steps through the threshold of my room and turned on the lights. As soon as I did, I noticed Liz in my bed, under my covers, wearing what appeared to be nothing but a shit-eating grin and sucking on an orange slice.

"What the fu—"

"Turn the lights off, shhilly!" she whispered loudly.

I slapped my hand over the switch and took a quick breath as the room went dark again.

I spun around and closed the door behind me, my heart beating fast. "What are you doing here? You need to leave. Now."

"Come schit thown with me. Right here, Jackie," she slurred.

I ran my hand through my hair, placed my bag on the floor, and tried to remain calm. "Liz, you need to get out of here right now." I flicked on the closet light, so I could see her face. "Are you dressed?"

She proudly shook her head and patted the bed for me to join her.

I could see her clothes on the floor, so I picked them up and handed them to her. "Get dressed, please."

She rolled over to her side and propped herself up on her elbow. Then, she smiled with the bright orange peel in her mouth and giggle-snorted. The blanket was draped dangerously loose over her breasts that so much as a sneeze would force those things to come out. I looked away.

"You're shoo adorable when you're nervous."

"I'm not nervous. I just want you to get dressed." I kept my eyes on the floor. "Are you drunk?"

"Maybe. Maybe not."

I looked over at the bedside table between the two beds, and there was a little bowl of fruit sitting atop it. I lifted it and took a whiff.

Vodka.

Liz smiled. "Brought you some from the wap party."

Wapatuli was a college drink where people dumped various bottles of liquor into a large container, typically a garbage can, and then added fruit and ice. After letting it marinate, people would then drink it and eat the fruit.

"We soaked the fruit for twenty-four hours this time! You can hardly taste the alcohol in the oranges, and the watermelon went down like…water!" She cracked herself up. "Come thit by me!"

I crouched down next to the bed, getting drunk off her breath. Upon closer review, I saw she'd smeared mascara and lip gloss all over my pillowcase. "I'm glad you guys had some fun, but we need to move this little party out of here. Okay? You need to get dressed."

"I have underwear on." She quickly lifted the blanket to show me. "But I don't imagine they'll be on for long."

"Underwear is an excellent start, but let's get the rest of these on." I tapped her clothes.

"I've been thinking about you," she said, ignoring my requests. "In fact, looks like I'm not the only one." She laughed and waved a dismissive hand.

"I'm going to step out, and I'll meet you in the rec room. We can finish this conversation in there."

I went to stand, but she pulled me on top of her with more force than I had expected from a girl her size.

"Kish me." She sat up, and the blanket dropped.

As she pressed her lips to mine, she took my hand and placed it on her bare breast, holding it there. Her liquored citrus tongue tried to find its way inside my mouth. I pulled back and put both my hands on her shoulders, straightening my arms. A nervous laughter escaped my throat as I held her at bay, and I moved my feet off the bed and onto the floor.

"Come on, girl. Let's cover you up and maybe get you some alcohol-free food. Or coffee. Or sleep."

She sat up and thankfully held the blanket over her chest. "Jack!"

"Shh," I warned her.

"If I wanted to just *talk*, I wouldn't have wasted all this time waiting for you. Now, please come sit down before I scream."

I looked over my shoulder at the door, and then I walked over and sat opposite of her on Will's bed. My body temperature was rising with every syllable that came out of her mouth. I couldn't tell if she was being facetious by threatening to scream, so I leaned forward and spoke carefully, "I have to meet Bob in his office. I can't have you lying in my bed, all drunk—naked or clothed—while I'm gone. I think you know that."

She giggled.

"We can't do this, Liz. Come on. I know you don't want to get both of us in trouble."

She pondered that for a moment.

Thank God.

But then, she dropped the blanket again. At that point, there was no looking away. As much as I wanted to, a man's eyes were simply going to look at a woman's bare breasts, regardless of the circumstances.

Liz lowered her chin and leaned forward, placing her hand on my thigh.

Holy crap.

"I need to get you out of here." I stood and paced. Then shoved a handful of the drunken fruit into my mouth.

Liz's forehead crumpled between her eyes while the corners of her mouth turned down with humiliation, which was a huge red flag. I knew the drunk-humiliated combo would cause this situation to go from bad to worse if she turned her infatuation into mortification.

"Hey"—I knelt before her—"let's get you dressed and outside. Then, I can talk with Bob really quick, and afterward, you and I will meet up down by the boathouse. Okay? We can talk."

She smiled and nodded.

Thank God.

"I'll meet you outside," I said.

She slid another orange slice into her mouth and then lifted her shirt off the bed. I turned the closet light off, so the room would go dark and give her some more privacy. Just as I was about to put my hand on the doorknob and exit the room, the door flew open, and Bob was standing there. Liz puked almost on cue.

There was no mistaking the sounds of chunky vomit hitting the ceramic floor tiles.

The next few seconds were a series of, "Oh my God," attempted neck craning, me blocking Bob, me whacking Bob on the forearm as he tried to turn on the light, necks whipping back and forth, and utter emotional chaos. It ended with me shoving

Bob into the hall and slamming the door before he ever got his head past the threshold.

Bob backed out of the room as quickly as he'd entered, and I followed.

"What's going on in there? Who was that?"

I couldn't believe he hadn't seen her face. "I can explain."

Bob hiked his shorts up so high that I thought he might split his torso in half, and then he stomped off. Once he was at the end of the hallway, he looked back at me and pointed. "Bring whoever is in there with you to my office."

"I had no idea anyone was in there before I entered."

I started to go after him, but he raised a hand to silence me.

"Do you really expect me to believe that?"

I threw my hands up. "Yes! Yes, I do because it's the truth. I was on my way to meet up with you."

"But you didn't. You never came."

That part is true, I thought to myself.

"And you said you had to wash up or some other bullshit while I sat, waiting for you, and you were...you were..." He waved me off. "Ah, hell!"

"Ah, hell is right," I said. "I'm not going down for this, Bob. I had nothing to do with it."

"I find that hard to believe." He stopped with his hand on one of the swinging double doors and wiped his brow. Fifty years of bacon cheeseburgers, cigarettes, and sugar addiction were catching up to him.

My teeth gritted so tightly that I thought they all might splinter under pressure.

He was about to say something else when he looked over my shoulder and let out a sigh instead. "My office. Thirty seconds!"

I walked away from my room and down the hall toward the main entrance. Once there, I dropped my head and debated on shoving my fist through the glass panel on the door, but I thought better of it and walked through it instead. Once outside, I paced the ground and waited for Liz to exit the building.

She walked out about two minutes later. "Well, that was a close one. I cleaned up the puke with a towel I found on the floor of your closet, but you might need some Windex or something. Sorry about that." She wrapped her arms around herself.

My back was to her as I stared down the path leading to The Cove, lit by the moon and the lampposts. The camp was disturbingly quiet in that moment, the type of quiet I'd thought I'd never experience until ten minutes ago. I looked down at my shirt, stained from campfire nachos, and thought about how those nachos had led me to where I was now. If I hadn't insisted the girls use refried beans, then the nachos wouldn't have been as messy. Therefore, I wouldn't have dribbled a series of them down the front of my shirt, causing me to go to my room and change before heading to Bob's office for whatever BS he needed to berate me about.

I turned to face her. "It's na-cho fault," I said.

She coughed and clutched her stomach. "I'm so embarrassed, and I don't feel good. I need some Advil," Liz told me.

"Bob wants us in his office."

She shook her head while wiping away the smudged makeup beneath her eyes with her middle fingers. Liz was someone who was all about appearances, and I could tell she was not too happy with hers at the moment. A smart, pretty-enough social girl with great tits, she had a talent for overhand serves and making friends, but she was fiercely insecure.

She refused to look me in the eyes. "I'm not going in there. Does he know it was me in your room?"

"I don't think so, but he knows someone puked when he tried to walk in and that it wasn't me. I need to produce a body."

"Very funny." She untucked the hair from behind her ears and let it fall in front of her face like two curtains.

I gently reached for her hand. "Come on. Let's get this over with."

We started walking, but then she whipped her arm away from me.

"Jack, I'm sorry. But what should we say to him?"

I halted my stride. Any trace of chivalrous restraint was gone. "What should *we* say? Seriously, Liz? Don't you mean, what should *you* say? I just finished up with the Voyagers and came back to my room to find you lying there, naked and wasted. I was as shocked as Bob was that you were in my bed, and you are going to tell him that." I stepped toward her. "Do you understand?"

She crossed her arms and pouted, which only made me angrier.

In a huff, she took a rubber band off her wrist and smoothed her hair into a ponytail while trying valiantly to keep her balance on two feet, and then she started to cry.

Shit.

I looked over at the office building where Bob was waiting to rip me a new one, and then I embraced her. "I thought we talked about this, about us," I said quietly to her. "I thought you and I were on the same page."

She sniffed and abruptly pulled away from me. "I'm not going in there." She pointed at the building behind me. "I've had enough humiliation for one night."

Then, she took off running.

"Liz!" I shouted after her.

But she kept going. I placed my hands behind my neck and looked to the sky for some answers written among the stars, but I found only mosquitoes instead. Up ahead, Bob walked out onto the covered porch of the office building and spastically waved me over like I was about to miss my train.

Once I reached the porch, I pushed past him and took a seat in his office. I was relieved to see Aunt Sally there with a nonthreatening what-have-you-done-now look on her face.

Much like Bob, his office was a mess. You would think it belonged to someone who ran an automotive shop rather than a summer camp. There was a black-and-white TV resting in the corner atop a file cabinet that had been missing two drawer pulls for eleven years. A neglected potted fern hung in the corner near the windowsill, which held a cinnamon candle that poorly masked the times when Bob would sneak a cigarette. Also displayed were four framed photographs—three of Tabitha and one picture of his beloved dogs, Squidward and Plankton. Speaking of, their two-gallon-sized dog bowls were underneath the corkboard on the far wall. In short, the room smelled of tobacco, cinnamon, and Purina Chicken & Rice—and BO, if Bob were in there.

"Can I grab a water?" I pointed to the mini fridge in the corner.

"No!" Bob said.

"Of course." Sally handed me a tiny eight-ounce bottle that I emptied in two gulps. "Bob told me what happened."

I tossed the empty bottle into the trash can next to Bob's desk. "Did he also tell you that I had nothing to do with it?"

Bob looked at me like I was trying to convince them that the Earth was flat. His lips pressed together, making him look like a duck, and he folded his arms, resting them on his gut.

Sally looked at him and then at me. She was never very good at standing up to him or standing up for me, but at least she'd try. "We're having some issues with Liz," she started.

I honestly had no idea whether Bob knew it was Liz who'd just hurled a wet pile of bile and alcohol-soaked fruit in my room or not.

"And that's why Bob called you in here earlier," she continued. "She's been going around telling people that the two of you are dating." Sally sighed. "I wouldn't have such a big issue with it if she wasn't sharing this information with the campers."

I opened my mouth to defend myself, but she silenced me with her hand.

"But that's not all."

She took a breath, and Bob threw himself into his century-old desk chair, causing the wheels to shriek and holler in agony as he landed. He threw his thick ankles up onto the desk.

Sally continued, "She's also been telling some of the staff that Will has been making unwanted advances at her, too. She said he came on to her the other night after the Rock 'n' Roll bonfire, and he wouldn't take no for an answer."

"What? Will has never—" I caught myself as I remembered that Will, in fact, had been busy raiding Tabitha's panties in the pantry after the bonfire, so he couldn't have been with Liz, too. I left that detail out. "That's bullshit. She's crazy. We're not dating, and Will has no interest in her. I promise you that. She's insane and making all of this up to get attention." I sat back in the vinyl chair and rested my forearms on the wooden armrests.

Sally walked over and placed a hand on my shoulder. "Where is Will? We wanted to talk to both of you. We just need to be very sensitive with this. Liz's family has been a longtime financial sponsor of the camp, and she's been coming here for many years, as you know, so we have a close relationship with her parents." She looked at Bob. "We don't want to upset things. We just need to make sure you and Will are behaving, and we'll handle Liz."

Good luck with that, I thought to myself. "Are you going to believe her or us?" I asked.

"We are going to talk to everyone. I know you're a good boy, sweetie—"

Bob grunted.

"But these girls can be led on easier than you think—one too many hugs, one too many piggyback rides. I know we've talked about this before, but it bears reminding," Sally concluded softly.

The first time Sally had sat me down and talked to me about leading girls on was when she got a phone call one summer from a parent of a nine-year-old. Fourteen at the time, I had been the junior swim instructor that summer. The little girl's name was Nicole—Nikki for short—and she'd adored me. She would sit on my lap during the bonfires. She'd latch on to my neck like a cape during free swim, and she'd spend all her canteen money on buying me gifts. As it had turned out, I'd thought I was doing a stellar job with her until her mother had called the camp and said that all Nikki's letters home were about me and how handsome I was and how I promised to marry her one day and could her parents drive up to meet me and could she invite me to sleep over—in her bed, with her.

The second time was just last year. An older counselor named Kirsten, who was twenty-two and a recent college graduate, had come down to the docks one night when I was cleaning the boathouse. I had been wearing my swim trunks, and she had worn a raincoat. She had been one of the senior staffers, and I had felt slightly intimidated by her, but I'd been mostly fascinated—especially when she'd removed her raincoat and stood there under the spotlight on the dock, naked.

"I'm ready for you, Jack," she said.

I dropped the hose into the lake and just stared, slack-jawed, at her breasts.

"Are you ready for me?" she added.

I swallowed hard and managed to look her in the eyes. She walked toward me, her bare feet padding on the wooden planks, and she slowly began to pull my shorts down before I stopped her.

"What are you doing?" I asked, nervous energy racing through my veins.

"What do you think I'm doing?" She placed her hands on my cheeks and pulled my face down closer to her.

Our bare chests pressed against each other. I closed my eyes, my arms at my sides, and we kissed long and hard until I heard a cough and then a voice behind her.

"You okay, bro?"

I looked up to see Theo standing there. Kirsten scurried behind me, and Theo stood there until she put her coat back on.

He and I both went straight to Sally, and Kirsten was sent home the next day. Apparently, she'd been sleeping with James, the cook, too.

Good times.

I looked at the 7UP clock hanging on the wall behind Sally's head. "I get it," I said.

Bob made a sound. "Oh, he gets it all right. He was just about to get it before I busted things up. Just too good-looking for your own good, is that it? Can't help himself, I guess." His comments were laced with sarcasm, but he sucked at it, so his words came out as a jumbled, confused string of thoughts.

One needed to have some semblance of a sense of humor to pull off mockery.

I slapped my hands down on the armrests. "I have my Voyagers overnight tomorrow, so I really need to get some rest."

"Are you going to tell us who was in your room just now?" Bob asked incredulously.

Sally spoke before I could, "I'll walk you out, Jack."

The two of us pushed through the flimsy screen doors and walked down the front steps.

"He's just looking for something to pin on me. He's always trying to bust me for something," I said with my back to her.

"That's not true."

I spun around. "Yes, Sally, it is."

I took a step forward and gave her a hug. She said nothing as I sauntered off.

FIFTEEN

Julia

Liz stumbled into our cabin after we'd all gone to sleep, and she spent the next couple of hours puking in her and Maggie's private bathroom. Unfortunately for the entire cabin, the walls were paper-thin. Needless to say, I didn't sleep much due to her stomach flu and my nerves about the solo overnight.

Emma met me at the bathhouse before breakfast the next morning. "You excited about tonight?"

"I'm freaking-out nervous."

"Me, too! I didn't sleep a wink. I'm, like, pissing myself, imagining bears and rabid wolves and shit."

"Jack said they've never, ever encountered a bear out there. And do wolves even exist up here?" I asked.

"Hell if I know. All I know is that I'm sneaking snacks in my butt crack if I have to. I'll starve without Franteen." She loaded her toothbrush with toothpaste and began scrubbing.

"That's what will attract the bears, you moron."

"Morning, ladies." Brittany walked in with her pink shower caddy and pink towel wrapped around her pink sun-kissed shoulders. "You both look exhausted."

"Not as exhausted as this conversation," Emma said after spitting into the sink.

"I was wondering if you and I could talk outside—privately," she said to me.

I finished dragging a Noxzema-drenched cotton ball across my forehead. "I'm sure it's nothing that Emma can't hear."

Emma spit again for good measure.

Brittany removed her towel and draped it on a shower hook to save her stall. Then, she placed her caddy beneath it. "I just want to apologize to you, but I'd rather do it alone."

I shook my head. "No, thanks."

She placed her hands on her hips. "Seriously? You need this goon—"

"Watch it, ghetto Barbie," Emma interjected. "Don't get me mad before I've had my blueberry pancakes."

Showerheads were squeaking on and off behind us, and girls were dripping past on either side, elbowing each other to get in front of the mirrors.

I looked up at Brittany. She was attractive, wet or dry, and she knew it. But batting her lashes wasn't going to work on me.

"There's nothing you can say to make up for what you did, and one of these days, I'm going to get you back when you least expect it."

She raised an eyebrow and suppressed a grin.

"So, save your sham of an apology because I don't believe you're sorry for anything." I stepped toward her. "Except that Jack Dempsey pays more attention to me than he does to you," I whispered the last part, but she heard it.

Emma straightened her shoulders and craned her neck to make sure she'd heard what I said.

"Ha!" Brittany coughed out a manufactured burst of laughter and clutched her stomach in a dramatic fashion. "Oh my God!" More laughter. "If you think for a second that I'm, like, jealous of anything that has to do with you and your fucked-up life, you are even more ridiculous than that letter you wrote, begging for your mommy."

I was paralyzed with rage—all but my mouth, which dropped and hung in disbelief. *She's calling me ridiculous?* I wanted to hit her and pull her hair and have a bathhouse catfight, but the truth was that I was too scared of her, and I wasn't that girl. I wasn't a girl who said those mean-spirited things to other girls. I was a girl who never wanted to be the epicenter of anyone's jealousy or resentment or boredom or whatever reason Brittany and her useless twin were targeting me for. I'd done nothing to her. I'd done nothing to anyone.

Emma took my hand. "We gotta go," she said to Brittany.

She shrugged as if she didn't care.

After I was dressed, Emma and Amber and I walked to the mess hall for breakfast. One of the girls from our cabin had just set the mail down in the middle of the table, and there was a large envelope with my name on it. It was from Sharlene.

"What's that?" Emma asked.

"It's from my stepmom." Inside was an oversized greeting card with a photo of my father, Sharlene, and her kids at Disney World with Cinderella's castle in the background and my dad checking his phone. I opened the card and "When You Wish Upon a Star" began playing.

Emma nearly spit out her OJ. "Wow," she said.

I tossed it on the table. "I sent a letter to my dad last week about the Voyagers program and the solo overnight, and this is what I get back." I rolled my eyes and laughed.

Emma began whispering in my ear, "When you wish upon a star, in the woods is where you are, every Jack your heart desires will come to you."

I smiled and swatted her away.

At seven o'clock that evening, the six mildly fearless Voyagers met up on the steps to the office building. Jack was there, waiting for us, with a backpack and a huge duffel bag. Up to that point, we'd each accomplished lessons one through six, and tonight was our big night, our final test of endurance.

He smiled as we all approached. "Evening, ladies. Glad to see none of you chickened out. Who's excited?"

The twins raised their hands.

"That's a start," he said. "All right then, let's get this party rolling. Follow me."

Jack took us on a one-hour hike, far into the woods surrounding the lake, and we could almost see the lights from the camp across the water. We were farther than I'd thought we were going to be.

Eventually, he stopped under a large evergreen, set down his duffel, and grabbed a folder from his backpack. "All right, from here, I'm going to walk each of you out to your own spot, away from each other, and I'll give you a series of choices. Once you've made your choices, I will leave you for the night. Got it?"

We all nodded with little confidence, like baby chicks—except for Brittany.

Her hand went up, and her chest went out. "Can I go first?" she asked.

"Sure," he said. "I'll take Brittany first. You all figure out what order you're going in by the time I come back. And in the morning, everyone is to stay put until I come and get you."

Jack shifted his backpack onto his other shoulder and turned his baseball cap around, glancing at me before walking away.

I took a deep breath. "I'd like to go last," I told the group.

No one else really cared when they went. Along with the remaining girls, I sat under the tree next to Emma as she bit her nails down to the nubs, and I waited my turn.

When Jack came back after dropping the last girl in her spot, we were alone, and he extended his hand to me.

"Off your ass, lazy bird," he said, pulling me to my feet.

We officially held hands for a second or two.

"You ready?" he asked, lowering his chin.

I nodded.

"Come with me." He grabbed the duffel bag.

I walked next to him for about ten minutes. He had one hand gripping the strap of the bag and the other dangling precariously close to mine. It was so close that I simply couldn't resist the urge to swing my arms a little harder than normal and brush my skin against his. He pretended not to notice, which made me question my abilities as a flirt, so I crossed my arms.

We stopped walking in the middle of nowhere. In fact, there was nothing about where we stopped that resembled a place where anyone would stop for any reason.

I looked at him. "You're kidding, right?"

He shook his head and lowered the duffel off his shoulder. "No, I'm not kidding. This is your spot."

I looked around. My stomach turned, and I began to perspire. "I'm nervous," I said quietly.

Jack paused what he was doing and stood straight. "I know, but you're going to do great." His eyes were fixed on mine.

"It's only one night," I told myself aloud.

"That's the spirit, Pearl." He placed his hands on his hips. "You've got this."

I nodded.

He knelt beside the bag and returned to the task at hand. "I've got a few necessities for you, but first, you get three choices. First choice, tarp or blanket?"

"Blanket."

"Bug spray or matches?"

I looked around and took a moment to assess the skeeter factor. I hated bugs, but I'd also failed the build-your-own-fire challenge on my first three tries. "Matches," I said.

"Last but not least, flashlight or Swiss Army knife?"

"Flashlight. No contest."

He handed me my three items, zipped up his bag, and then stood. I watched him look around for a moment, and then he started kicking some of the dirt and rocks beneath his feet, clearing a spot for me near the base of a tree. He bent down and broke off a few low-lying branches.

"This will be a good place for you. Once you gather enough wood and rocks, just clear that spot I started with my feet, and make your fire there. Not too big, okay? Just like we learned."

The sun was just on the cusp of its descent, illuminating his eyes as he spoke. It was hard for me to concentrate when I had his full attention. The only reason I'd agreed to be alone in the woods was because of him, and now, he was going to leave me there.

"What if something goes wrong?"

"Like what?" he asked.

"Like, a bear comes and eats me."

"Then, we'll all have to mourn you, and Emma will get first crack at your clothes and canteen money."

I didn't comment.

He smirked. "They're really more prevalent in northern Wisconsin. Hell, the only bear around here is a forty-foot statue that welcomes visitors to a water park. Next question?"

"What if I run out of water?"

"That would require the lake to dry up in twenty-four hours, and I promise you, that's not going to happen. Next?"

"What if I have a panic attack? Can I throw in the Voyagers towel if something crawls on me? I hate being left alone." It was the truth. I just rarely admitted it.

Jack took a step closer and narrowed the space between us.

If he agreed to stay with me, then I'd be fine. We could brush dirt together, play Spin the Twig, tell ghost stories, and do hourly tick checks. I could use his rock-hard abs as a pillow and rest easy to the sound of his beating pectorals. I never felt more at ease than when he was near me. Even yards away, I could always sense his presence. Jack could put a smile on my face before I even saw him, like the scent of cotton candy in the air or music playing in the background.

He placed his hands on my shoulders and squeezed. That was his signature move that said, *Look, I'm touching you but at arm's length.*

"If you have a panic attack, I will come for you," he assured me.

"You will?"

"Yes." He removed his hands, reached inside his pocket, pulled out a whistle, and handed it to me.

"What's this?"

"A whistle."

I rolled my eyes. "Thank you, master of all that is obvious and relevant. What's it for?"

"It's your emergency signal. Just whistle if you need me."

I stared at the whistle in my hand. "Does everyone have one?"

"Yes, Julia, everyone has one."

"Are they distinctive? How can you tell my frantic whistle from, say, Tweedledum's or Emma's?"

"Be nice. And, yes, they each have a distinct sound." He paused for a moment. "Well, two or three are the same, but it's fine. I know what whistle everyone has and exactly where they're located."

"Has anyone ever blown their whistle?"

"Not as long as I've been doing this."

"How long is that?"

"This is my third year running this program. I created it as a way to get people to open up and be more comfortable with themselves and the outdoors. Everyone is so scared to be out here, alone, at first, but in the morning, you will feel a huge sense of accomplishment. You'll be really proud of yourself, and I'll be equally proud of you." Jack gestured to the tree. "Come sit with me for a sec."

I followed and took a seat next to him.

"You're a champ. I know it. If you can believe in yourself half as much as I believe in you, you're going to have no trouble at all." He tapped his head. "It's all up here. The mind can be your best friend or your worst enemy. Instead of asking what-ifs, why not ask what it's going to take for you to get through this? What, in your head, is making you paranoid? What is blocking you from being the strongest, best, fiercest, toughest person I know you can be?"

I smiled. If only he knew how hard I'd fallen for him, he probably wouldn't be spending so much time with me—alone and in the woods. All I could think about was how I might never get the chance to tell him how much he meant to me or how comforted I was when he'd just glance my way or give me a nod.

He kept on talking, and I kept right on staring into his eyes, soaking up every word. He cared about me, about all of us. I refused to believe he'd had the same heart-to-heart with each of the other girls out there. It would help me be strong if I thought he'd reserved those words of wisdom for me alone.

"Thanks, Jack."

We stood, and before I could say anything else, he spoke, "The pleasure's all mine."

"How far will you be?"

"Not too far. Somewhere in the middle of everyone," he said.

Then, slowly, without removing his eyes from mine, he leaned toward me and placed his palms against my cheeks. I swore I'd heard him catch his breath. He pulled me to him, bent down, and rested his forehead on mine. My lungs were working hard to maintain composure as they nearly beat out of my skin. I kept my arms at my sides, trembling. I wanted to wrap them around him like a snake and hold on for dear life, but I didn't dare.

With his hands still on my face, he placed his flawless lips in the spot where our heads had just been touching. His lips were soft and warm, and he let them linger there for a long time—but not long enough.

He opened his eyes and smiled. "I'll be positioned closest to you, Pearl. You won't even need your whistle." He embraced me tightly. "Just whisper if you need me."

Sixteen

Julia

The sun was setting as though someone up above had dimmed the lights. Jack had encouraged us to each build a small fire—not for warmth, but for practice. Each of us would then have to put the fire out before going to sleep, but since I didn't intend on sleeping much, I was going to gather as much kindling and wood as I could find.

First, I had to start by clearing away any dead grass or vegetation about eight to ten feet around my spot so that there was nothing but bare ground. Then, we had been taught to dig down a couple of inches into the cleared soil to create a little pit for the fire to keep it from spreading. Jack had suggested keeping the extra dirt in case of an emergency since it could help put out the fire.

Once I had my pit, my hands were caked in dirt, so I walked down to the lake to rinse off before looking for kindling. To my right, I could see the tiny glimmer of a fire from one of my fellow Voyagers, but I wasn't sure whose it was. Jack had warned us that if we snuck over to each other's camp or called out for one another, we'd be disqualified, and we would have to do it again another night.

I gathered an armful of branches and retreated back to my spot where I set them down next to the pit.

In addition to the blanket, matches, and flashlight I'd gotten from Jack, we had also been allowed to bring water bottles and a change of clothes. No snacks were allowed, so we wouldn't attract any hungry critters. Emma had begged for a roll of toilet paper, and Jack had just shaken his head.

I had worn jeans, a T-shirt, and a hoodie. To sleep in, I had brought a long-sleeved shirt, sweatpants, and an extra pair of socks. I also had a second sweatshirt that I intended on using as a pillow.

Lastly, we had been told to bring a pen and a piece of paper to keep a journal of our evening. Jack had wanted us to keep track of our thoughts, whatever was going through our heads. He'd promised we wouldn't have to share it with anyone, but the memories would be something we would have forever. By chronicling the experience, it would always be with us—or so some professor had told him in a psych class.

"I encourage you all to take this seriously and write down everything you're feeling. Describe your emotions and your fears and your triumphs," he'd said.

Before I started my fire, I sat down and drank some water. Then, I took my pen to my paper and wrote, *I'm alone in the woods, and I'm not afraid.* I put it aside.

I looked around at the many different trees and marveled at their sizes and their strengths. Some of them were over one hundred years old. I leaned back against the one where I'd set my things and looked up. I could see leaves and branches for miles, and they were all there to provide shelter and watch over those who came to them for protection—squirrels, birds, rabbits, me...and countless others throughout their lifetime.

As soon as the sun had completely disappeared, the crickets got louder, and while their chirps sounded threatening, their clandestine presence gave me some reassurance—as if, in the woods, an army of camouflaged critters existed, ready to serve and protect as necessary.

I thought about my mom and how she'd vowed to protect me, how I'd believed in her and trusted her and had put my mind at ease for so many years because she'd assured me. But she'd failed me.

How could I ever trust anyone else to keep me safe? I couldn't.

It was up to me, and there was no better test of my own endurance and power to protect myself than what I was doing now. I smiled and took a deep breath. The air was so crisp and clean that I could smell everything—the spray of the lake, the pine needles, the musty bark of the trees. All of it was so much more alive and vibrant and tangible when nothing was there to distract me from it.

I reached for my pen and paper, and underneath the first line, I wrote, *No one can protect me, except for me.*

Passing time alone in the dark was like waiting for a train that would never come, standing at the platform with no clock and no other travelers. It was just you and the uncertainty of whether you'd ever make it out of there or not.

Every once in a while, I'd flick my flashlight on just to remind my brain that my eyes were open. It was so dark that it was hard to tell. There were a few noises besides the crickets—leaves rustling periodically with a soft breeze, water lapping in the lake—but for the most part, it was silent. Only the thoughts in my head were loud and clear, and all of them were about Jack—how I was both nervous and relaxed when he was around; how he was the first person I'd think of every morning and the last person on my mind as I'd drift off to sleep; how he'd brought me to this place, both literally and figuratively, where I had to face my fears and focus on only what mattered; how I was falling in love with him.

My shoulders were propped at the base of the tree with my head resting on my balled up sweatshirt. I knew I would eventually fall asleep, but being present in the quiet, calm dark woods that night soothed me. There was something peaceful about not being concerned with the passing hours, minutes, seconds. None of it mattered. The only thing that mattered was me, being in control of myself and being comfortable alone.

Until I wasn't.

I sat up when I heard footsteps, and I fumbled for my flashlight.

Jack was kneeling before me when I turned it on. I shivered at the sight of him but remained silent. I laid my flashlight on the ground between us, and it created a dim ray of light, like a tiny candle illuminating his face, as I waited for an explanation as to why he was here.

My heart beat faster as he moved closer, and his face emerged from the darkness. Slowly, keeping his eyes on mine, he leaned forward and placed his hand on my cheek, like he'd done earlier. I pressed my face into his palm and closed my eyes. His hand was warm, and the scent of him flooded through me like a drug. He caressed my cheek with his thumb and then moved it over my lips.

I heard him inhale before he removed his hand, and then he sat cross-legged in front of me. No words were spoken.

I sat up straighter and could see him perfectly through the glow. Our eyes met again, and his face was serious now—eyes fierce, lips tight—and then his expression changed. It softened, and there was a new eagerness in his eyes that I'd never seen before.

His eyebrows rose. "I came to see if you were all right," he whispered.

I hesitated before answering, allowing only a hint of a smile. Inside, alarms were ringing in my head, fireworks were exploding, brass bands were playing in the streets, and I was soaring above all of it with the wings of an eagle. "I'm good."

He smiled with his lips together. "I came to ask you something else, too."

My breathing intensified to short gasps.

He searched my eyes, and then he reached for my hand and lifted it to his mouth. "Can I kiss you?" His determined low tone was everything.

My entire world was spinning with those four little words flashing in my brain. Time didn't exist out here, only dark, moody, sexy, mysterious moments. And this was one I would never let go of.

I nodded.

He kissed my hand and pulled me to him. Then, he placed one hand at the base of my neck and drew my mouth to his, kissing me. I straightened my legs, and he gently laid me on the ground with his chest hovering over me. His lips were firmly planted on mine, and our bodies were touching.

I wrapped my arms around him and released every ounce of myself into that kiss. Every emotion, every ache, every insecurity, and every hope I had for him emanated through me and came out in that kiss. It didn't matter that my hair was in the dirt or that we were breaking every code of conduct rule. All that mattered was that he'd wanted to kiss me as much as I'd wanted to kiss him.

His hand slid down the right side of my body, moving under my arm, past the curve of my waist, and to the back of my knee, and then he pulled away. His eyes hung an inch or two from mine, and once more, he brushed his thumb across my lips. My reaction surprised both of us as I grabbed him and pulled him to me again. I'd had a taste of him, and I wanted more.

He whispered something—it didn't matter what—and then he sat up and reached for my hand to pull me forward. He pressed his lips to my forehead and then lowered his chin to meet my gaze. "I guess you're all right."

I couldn't speak. I just bent forward into his chest and wrapped my arms around his waist. He caressed my hair and put his legs out in front of him as he leaned back against the tree.

After a moment or two, I sat up straight. "This had better not disqualify me," I said.

"Never."

"Okay, good. Are you staying here all night?" I asked, hopeful.

He shook his head. "I can't," he said.

We stood up together. I reached for the flashlight and held it between us.

His expression was concerned. "I probably should have thought this through. I'm sorry if I did something I shouldn't have, but I'm not sorry I got to kiss you."

"Please don't be sorry. I wanted you to kiss me, and I've been thinking about you for most of the night. I understand that it was impulsive, and I won't hold it against you if you never do it again." I meant it. If I was only allowed to kiss Jack Dempsey once in my lifetime, I was glad it'd happened under the stars in the dark woods, next to a smoldering campfire while being serenaded by chirping crickets.

He blinked and then put his hands in his pockets. "Good night, Julia," he said quietly. He gave me one last peck on the cheek.

"Good night, Jack."

I lay beneath the blanket at the base of my tree and savored the scent of him that lingered on my lips. My mind was giddy, replaying the events over and over, like a scene from a movie. First, the startling noise, and then the realization that everything I'd ever wanted was in front of me, asking my permission for the one thing my heart had been aching for. Then, the passion had happened, fast and furious, yet at the same time, it had been slow and intense. Both of us had concentrated on each other, moving and breathing as one, before the intensity had subsided, and we'd loosened our embrace to gaze into each other's eyes. The music had started, and the credits had rolled to end the show. It was time to leave the dark theater and wander out into the bright, sobering lobby of life. Popcorn not included.

There would never be a moment in my life that could top this. I couldn't conceive of anything ever causing such a seismic shift in my world. I would never be the same. I might never be intimate with Jack again, but I was forever changed by it, and that I knew for sure.

Is it love? It has to be.

He hadn't said he loved me, and I could live with it either way because I knew he felt something for me, something magnetic and awesome.

Maybe I was being way too dramatic about the whole thing? *Nah.*

I picked up my pen and paper and wrote, *I'm in love with Jack Dempsey.*

Then, I leaned back against the tree. I'd survived my first *real* kiss. I would most certainly survive the night.

Seventeen

JACK

Julia could have told me to stop, but she hadn't. She'd arched her back and opened her mouth for me, and I had felt her heart pounding beneath her sweatshirt. It had taken every ounce of self-restraint for me to stop.

From the moment I'd seen her, I'd felt compelled to look after her. Seeing her asleep on the bus with no interest in waking up and not one ounce of eagerness in those ridiculous blue eyes of hers had killed me. I had seen myself in them. She'd had that void, dim look on her face, as if nothing or no one could brighten things up for her. But there was a force of empathy between us, and without even knowing how or why, I had known she was lost and abandoned like me.

And I loved that about her.

As I'd sat back against the tree and she'd laid her head on me, I could only hope I hadn't made the wrong choice. I would not only need to protect her from then on, but I'd also have to trust her. That was something I had never been very good at and something that had destroyed me in the past.

Five years after my parents had died, a man had come to my aunt and uncle's house where I was living and placed a large trunk in the foyer. I was ten years old at the time, and I had heard most of the conversation between Bob and the man. The contents of the trunk had belonged to my mother and had been in the possession of my grandmother since the accident. My Grandma Judy, who was in the process of moving to Florida, had asked that the trunk and its contents be given to me.

I watched my uncle look over at the trunk and then at the man. "Is there anything worthwhile in there?"

The man wiped his brow with a handkerchief. "I haven't opened it, sir."

Bob turned to face me as I approached the trunk. "Hold up," he said. "Sally and I will go through it first."

"It's meant for the child," the man interjected. "Miss Judy, who sent me, wanted to make certain I gave it to him."

Bob forced a smile. "Of course, yes. Well, as his guardians, we will obviously oversee the process. His best interest is our only concern."

The man nodded at me.

I stopped and ran my hand over the worn metal corners of the chest, imagining what was inside and wishing my mother could have been here to open it with me. I strained to picture her face, envisioning her lifting the lid and taking each item out one at a time, attaching stories to every keepsake.

Once the man was gone, Bob called for Sally and told me to go outside with Tabitha.

"I don't want to go outside. I want to see what's in the trunk. The guy said it's for me."

Bob stood with one hand on his hip and the other pointing to the back door. "Get outside! Now!"

"No."

Bob wrapped his sweaty fingers tightly around my forearm and dragged me to the yard. "Stay here until I call you, or you will never see what's in there."

"But it's mine," I said.

The door slammed behind me.

Tabitha sat with me on the porch, and we pressed our noses up against the dirty screens, but we couldn't make out any details.

About an hour later, Tabitha and I were allowed to go through the trunk. Its lid was open, and the contents were disheveled, but I didn't care. It was like finding a pot of gold at the end of a rainbow. I found old clothes of mine, baby clothes for my brother who had never been worn, an old quilted blanket that I recognized like the back of my hand, some random toys and markers and faded drawings with my name scribbled on the bottom, and books. There were a bunch of books, including her favorite, Charlie and the Chocolate Factory. *I didn't want to open the book, thinking it didn't feel right to turn the pages without my mom next to me.*

Tabitha and I spent hours going through everything, just the two of us. Then, I tucked the book and the trunk in the back of my closet and left them alone.

Years later, when I had been about to leave for college, my grandmother had sent me a card, congratulating me. Inside had been a check for one hundred dollars along with a note.

Dear Jack,

Your mother would be very proud of the young man you've become. I know I am. I think about her every day, and I hope you do as well. She deserves to live in your thoughts and your heart. She loved you so much.

One day, you will meet a woman and fall in love, and I hope I'm alive to meet her. If she is deserving of you, be sure and give her your mother's ring that was among her belongings. I trust you've kept it safe. That way, you will have a part of your mom beside you, looking after you, upon the caring, loving hands of your wife forever.

—Grandma Judy

Confused, I went to the back of my closet and dragged the trunk out. I hadn't touched it since I was ten. Once it was in the center of my room, I tore through it. I dumped out every toy and shook out every piece of clothing, even the ones still in its original packaging. But there was no ring.

Had she forgotten to include it?

I ran downstairs with the letter and showed it to Bob. His face went pale, and then I knew.

"Where is the ring?" I asked, my chest on fire.

"It was a long time ago, and we did what we had to do," he said after a long pause.

Before I knew it, I was towering over him with my hand around his throat and his back pressed up against the wall, watching his face turn red.

"What did you do with it?" I shouted and spit.

Bob choked and ferociously kicked the wall until Tabitha came running, screaming, pleading for me to let him go.

I released my fingers, and he gagged and crumbled to the floor, cursing my name.

I watched Julia's flashlight go dark before walking away and turning on my own. As I walked, I thought about what I had done, about the noises she'd made and her soft breath on my neck, about the way she'd smelled of aloe and baby power, about how I'd wanted to lie with her in the dirt for hours and undress her right then and there, about how she'd never tried to bat her eyelashes at me or shove her cleavage in my face or show up drunk and naked in my bed. She was refreshingly real. The urge to go to her tonight had been unbearable, and I clearly hadn't had the mindset to fight it, as I probably should have.

Once I returned to my campsite, I lay down, crossed my arms over my chest, and covered my face with my baseball cap. Never in all my years at Hollow Creek had I made the moves on a camper. I cleared my lungs. I could kill someone in a waterskiing accident, and Bob would look at it as more tolerable than what I'd just done.

But I couldn't help myself. I had been certain that she wanted me, and I had to know. It'd turned out that I was right. She'd said it herself that she'd wanted to kiss me. She'd looked surprised to see me but excited. Her eyes had gone wide, and she had smiled more than I'd seen her smile before. She could have said no when I'd asked her, but she hadn't. She could have told me to stop, but she hadn't.

I would look out for her...and I knew I could trust her to look after me, too.

EIGHTEEN

Julia

I was half-awake when a nut hit me on the head.

"No, thanks. I'm allergic!" I shouted into the branches above, swatting the nut away from me.

The sun was up, so I knew I'd made it. With the rising sun came confirmation of my achievement and so much more. At some point after Jack's visit, I had fallen asleep and dreamed of being on a boat with him, eating popcorn.

Weird.

I sat up and thought about our kiss and how badly I wanted to tell Emma. He hadn't said not to tell anyone, but I was sure he would want me to keep it to myself.

If he'd gone and kissed Brittany, the whole camp would have known about it by now.

The thought of him kissing me instead of her pleased me to no end. But I wasn't going to be one of those girls who lost all hold on reality and let our kiss, our moment, surpass everything else in my little world. I refused to be dramatic.

Overnight, I'd thought long and hard about appreciating it for what it was—simply the best thing ever.

My next thought was, *Get me the hell out of here.*

I'd had just about enough of that tree, and the squirrels had had enough of me. I took a swig of water, swished it around my mouth, and then spit it out. Then, I needed to pee badly. There had been no way Emma and I weren't going to sneak toilet paper out there. The only problem we'd had was, what to do with the toilet paper once we used it.

"Don't leave anything behind!" I could hear Jack's voice in my head.

So, Emma and I had tucked some toilet paper into our bras along with a couple of plastic baggies for our soiled tissue.

When I was squatting, I heard his voice calling my name.

Seriously? This very second?

I squeezed my pee out as fast as I could. As I was trying to balance and get the toilet paper out of my bra, I fell backward, my bare ass hitting something sharp. "Ow! Shit!"

"Julia? You okay?" he hollered.

"Stay there! I'm fine. Don't come over here."

His footsteps stopped. "Whatcha doin'?"

I could almost hear him smirking.

"I'm using the ladies' room!" I scooted backward like a crab and then got to my knees, so I could assess my ass. My butt was bleeding but nothing too serious, so I wiped myself and pulled my pants up. Then, I shoved the baggie in the front pocket of my sweatshirt.

"Good morning," I said as I walked toward Jack.

He was wearing a baseball cap, a thick fleece jacket, and jeans. He looked glorious. Naturally, there was a second or two of awkward silent glances, and then he hugged me. I really didn't want to have a conversation about last night, and thankfully, neither did he.

He pulled back with his hands resting on my shoulders. "You okay?"

I nodded.

"I'm really proud of you."

"Thanks. It turned out to be a great night."

Jack winked and lifted my backpack up onto his shoulder. He walked me back to the meeting point where I was the last to arrive.

Emma threw herself at me and gave me a huge squeeze. "We made it, sister!" she screamed.

She hugged me, and we jumped in a circle like crazy people, causing my pee baggie to fly out of my sweatshirt pocket and land at our feet. Emma laughed as I scrambled to pick it up.

Jack rolled his eyes when he saw it.

"Are you kidding me?" Brittany said. "That is disgusting."

"Shut up," Emma said to her.

"Enough, please," Jack chimed in. He began walking away with Emma in his ear.

I could hear her rattling on about how hard the ground was and asking if he could check her for ticks.

Just as I was about to lift my duffel, Brittany stepped on the strap. "Good job, Julia. I didn't think you'd survive without your mommy."

Brittany looked as bad as I'd ever seen her. She had her hair in a rat's nest of a ponytail and a baseball hat pulled down so far that I could hardly see the dark circles under her eyes. But they were there. She did not have the look of someone who had been kissed by Jack Dempsey last night.

Thank God.

"Get your foot off my bag."

I gave it a tug, but she didn't budge. We were the only two left standing there.

"Let me guess. Writing notes to her in your journal gave you the strength to make it through the night. *I can do this for Mommy and make her proud of me!*" She laughed.

I yanked again and set the bag free. "Leave me alone, Brittany. You sound about as stupid as you look right now." I scanned her hair and snickered.

"You're so obvious that it's sad. The way you drool over Jack and try to act like you're not interested in him, but then you follow him around like some sort of groupie. It's laughable." She crossed her arms. "But what's more laughable is that you even bother to waste your time, that you even think he'd be interested in *you*." She dragged the word *you*.

The wind picked up and rustled some leaves at our feet.

"What I think is that you spend more time thinking about me and Jack than I do. If I am so sad, then why are you so obviously threatened by my friendship with him? Seems like you're the one wasting your time, worrying about me. Maybe you should have written in your journal about your jealousy last night, and then we wouldn't be talking right now."

She pursed her lips and smiled. "You're pathetic," she said with the clarity and assurance of someone who knew everything about everyone. Then, she turned and skipped off toward the others.

I stood there, alone, and let out a deep sigh. Talking to her was like diving under water and holding my breath, desperate to come up for air and panicking because the surface was farther than I had anticipated. Every ounce of my being saw her for who she was, but my self-esteem would let her win, and her words would crush me every goddamn time.

By the time the group was gathered at the edge of the campgrounds, Jack clapped his hands to get everyone's attention. "Real quick, I know you're all dying to get back and brush your teeth and your hair and get some grub, but sit down and give me two more minutes."

We did as he'd asked.

"I just want to start by saying how proud I am of this group. Let's give each other a round of applause."

We all clapped and hollered and squealed.

"Now that it's done, maybe it doesn't seem like such a major undertaking, but it was. I hope you all took the time to write something in your journal. Those are the thoughts and moments and memories that you will have from this experience forever." He looked around the circle. "Again, you all make me very proud."

"Cheers to our fearless leader extraordinaire, Jack!" Emma shouted.

We all clapped and screamed again.

"One last thing, we'll be having our Voyagers completion party tonight, so instead of dining at the mess hall, the seven of us are going to have a special celebratory awards dinner down by the docks. You'd better all be there!"

The hot water on my face felt amazing. Every crevice of my neck and arms and legs were covered in a black soot-like dust, so I stood in the shower stall and soaped and scrubbed for as long as I could.

When I stepped out, I towel-dried my hair and thought of Brittany and her half-ass attempt to apologize, followed up by her full-ass attempt at making me feel like shit.

Mission accomplished.

I knew Jack had a great night planned for us, so I thought I would be the bigger person and try to clear the air with Brittany. There was no reason we couldn't get along—for him. The tension between Brittany and me was stupid, and I didn't give a shit about her anyway.

So, why not get along for at least one night?

As she was leaving the bathhouse in her shower sandals with a towel rolled up on her head, I approached her. "Do you have a second?"

"Not for you," she said, walking right past me.

I rolled my eyes and swallowed my pride for Jack.

"Brit." I gently grabbed her elbow from behind.

She stopped walking and looked down at me. "Please don't ever touch me."

I took a deep breath and crossed my arms in an effort not to slap her. "Look, we don't have to be best friends—"

She snorted like a pig, very much like a pig I decided.

I continued, "But there's no reason we can't coexist, right? I mean, it's summer camp. We don't go to the same high school, we don't belong to rival lipstick gangs, and we don't have to spend the holidays together."

"Yeah, because my family celebrates Christmas, not Hanukkah."

"Wonderful!" I said in a tone befitting an adult praising a child who had just gone poop on the potty for the first time. "I bet Santa is watching us now, and he sees what a good little girl you're being by pausing to speak with me."

She glared at me.

"If you hate me, that's fine. I'm not your biggest fan either, but that doesn't mean we need to ruin the night for Jack and everyone else who is looking forward to the Voyagers dinner."

More glaring.

"Right?" I asked.

She looked around and adjusted the towel on her head before answering, "You don't ever need to tell me how to behave or whatever." She flailed her hand at me. "I am fully capable of ignoring you and enjoying myself at the same time."

"Perfect." I clasped my hands together. "That's perfect. All I was trying to do was—"

"My hair is going to frizz if I don't get to my blow-dryer," she said. "But if you're truly concerned with me having a good time, then you should skip the dinner." She nodded and walked off.

Her words hit me like a fist to the gut. I'd put so much energy in being strong around her, convincing myself that she and her sister were insignificant, working up the courage to be the bigger person. It was exhausting.

Emma came up behind me. "What was that about?"

I squeezed some water off the ends of my hair. "I'm not going to the dinner tonight."

"Like hell you're not."

"I'm not. I don't need to deal with her bullshit, and I don't care about the stupid dinner. Besides you and Amber and Jack, I'm not dying to celebrate with anyone there. So, what's the point?"

I walked away, and she ran after me.

"What did she say to you?" Emma grabbed my arm, and the towel fell off my shoulder.

I bent to pick it up. "Nothing. I just have no desire to spend the evening with her and Brianna. I'd rather spend all night using a spork to scrape mold off of some chick's underwear that has been hanging on the clothesline for three weeks."

She dropped her arms to her sides. "You are going to the dinner. You earned it."

"I'm not," I said in a bratty don't-tell-me-what-to-do tone. On the verge of equally childish tears, I stomped off.

Emma didn't follow me.

I skipped my first two morning activities, which were swimming and drama, and stayed in the cabin, writing a letter to my dad about the overnight. I left out the part about Jack kissing me...and the part about Brittany calling me pathetic...and the part about carrying my urine in my pocket. Instead, I proudly mentioned how accomplished I felt even though it was only one night.

The cabin was empty because most of the girls were at lunch, so I borrowed one of the many magazines my bunkmate had received in her weekly care package.

I was almost asleep when there was a knock on the door, and Jack peeked in.

I hopped down and hurried to him. He wasn't allowed inside.

"Hey," I said, beaming. "What's up?"

"Do you have a sec?"

I nodded and walked out of the cabin. Then, I stood with my back to the door.

Jack's sunglasses were buried in his hair, and he was wearing swim trunks with a hoodie hanging open and nothing underneath, daring me to reach out and place my hand on his chest.

"Emma tells me you're not coming to the dinner tonight, and since I didn't believe her, I came to see for myself."

I looked up at him. "I just don't feel like it."

He pulled his head back. "Too bad. It's a mandatory invite."

"No, it's not. What? I'm not getting a Voyagers certificate if I don't go?"

He shifted his weight and narrowed his eyes. "What's the matter with you? Obviously, something happened between this morning and now to make you upset. So, what gives? Out with it. And if it has anything to do with Brittany, I'm going to be pissed— at you, not her."

I leaned against the wall for support. I could hardly look him in the face. The air outside was quiet, except for a few distant squeals coming from kids splashing in the lake.

"Please don't be mad at me. I'm just not comfortable around Brittany and Brianna. I promise you, it's as simple as that. No catfight drama, no bruised ego. I just really don't have any interest in being with them and putting on a fake smile and singing 'Kumbaya.' I can't celebrate anything with Brittany there. I wish you could understand."

It wouldn't do me any good to tattle on Brittany because it would only fuel her hatred of me, and nothing would come of it anyway.

One year in school, an upperclassman, a girl, had been rude to me. She'd slam my locker shut after I'd just finished unlocking it, and then I'd have to spin through the combo again, all flustered, while her and her friend would stand over me and watch. After the third time it had happened, I'd told my advisor about it, and she'd told their advisor, so they'd stopped messing with me when I was opening my locker. Instead, they'd just squirted maple syrup through the vents, getting it all over my jacket and books. I hadn't wanted to tell on them for the syrup, only to later have them fill my backpack with used tampons. So, I had kept my mouth shut.

Truth be told, I'd been just as obnoxious to Brittany and Brianna in my own way, so I had to just deal.

Jack lowered his chin and looked at me. He had a way of smiling sideways that made me cross my arms and fidget. He looked around and then took hold of my hand. I nearly fainted at the boldness of his move.

"It's not up for debate," he said. "Forget the fact that you've earned this celebration as much as anyone else. I want you there with me tonight. It won't be the same without you, so please come. For me." He squeezed my hand and lowered his voice as he said, "Have you thought about last night?"

I nodded.

"Are you okay with everything?"

"Yeah, it was amazing."

I hoped he would lean forward and kiss me again, but he didn't.

Instead, he let go of me and pushed his hand through his messy hair, fishing for his sunglasses. "I'm counting on seeing you again tonight."

How can I refuse him? I wouldn't. "Okay, I'll be there. Sorry...it's not that I didn't want to be with you—"

He shook his head to silence me. "Just be there, please. I'm looking forward to us hanging out."

"Me, too."

Jack put his sunglasses on and then stuck his hands in the pockets of his sweatshirt as he took a few steps backward. I watched him walk off, smiling at me, before he disappeared behind the cabin. My heart was full, and my head was light, like that time Jimmy Scarpino had dared me to chug a beer.

When I headed back in, the screen door got stuck on the bottom of the frame, as it probably had for years. I pulled harder, and it slammed against the exterior wall because of the neglected springs. The cabin had been empty when I left, but when I walked back in, Liz was standing there with her hands on her hips. She'd apparently been asleep in her counselor quarters.

"Oh my God!" I gasped, throwing my hand on my chest. "You scared me."

She glared. "What the fuck was *that* all about?"

Nineteen

JACK

My flip-flop busted as I was running back to the mess hall, so I tossed the pair in a garbage can. Lunch was over, and the place smelled like ammonia and ranch dressing. I headed to the back, looking for James.

"Put some shoes on, you filthy animal," he said.

I found him scraping some nasty-looking black residue off the griddle. "Dude, I'm sorry. They just broke. Are we all set for tonight?"

James gestured with his head, an unlit cigarette hanging off his bottom lip. "Your cooler is in the cooler. You'll need to get your own plates and shit for however many people you have."

I slapped him on the shoulder. "Thanks. I appreciate it." I grabbed a handful of baby carrots off the mobile salad bar before heading back to my room.

After a long hot shower, I pulled on a pair of jeans and a T-shirt and sifted through the back of my closet for some shoes. One sniff of my laceless Chuck Taylors, and I had my outfit. Just as I was shoving a tin of Altoids into my pocket, there was an aggressive knock on the door.

"Come in," I said over my shoulder.

The door flew open, but Liz just stood there with her arms crossed, the expression on her face looking like she wanted to puke on my floor again.

"What's up?" I asked.

She shrugged. "You tell me."

I shut my dresser drawer and grabbed my keys. "I don't have time for this right now. Is there something you need from me?"

She took one step forward and cocked her head. "I just happened to be napping when you came by to talk to Julia."

"So?" I responded quickly, scanning my brain for any incriminating evidence I might have left behind. It wasn't like I'd dropped off a bouquet of roses.

She threw her arms up. "So? So, I heard your whole conversation. The walls are made of tissue paper."

"Look, I don't know what you think you heard, but all I was trying to do was make her come to the Voyagers dinner tonight. You know that Brittany has been teasing her for whatever reason, and I wanted Julia to know she deserved to be there." I paused, trying to think if she could have seen me holding Julia's hand, but it wasn't the biggest deal anyway. Hugs and hand-holding were as common as mosquitoes around this place.

"You know you'll get kicked out for this."

"For what?"

"For *frater-ah-nizing* with a camper." She completely butchered the pronunciation of the word. That pissed me off.

"You don't know shit about anything. I gotta go." I pushed past her.

"You know I'm obligated to report something if I see inappropriate behavior going on."

"You do what you think is right, Liz." I left her standing there.

TWENTY

Julia

At five o'clock, Emma came to my cabin to pick me up before heading down to the lake.

The kitchen had prepared a special dinner on the dock for the Voyagers, and then Jack had promised us a bonfire and s'mores afterward. My preferred uniform for almost every camp occasion was a tank top, a sweatshirt, jean shorts, and flip-flops. But that night, Emma had talked me into wearing a sundress. She and I had picked one out—a yellow halter-top style. Plus, it was the only one I'd brought.

I couldn't get the encounter with Liz out of my mind. Her face had looked so skeptical as I explained that Jack was just being nice to me. I had gone on and on, exaggerating about how Brittany and Brianna had tormented me after the overnight and that I couldn't bring myself to celebrate with them. She'd listened to me with narrowed eyes and pursed lips and little sympathy. Then, she'd just sort of blinked and walked away when I was through talking.

"You look delicious. Good enough to eat!" Emma squealed when she saw me. "And wear your hair down for once. It's always in that godforsaken braid."

"I like my pony braid."

"It makes you look like you're six years old."

"Every time I wear my hair down, I always end up playing with it, and then it gets greasy. I'm much more comfortable with it out of my face."

She stepped behind me and pulled the rubber band out of my hair. Then, she took her hands and fluffed the sides of my head. We both studied me in the mirror.

"Okay, so you need a brush, but you're looking a decade older already. Almost Jack's age." She winked.

I rolled the rubber band onto my wrist. I was desperate to tell her about the kiss, but I knew I should keep it to myself until he and I talked. "I really like him."

"I know you do."

I sat on the bottom bunk. "No, I mean, like, really, really like him. Like, when-you-can't-think-of-anything-else like him. It's bad."

"Why's it bad?" she asked.

"You know why. Because I'm not allowed to like him." My eagerness to talk about him couldn't be suppressed.

She sat on the floor, cross-legged, and faced me. "It's not forbidden for you to like him. It's forbidden for him to like you— or rather, for him to act on it. I know he likes you."

My head shot up. "How do you know that?"

"I can just tell."

"How?"

Emma rested her elbows on her knees. "I remember when my older brother, Tom, fell in love with this girl, Phoebe. She lived down the street from us and worked part-time at our local pharmacy. After work, she'd ride her bike home at the same time every day, and Tom would be out there, performing some ridiculous yard task, when she did. He'd wash the car, mow the lawn, walk the dog. Only, he never actually walked the dog. He'd just sit with her in the yard until *Phoebe* rode by and waved or stopped to talk to him. Tom's entire demeanor would change when she appeared. He'd become bashful and sweet, and he'd move his feet a lot when she spoke to him. It was like he couldn't stand still when she was near. He'd fidget and place his hands in his pockets or remove his baseball hat, anything to keep him from leaping forward and shoving his tongue down her throat."

I blinked. "But Jack is not like that at all. He's the pillar of all that is calm, cool, and collected."

"He doesn't fidget like Tom did on the outside, but Jack acts the same. When you walk up, I can see it switch on like a light bulb."

I smiled and shook my head. "I don't know."

"I do, and you can get his number and keep in touch with him when camp's over."

I lifted my arms. "Oh, yes, I'm sure every guy in college—especially one as good-looking and amazing as Jack—is dying to date a junior in high school."

She shrugged. "Tom was."

"Who's Tom?"

She slapped my leg. "My brother, you narcissistic moron!"

"Ow." I laughed. "Oh, okay. I'm sorry. I was lost in the story, not the names."

"Tom is three years older than Phoebe, and they've been dating for two years. She was fifteen when they met. You never know."

"You never do, do you?"

We arrived at the dock right on time—me in my bright yellow dress with my hair down and Emma in jean shorts and a tank top.

Jack smiled as we approached.

"Doesn't Julia look pretty?" Emma said.

"Please don't," I whispered to her.

"She does. You both do." He smiled wider. "Take a seat. We're just waiting on the twins."

I could swear he looked at me, daring me to say something, but I just smiled, and so did he. He had to be wondering if I'd spilled the kissing beans to Emma.

Once Brittany and Brianna arrived, we were treated to cheeseburgers and ears of corn on the grill with sides of potato chips and fruit salad that consisted mainly of watermelon and grapes. Emma challenged me to find more than three blueberries in the salad. I couldn't. All foods had been approved for us to eat.

"Let's all raise a glass of bug juice in a toast," Jack said, standing.

We all elevated our plastic cups.

"This is only my third year as the director of the Voyagers program, and I couldn't be more pleased with this group. Cheers to you guys!"

We each took a sip and placed our cups back on the table.

Jack remained standing and then turned to each of us. "Emma, let's start with you. I have to admit that I really thought you were going to bow out of the solo overnight after that tick bite. I'm especially proud of your bravery and your willingness to never give up. To Emma!"

We all cheered.

"Brittany," he began, "I've known you for a few years, and you're one of the last people I thought would join this program— not because I thought you couldn't do it, but because I don't think you give yourself enough credit."

Oh, she gives herself plenty, I thought.

Jack continued, "So, I'm very glad you challenged yourself, and I hope you're pleased with the results. To Brittany!"

We all cheered, and I made an extra effort to raise my cup and smile at her as sincerely as I could.

"Julia…" He looked me square in the eyes. "You've overcome some serious self-doubt, and it's been an honor for me to watch you become a stronger, more confident…woman," he said.

But I interpreted it as him saying how much he wanted to kiss me again.

Maybe I really am a narcissistic moron like Emma said.

Once he was done with everyone, we ate our feast, and then Rebecca and Amber followed Jack into the woods to look for sticks for s'mores. Emma stayed with the twins and me to clean up and prepare for dessert. We knew we had to be diligent, as night critters were especially fond of messy campers who left their food outside.

Once we were through, Brittany pulled a small container of cookies from the cooler along with a separate tray of chocolate bars, marshmallows, and graham crackers.

She and her sister each took one cookie and then offered me the tray. It was a standard foil-serving container from the mess hall, same as what all the other food had been in. Since I was slightly floored by her kind gesture, I grabbed a cookie, thanked her, and ate it.

The twins and I were sitting at the picnic table, eating our cookies in silence, as Emma was tying up the garbage bag. Just as I was a little over halfway through with mine, I heard a snicker. I swallowed and then made eye contact with Brianna as she snorted and exchanged glances with her sister, who was covering her mouth and giggling.

"What's so funny?" I asked.

Neither of them answered me. I thought I saw Brittany shrug, but then Emma walked over and noticed the awkward exchange going on between the sisters.

Her head went back and forth from me to them. "What's going on?" Emma asked as she sat beside me.

I just looked at her, my eyes saying, *I have no clue.*

"How was the cookie?" Brittany asked me with a raised brow and a wicked grin.

My stomach tightened with her words. I released my grip on the remainder of the cookie, and as if in slow motion, it fell to the table. My forehead began to perspire, and I looked at Emma with desperation in my eyes. I felt dizzy and scared.

And then I tasted it.

Emma sprang to her feet and dumped the cooler, looking for the container that had held the cookie I'd just eaten. "What did you give her?" she shouted at them. "Brittany!"

Emma dropped the cooler and then forcefully threw Brittany off the bench and onto the ground. Then, Emma sat on her.

"Ow! Get off me, you cow!" Brittany screamed.

I blinked my eyes and looked over at Brianna. She'd stopped laughing, and she was staring curiously at my face, specifically my mouth.

"Her lips," Brianna said quietly, pointing, not sure if she should still be laughing or not.

"What did you give her to eat?" Emma shouted.

Brittany just screamed and screamed for Emma to get off of her, but Emma wouldn't budge.

"Help!" Emma yelled from atop Brittany's stomach. "Jack, Amber, Theo! Anyone!"

Then, she looked at me, and I knew.

"Oh my God! We need an ambulance!" she shouted. "Somebody, help us!"

TWENTY-ONE

Julia

One time, when I was young, five years old maybe, my mom and dad had been about to take me to a doctor's appointment to test the severity of my allergy. They had sat me down and talked to me at length about how my body might react and how I should try not to be afraid.

"This is a standard test, sweetie," Mom said. "We know you have some allergy. We just don't know how bad it is, so the doctor is going to test you in his office. That way, he and I will protect you if anything happens. Okay? I don't want you to be scared."

I nodded.

"What kind of kid can't eat peanuts?" Dad asked.

From the way he'd said it, I felt like something was wrong with me.

It turned out there was. After the test, my pediatrician, Dr. Taxman, said I was the worst case he'd ever seen. In fact, my condition was relatively rare.

In his office, I began wheezing and coughing, and eventually, I threw up the Benadryl he had given me. I broke out into a few hives, mostly around my mouth, but that was all. We stayed there for a few hours, so Dr. Taxman could monitor me, and he said my mom should sleep on my bedroom floor that night to make sure I was still breathing.

Thankfully, that had been in a controlled environment. But this one in the woods, courtesy of the evil twins, was far from it.

I turned my head, and my attention went back to the cookie.

So, that's it? A fucking cookie? I thought, narrowing my eyes to try to focus on it. *That's what's going to kill me?*

I tilted my head to one side and stared. I watched, awestruck, as the cookie came alive and began to morph into shapes of various weapons made out of dough—first, a gun, a knife, and then a large peanut. It was confusing yet fascinating.

My whole life, I'd been careful to avoid my deadly allergen, preferring to believe I'd grow old and get dementia and die in peace like my nana. Or maybe I'd be parasailing off the coast of Mexico and die from a horribly unfortunate crash on the side of a mountain due to a negligent instructor who was employed by the fancy resort I was staying at, and they'd never bothered to check his credentials. *Bastards.*

Am I really going to die from the one thing I've avoided my whole life?

The one thing I knew could kill me was never the thing I'd actually thought would kill me because I'd taken such pains to avoid it.

I reached for the cookie on the surface of the table where I'd dropped it, but it fell to the ground when I went to pick it up. I squinted some more, still trying to focus on it once it had hit the dirt, but my eyes were itching like crazy. I could still hear Emma and Brittany shouting at each other, but their voices were muffled and distant. I looked back at where Brianna had stood, mocking me only seconds before, but she was gone.

Finally, Emma stood and rushed to my side. "Lie down! You need to lie down. I'm going to get the bags." She looked over my head. "Where the hell is everyone?"

Emma lowered me to the ground. Brittany had stood up and was brushing off her clothes. Her demeanor had changed, and she was lurking around us, like a vulture scavenging its prey. Only, she wasn't giggling anymore. She was just silently staring at me and observing my metamorphosis on account of her actions.

My eyes were stinging and watering, and the skin on my face was tightening fast. The sensation was unbearable. I could feel myself inflating like a balloon, and there was nothing I could do to loosen the pressure. My hands were pawing at my neck and face in a frantic attempt to bring some relief.

"Brittany, run as fast as you can and find Miss Alice before she dies!" Emma said to her.

"Dies?" she questioned.

"Yes, *dies*, you goddamn idiot. *Run!*" Emma was hysterical.

Brittany took off, and so did Emma. One went toward the camp, and the other ran into the woods.

Then, I was alone. I curled into the fetal position but with my neck extended like I was underwater, gasping for air. The walls of my esophagus were closing up, and it was getting harder and harder to breathe. I'd never worked so hard for one tiny breath. My fingers clawed at my throat as if I were trying to undo a noose around my neck. My lids fell shut, and I imagined myself on the floor of an elevator, watching the doors close, trying to get my arm in between them. I was both conscious of what was going on and simultaneously having delusions.

I brought my hands in front of me for a moment and saw that the hives had started to spread. It had been so long since my mom was around to help me that I surprised myself by shouting for her. I knew she wouldn't come, but I repeatedly called out for my mom.

Then, I vomited twice.

After who knew how long—less than a minute maybe— Emma, Jack, Amber, Rebecca, and Brianna emerged like bullets from the woods, and the next thing I knew, Jack was over me. I tightly closed my eyes, wishing that I could prevent him from seeing me this way.

"Oh my God, Pearl. No," he whispered loudly just one time. He was shaking his head, panicked and afraid to touch me.

From what I could tell, Emma handed him something, and then he began to move my body around with great force, but I barely felt his hands on me. Emma was crouched by my side with her hand over her mouth, rocking back and forth, muttering and sobbing.

Then, the needle went into my thigh, and everything went black.

The first sound I heard when I came to was Emma wailing.

The second was the sound of my own voice in my head, telling me, *You're not dead.*

I closed my eyes to let that sink in.

Holy crap! I didn't die!

I'm alive!

I survived the Cookie of Death!

Or so I hoped.

My mind was racing. I couldn't believe I was still alive. I'd thought for sure I was a goner.

And as soon as the severity of what had happened hit me...as soon as I had seen the look on Brittany's face—no, wait! I must rephrase that. As soon as I had seen the look on Brianna's face, I had known I was going to die.

I knew because Brittany's initial expression after I ate the cookie had been one of deception, while Brianna's had been one of deep regret.

She and I had looked at each other, and we'd both known things were about to get ugly for me, fast.

My head was filled with questions, but I needed to concentrate on breathing. I didn't think I could blow enough air out of my lungs to shift a feather.

Twenty-Two

Jack

Everything had happened so fast. One second, I'd been in the woods with Amber and Rebecca, climbing trees with my hunting knife, in search of the perfect marshmallow skewers. Then, the next minute, Brianna had screamed for me, panic-stricken. I couldn't even understand what she had been saying at first, just that I'd needed to hurry.

"Jack!"

I heard Brianna before I saw her.

"Jack!" She tripped over her own feet, running to us, and then she paused for only a second to catch her breath. "Julia broke out in hives, and her lips are swollen. You need to come back now. Hurry!"

"She what?" Amber asked, unfazed.

"She ate something, and then she started to break out. I think she needs help."

I threw my knife to the ground and jumped out of the tree. "What did she eat? Is she choking?" I was fully aware that the cooler had been packed by the kitchen staff and approved for both Julia and Emma.

Brianna glanced down. "A cookie."

I hadn't remembered there being any cookies in the cooler, just the s'mores. "Okay, let's see what—"

"Jack!" Emma shouted as if being chased through the woods by a rabid wolf. "Julia is dying! They gave her peanuts. She can't breathe. She's dying. They gave her nuts. They tried to kill her!"

All I heard was, "Julia is dying," and the words were nearly impossible to conceive.

You never really knew how your brain would try to make sense of a statement like that, and mine simply turned it into disbelief, as if the girls were playing some twisted evil joke on me.

I sprinted back to the table, and as I spotted her, my insides crumbled and then erupted. My mind and my heart had just been getting used to the idea of caring about her and being with her yet coming to terms with the fact that I was forbidden to do so.

I wanted to cry, but there was no time for that. She was barely moving, and she needed me to look after her like never before. Her body was on the ground in an unnatural position with her limbs all stiff and bent at odd angles. It looked as though she'd been knocked unconscious and then fallen off the picnic table.

I was too late.

I fell to my knees and crouched beside her. She looked worse close-up, but at least she was moving. Her hands and face, mostly around her mouth, were covered in circular red hives, and her lips looked like that of a cartoon duck. Swollen and foreign in shape, they didn't belong to her face—or any other human's face for that matter.

"We need to get her to the nurse. Now!" I said.

Emma slid beside me with her bag and handed me something that looked like a glue stick. She was hysterical. "Here, here. She needs this first. In the thigh!"

I took it from Emma. "What is this? I don't know what to do with this!"

Emma took the safety cap off and handed it back to me. "It's her EpiPen. She needs it now, or she will die for sure!" Her breaths were coming fast and furious. "In her thigh, in her thigh, in her thigh. I can't do it!"

Instinctively, I turned Julia on her side like I was roping cattle, and without a second thought, I jammed the needle end of the EpiPen into her thigh.

I held it there until Emma yelled, "Enough!"

It was hard to tell if Julia felt anything at all. She was clutching her throat, confused about why it was so hard to breathe.

I scooped her up into my arms and ran toward the infirmary. Bob, Alice, Liz, and some of the other camp staff came running toward us. Everyone's panic turned to horror as soon as they saw Julia. Not one of us had been prepared for the gruesome sight of beautiful, sweet Julia.

"Over here!" Bob shouted, waving me toward the front of the building.

I dropped to the ground with Julia in my lap as Alice did her best to administer some medication.

"I gave her a shot in the thigh. Emma gave it to me. I don't know if I did it correctly, but it seemed to go in. She didn't flinch." I was out of breath. "I don't think it worked. Nothing happened."

Alice placed her hand on Julia's forehead. "Oh, dear." She brought Julia's hand to her mouth and then looked at me and squeezed my arm. "You did the right thing, sweetie. Thank the heavens you were there."

Julia finally shifted and spit a little. It was torture, watching her gasp for air like a fish out of water. She was wide-eyed and confused.

"What happened?" Bob said, incredulous.

I was shaking my head. "I don't know. We were having our Voyagers dinner"—which he'd known about—"and I was getting some sticks for s'mores when Brianna and Emma came to find me. I wasn't there when it happened. I guess she ate a cookie or something."

The sound of someone howling interrupted me, and our attention turned to Emma.

"They did this to her!" She pointed at Brittany and Brianna, who were inconspicuously gathered with a group of onlookers.

Brianna was crying, and Brittany was somber and pale.

"Brittany tricked Julia into eating something with peanuts." Emma's voice was hoarse and guttural. "I saw the whole thing go down. They tried to kill her." She threw her arms up. "And they might have just succeeded!"

Everyone's eyes went to the twins, but mine went to Julia.

Please don't die. Please don't die. Please don't die, I repeated to myself. The burden of those words weighed heavily on me.

It was inconceivable that this girl—who'd come so far, who I'd just kissed less than a day ago, and who'd touched my heart like no one else had—might take her last breath in my arms. I fought back tears of my own and held Julia close.

The ambulance arrived, and I struggled to relinquish her to the paramedics.

Theo ran over and scooped her up, carrying her the rest of the way. He had to pry her fingers from me.

I stood, but before I following Julia, I went over to Brittany.

"What did you do? Is it true—what Emma said?" I asked.

She just shook her head. Her arms were wrapped around herself as if she were in a straitjacket.

"Did you have any part in this?" I asked, louder this time.

Girls were crying and hugging each other on all sides of us. Will was standing on the steps of the office building with his arm around Tabitha's shoulder as they both surveyed the scene in horror.

"We just thought it'd be funny," she whispered in a barely audible voice.

She glanced at Brianna, but Brianna was a pansy, a follower. There was no way this had been her brainchild. Brittany and I both knew it was all her idea.

I grabbed Brittany's shirt by the neck and rolled it into my fist with little concern for who was looking. "You thought it would be funny? To kill someone? To watch her suffocate at your feet?"

She shook, tears streaming down her face. "We...we just thought she would get all puffy and break out in hives," she said between sobs. "We didn't know she could die."

I released her with a forceful shove. "Does it matter? Really, does it matter that she might die now? Does that change the sheer stupidity and the cruelty of it?"

I wanted to spit on her. Instead, I turned in disgust and disbelief at what she had done. There was no explanation that would suffice, and I couldn't conceive of explaining this to Julia's father or anyone else. There was no way to make sense of this.

Bob ran over to me, his face exasperated, searching for answers.

"I think we have a problem," I said.

"That's putting it mildly!" he shouted. "How could this have happened?"

I took a deep breath and started walking toward the ambulance. "I think the twins did this to her."

"What?" He latched on to my arm, trying to stop me.

"I need to get to the ambulance."

"You're not going anywhere. We need to get to the bottom of this!"

I dragged him along for a few steps as I picked up my pace, and then I finally yanked my arm away.

"I'm going with her."

"You're not going anywhere."

Bob reached for me again, and I smacked his arm with as much force as I could.

"Don't fucking touch me." I stepped in close and looked down at him. "I'm going with her, and you'll meet us there. Don't touch me again." My face was hot, and my chest was pounding.

Once Julia was strapped into the back of the ambulance, I jumped in beside her.

Does she know what happened? Does she know the twins poisoned her? Did she trust them and me?

I had so many questions but needed to focus on Julia and keeping her alive, but there wasn't anything I could do, except for pray.

As soon as we were mobile, the paramedics gave her another EpiPen while I sat next to her, searching for any signs of life in her eyes. She blinked at one point, and when the paramedic loosened her oxygen mask, she was able to get a few sentences out, all of which had to do with *Charlie and the Chocolate Factory*.

For the second time in years, I wanted to cry.

TWENTY-THREE

Julia

I opened my eyes and noticed that I'd been moved. I was lying on my back with strangers staring down at me. The look on their faces did little to ease my fear.

Once I was secured inside the back of the ambulance, the voices around me got louder and more urgent. There was so much chatter that I wondered how anyone could manage to focus on anything.

I was saying Jack's name, calling out for him, but the oxygen mask was preventing anyone from hearing me. I attempted to lift my hand and feel my face, but one of the paramedics stopped me and shook his head.

The chaos in the back of the ambulance was like a scene on TV.

Bob the Slob Hanson was talking to one of the paramedics and Miss Alice as they were quickly trying to get me out of camp and to the ER.

Then, like the sun peeking through the clouds, I saw Jack's face. He handed something to Bob and then hopped into the back of the ambulance next to me.

One of the paramedics climbed in after him and closed the doors, and then we were off.

"I'm right here," Jack said as he gently moved some loose hairs off my face. He shook his head while gazing into my eyes. "Just whisper if you need me." He winked. "You're going to be okay," he assured me with an expression that accompanied his statement, but there was little confidence behind it.

Vanity got the best of me as we drove, and I became more conscious of just how swollen and rashy I'd become. I mumbled something through my mask.

Jack looked at me and furrowed his brow. "She's trying to say something," he said to the paramedic.

The man leaned over and shifted my mask to the side, so I could speak, but I couldn't get the words out.

"Shh," Jack said. "Don't try to say anything. You need to relax."

I closed my eyes and struggled for air, less so than before when I had been lying in the dirt, but it was still difficult. I opened my eyes, and Jack was still looking at me.

"I'm Violet Beauregarde," I whispered.

Jacked leaned in as close as he could to my face. "What? Are you okay?"

"I'm Violet Beauregarde," I repeated.

Jack looked up at the paramedic and shrugged, frustrated. Then, he reached for my hand. "You're what?"

I swallowed carefully. "Violet, from *Charlie and the Chocolate Factory*. Ever heard of it?" I attempted a swollen eye roll to no avail.

He let out a breathy laugh.

"She's the one who eats the three-course meal gum and then swells to a one-ton super-human blueberry." I gasped and managed a bloated smile despite my puffy cheeks' attempt to suppress it.

He gently squeezed my hand and rubbed the back of it with his thumb. "You do look extra juicy right now." His eyes scanned my face, and then he lowered his forehead to mine before sitting up and looking back at me. "I've never been so scared in all my life."

I closed my eyes. I hated that he'd had to see me like that. "Me neither," I whispered.

"You know, in the book version, Veruca Salt doesn't go down the bad egg shoot in the goose room like she does in the movie. She gets attacked by squirrels in the nut-sorting room." He lifted a brow. "Looks like you might be more Veruca than Violet."

I kept my eyes closed. "And you're the candy man—the guy everyone follows around, drooling over," I said. Then, I leaned to the side and vomited again.

Twenty-Four

JACK

A team of doctors and nurses were waiting as the back doors of the ambulance flung open. Bob and Alice had driven separately and were also there. Julia was taken into the ER, and we all followed behind, not knowing if she would emerge alive or dead.

"Who is the adult in charge of this girl?" a female physician asked, looking at Bob, Alice, and me.

Bob raised his hand. "I am, and this here is Alice Darwinkle, our camp nurse."

Alice was visibly shaken. The poor woman had been trained to treat pinkeye, mosquito bites, scrapes, and bruises. She could also remove a tick in one fell swoop, but she was not equipped to watch one of her campers die at the hands of another. None of us were.

Alice was a kind older woman, maybe in her late fifties, but two big chunks of gray hair made her look much older than she was. She was a product of the sixties and a true flower child through and through, spreading her peace and love ideals to hundreds of patients over her past twenty-five years as a nurse. Rumor was she'd worn the same pair of Birkenstocks to Woodstock. Her work at Hollow Creek was purely on a volunteer basis. She'd retired previously, but she was an old friend of Bob and Sally's, and she loved kids.

She wrung her hands, looking very distraught. Her voice trembled as she spoke, "I-I did my best to give her some Benadryl, but she was unable to keep it down. Jack here, one of our counselors, administered an EpiPen a few minutes after Julia ate the cookie."

She looked at me for confirmation, and I nodded to the doctor.

"Very well." The doctor quickly turned to Bob. "She's severely at high risk for losing her airway, and I'm afraid we might need to immediately intubate her in order to keep her airway open in her trachea. Since this requires us inserting a tube between her vocal cords, we're also going to have to sedate her for what might be up to twenty-four hours." She looked over her shoulder and nodded at someone rolling an IV stand. "Have her parents been contacted?"

"They have," Bob said.

"She doesn't have much time, and we can't wait to get their permission, so we're operating under emergency consent to treat a minor. I've given the orders to proceed, but you might want to let her family know if you are able to reach them. Are they on their way here?" There was an urgency to what the doctor was telling us, but she was very calm and precise with her tone.

Bob nodded. "Yes. Yes, they are. We were able to reach her father, and he should be here in a few hours. They are just coming from Chicago."

I was grateful that Julia had made it to the hospital and that they had a plan for her, but the doctor had said nothing reassuring. There was no, *She's going to be just fine*, or, *She's in good hands now*, or anything like, *Let us observe her for a while, and we'll send her home.*

My stomach turned.

"I will be back as soon as we're through to update you on her condition," the doctor said before briskly walking away.

The three of us stood there, unsure of what to do, what to say, or where to go.

Bob wrapped an arm around Alice's shoulder to calm her nerves. "Let's have a seat and wait," he said.

We all took a seat in the waiting room where mauve-colored vinyl furniture was accented by plastic ferns, bi-level Formica end tables, and copies of *Reader's Digest*. Much like Alice's sandals, not much in here had changed since the sixties.

A whoosh of air escaped from the seat cushion as I sat.

Bob took a deep breath and rubbed his head with both hands. "How did this happen? How could this have happened?"

Twenty-Five

Julia

As soon as I'd gotten to the hospital, I had been whisked into the ER, away from Jack. Bob Hanson had already been there with Miss Alice. Both had been on cell phones and staring at me with the same worried look as I rolled past them. Miss Alice had blown me a kiss.

The paramedics had handed their paperwork to the attending staff and carefully transferred me off the mobile gurney and onto a hospital bed. I never got to thank them.

"Hi, Julia. I'm Dr. Akbarnia." She had dark hair and dark eyes and an exotic beauty about her, even in scrubs. "I hear you gave everyone quite a scare," she spoke quietly. Her tone was conversational, and her demeanor was calming, as if she and I were sitting at an outdoor café somewhere, sipping lattes.

I gave a small nod. Given everything I'd gone through in the past hour or so, I appreciated that there was nothing rushed about her behavior. Two residents were standing behind her, watching me, and a nurse walked in behind them with an IV bag.

"It looks as though you are improving slowly, but we'd like to get some additional medication in you to help you breathe. I don't want you to have to swallow anything right now because your esophagus is still pretty swollen." She looked at me for my approval. "All right then. Nurse Taylor is going to insert the IV."

The nurse walked around to the other side of the bed, across from the doctor, and asked me to make a fist and then release it.

I turned my head away from her and prayed she would nail it on the first try. She did.

I opened my mouth to speak, but I had to clear my throat before I could get any words out. "I didn't mean to…" I said quietly.

"What, honey?" The doctor moved closer to me.

"I didn't mean to cause all this trouble."

She placed her hand on my arm. "Of course. This was not your fault. Don't be silly. Try not to talk though." She smiled and patted the back of my hand.

"I know it wasn't my fault." I tightly squeezed my eyes shut and cringed at the lack of oxygen. "I was poisoned."

Dr. Akbarnia was slightly taken aback but managed to maintain most of her smile—maybe because she thought I was being dramatic, not because she believed someone would have done that to me.

She switched back to her café latte voice. "You have a nut allergy, I see here, and you ate something you shouldn't have. Is that correct?"

For the first time in what seemed like days but was likely less than an hour, I was able to swallow. "Could I have some water?"

"Of course," she said. She asked one of the residents, who was watching me deflate, to get me some water.

She checked my chart while we waited. "We have been seeing a rise in peanut allergies over the past two years. Have you had this condition all your life?"

"Pretty much."

She pursed her lips and nodded. "Well, thankfully, you had a quick-thinking counselor close by."

A nice-looking young guy in blue scrubs approached me with a cup of water and a straw. I took a tiny sip, choked a little, and then took a second one.

"He wasn't close by when it happened," I started to tell her, my voice working at about half its normal volume. "One of the two girls who tried to kill me ran after him when she realized what she'd done. Probably when my head turned into a pumpkin."

Dr. Akbarnia looked confused and exchanged glances with the water boy.

"I don't think anyone was trying to kill you," she said after a sip of her imaginary latte and a bite of her imaginary cranberry scone.

"What were they trying to do then?" I honestly hoped for the answer but assumed it wasn't going to come from her.

She studied my face for a moment and looked deep into my eyes. "Can you tell me exactly what happened?"

So, I did, but before I was able to finish, my throat tightened again, and I couldn't get any air. My chest was heaving, but my lungs weren't benefiting from it.

The next thing I knew, Dr. Akbarnia shouted some orders to the water boy and said something about intubation. Then, she turned to the nurse who'd just stuck me with an IV.

"We're going to need to call the police," the doctor said.

TWENTY-SIX

Julia

My father's best qualities were also his most embarrassing. He never entered a room quietly. He never lowered his voice for any reason, not even in a movie theater. And he never respected anyone's personal space—least of all mine. As usual, I heard him before I saw him.

"Julia, goddamn it. I only just turned sixty, for God's sake! My heart can't take this!" He burst through the curtain like an angry bull with his hand clutching his chest, causing Dr. Akbarnia to finally lose her signature cool.

He grabbed his head with his hands when he saw me, and I started to cry. I could never hold back my tears if something was wrong, and my dad was around.

When my ex-boyfriend Jimmy had broken up with me two days before prom and ended up taking that slushie-slut Karin Hanley to the dance instead, the only time I'd cried about it was when my dad asked me why I was staying home and why he'd paid good money for a new dress.

When I'd cheated on an algebra exam and gotten an A, my dad had sat me down and told me how proud he was, and I'd burst into tears.

When I had taken his car to the mall and someone rear-ended me, I'd called him in hysterics, and he had been pissed. He hadn't been mad about the damage to the car. He had been pissed because I'd scared him with my hysteria.

"Don't bother me with tears unless you're dying," he'd said.
Request fulfilled.

Sharlene raced past him and kissed my forehead. She had tears in her eyes and was clutching a wad of tissue. "Oh my God, honey, are you okay?" Her face was frantic with worry.

I nodded, surprised to see her so torn up about it.

Dr. Akbarnia moved over as my dad muscled his way in. He hugged me hard for a good long time, and I sobbed.

"I'm so sorry, Dad."

He pulled back. "Don't you dare apologize. We're going to get to the bottom of this, and heads are going to roll. Roll, I tell you! I'm going to own that godforsaken camp by the weekend."

I cringed, and he looked at the group of people in the room, which now included Bob the Slob Hanson, Miss Alice, Dr. Akbarnia, and three other hospital staff.

"Dad, please," I whispered.

Sharlene loosely held my left hand and dabbed at her tears.

"What?" He lifted his shoulders. "I'm sorry, sweetheart, but I just drove one hundred ninety miles in two hours, planning my only daughter's funeral," he spoke louder for effect. Then, he leaned in and whispered in my ear, "I didn't even have a chance to stop at The Brat Stop." He planted a kiss on my puffy face.

Thank God he never changes.

Dad turned to the group. "Who's in charge here?"

Sharlene played with my hair.

"I'm the attending on call," Dr. Akbarnia said. "And I believe Mr. Hanson here is the camp's director. I think we both would like to talk with you in private."

My father's hands went to his hips. "Clear this room, except for you two and my wife, please."

The uninvited guests scurried out, gladly, and left us alone.

"I want answers, and I intend on getting them, but let's start with what's most important here. Is she going to be all right? And by all right, I mean, exactly as she was—perfect."

The doctor nodded. "She suffered a severe anaphylactic reaction, but yes, she is showing all the right signs of improvement. We had a scare for a moment and thought we were going to need an emergency intubation on her, but we were able to keep the internal swelling down, and thankfully, we did not have to intubate.

It can be a painful procedure, and we would have had to sedate her for—"

"If you didn't have to do it, then why are we talking about it?" Dad interrupted.

"Mel, let the doctor finish," Sharlene scolded him.

"I'm sorry." He really must've been out of sorts because he didn't hand out apologies too often.

The doctor sighed as if there was no one that could surprise or derail her. "Bottom line is, we expect her to be perfect once again. We still have some tests to do, as all patients who undergo anaphylaxis need to be examined and monitored. There are cases where it's not always a single reaction. The symptoms can rebound, returning hours or even days after the epinephrine injector—the EpiPen—has been administered, so we'd like to watch her for a day or so."

"I really don't want to stay here," I said.

"You'll do what the doctor says," my dad snapped without looking at me. "You're sure she's going to be good as new?"

"I'm sure, yes. She was treated just in time, and she has rapidly improved, even in her short stay with us here."

"Her short stay with you?" He shrugged and sniffed out a chuckle. "It's like the Four Seasons here—only, some people don't check out. Was there a bath towel shaped like a swan when you got to your bed?" he asked me.

I glared at my father. "Stop it." I could see the Slob sweating in the corner, shaking like a naughty puppy that just peed on the floor.

"You." He pointed at the puppy. "How in the hell did this happen?"

Before Bob could answer, three police officers walked in.

"What's this?" Dad said.

One of them spoke, "I'm Officer McCaffery, and this is Officer McNeil and Officer Sullivan."

I could see my father desperately holding back an Irish crack.

"I couldn't have possibly offended anyone that quickly, could I have?" he said with a shrug.

Dr. Akbarnia made a move like she was about to speak, but I raised my hand to stop her. "Could I speak with my dad alone for a minute?"

She turned to the officers. "Her father has only just arrived. Perhaps we can give them a moment, and Mr. Hanson and I can speak with you outside."

Everyone agreed to that and left us alone. Sharlene was still clutching my hand and making me feel as though I were on my deathbed rather than rapidly improving as the doctor had just assured us.

Dad rolled a stool next to the bed. "Tell me why the police are here."

I took a deep breath. "I need you to promise to be calm."

"I can't promise that, and you know it."

I closed my eyes and tilted my head back. "Please, Dad!" I choked the words out.

Sharlene reprimanded him, "Enough of this nonsense, Mel! Your daughter is trying to talk to you, which is obviously painful for her, and she doesn't want a three-ring circus in here. No one does. Let's be thankful we found her in this condition and not worse off, as we had feared! Take a seat, and let her speak without any of your antics for five minutes."

Sharlene's support surprised me, and my dad went from an angry bull to more of an old but attentive German shepherd.

"Go on, sweetie," she said.

"Well," I began with something impressive, "I wrote and told you guys about the Voyagers program, remember? We passed all those survival skills, and I learned to take care of myself while alone in the woods."

"Ah, yes, and the first thing I hope to see on any new associate's resume at the firm is, *I can boil water.* Go on."

"Mel!" Sharlene hollered. Then, she looked at me with kind eyes. "Yes, Julia, we were so proud of you when we read all about that. I don't think I would last five minutes on my own. You've really impressed us."

Her sincerity surprised me, and I gave her an odd look.

Then, I continued, "Anyway, tonight was our celebration party. Jack, the leader of the Voyagers, threw a dinner party for the six of us in the group since we'd all passed." I swallowed carefully.

"With peanut butter sandwiches and hazelnut cookies?" My dad simply couldn't resist.

"No. The camp cafeteria had prepared and packed an approved meal for us, as they always do, but…"

His eyes widened. "But what?"

"But two of the girls, campers, tricked me into eating something I wasn't supposed to."

Sharlene let go of me, and her hands went to her mouth as she gasped. Across from her, the bull was back. In fact, I could have sworn that I saw actual steam coming out of my dad's ears as he paced the room. He nearly put his fist through the wall.

"Officer McFriendly!" he shouted through the curtain. "We're ready for you!"

Twenty-Seven

Jack

Seeing Julia's father storm the castle was more than I could handle. I left the waiting room and walked briskly down a brightly lit, sterile hallway, stumbling over my own feet, to the front of the hospital. Then, I went outside through the automatic sliding doors to the parking lot. My head was pounding. There was a bench a few feet from the entrance, so I lay down and bent my legs with my arms crossed over my face.

Some might say that having lost both my parents, the two people closest to me in the world, would have given me some insight into death, a unique perspective on life and loss, and that I'd somehow be more prepared than the average Joe who had made it to age nineteen without losing someone close to him or someone he loved. But I wasn't. I was only five years old when my parents had disappeared like snowballs under the hot sun, gone from my grasp forever.

Nothing could have prepared me for what had happened earlier today between the girls. And what puzzled me the most was that I couldn't figure out if I was so distressed that someone so young and beautiful had almost died in my arms…or if it was because that person was Julia Pearl. I thought the latter had hit me harder than the basic severity of the situation. Seeing someone I knew on the brink of death—unable to breathe, unable to ask for help, unable to trust the people around her to keep her safe—had been bad enough. But this was someone I'd come to really care about.

The image of her face, seconds before I'd kissed her, came to me—her fascinating blue eyes, her hesitant smile, her killer lips. I'd wanted more of her that night, and it had been torture to keep my cool. I wanted her again, now more than ever.

I rubbed my eyes and slammed the concrete wall next to me with my fist when I felt a hand on my shoulder.

"You okay, brother?" Will asked with Tabitha standing next to him. "You look like shit," he added.

I sat up and Tabby bent down to give me a hug. "Oh my God, Jack, that was insane."

I looked up at them and then leaned forward over my knees as I shook my head. It'd been a long time since I felt like crying, let alone acted on it. I lifted my head. "Where are the other girls? Emma and the twins?"

Tabby sat next to me, crossed her legs, and rested a hand on my back. "Most of them are in the lodge. Emma is with Theo and my mom in Bob's office. She tried to go apeshit on Brittany, so we had to separate them." She looked at Will and then at me. "Is it true that they did this to her?" Her face was incredulous.

I leaned back. "Do you have a smoke on you?" I asked Will.

"You don't smoke!" Tabby snapped.

"I do now."

"Sorry, brother." He threw me an apologetic look. "Rushed out too fast to grab anything."

The front of the hospital was a busy place. Cars were pulling up, followed by slamming doors. People were on their cell phones, talking loudly over each other. Doctors and nurses and various people clad in scrubs were pushing wheelchairs in every direction.

"Let's get out of here," I said.

The three of us walked through the parking lot and across the street to a large grassy area. It was meant to serve as a front lawn to the building, but it seemed to me like it only added extra drive time for the emergency vehicles.

We sat on the ground.

"They called the cops," I said.

Tabitha sat up straighter. "Who did?"

"The hospital."

She considerably slumped her shoulders. "How do you know?"

"Because three cops showed up, and Bob, Alice, and I didn't call them."

Tabitha sighed. "Were you able to see Julia? To get any information from her?"

I shook my head since Julia and I had only discussed the critical details in regard to what character she most resembled in *Charlie and the Chocolate Factory*. "But I did talk with Brittany just before I jumped in the ambulance."

"And?" Will chimed in.

"And I think she did it. I think she almost fucking killed Julia." I threw my arms up. "For all I know, she did."

The moisture came quickly to my eyes, and although I sniffed and looked away before letting go of one drop, Tabitha knew me all too well.

She inhaled, surprised by my emotion. "Jack, oh my God, don't get upset." She rested her hand on my knee. "It wasn't your fault."

I nodded. "I was in charge of them."

"Don't do this to yourself. Let's go in there, and check on her. She's getting the care she needs, and I'm sure she's going to be fine. Dad texted Mom that she was stable."

Tabitha always referred to her parents as though they were mine, too, but I always only called them by their first names. I guessed it was nice of her to make the effort though.

I nodded. "Did anyone talk with the twins?"

Will shook his head. "They weren't speaking by the time we left. Theo and Elaine and maybe Liz, too, had separated them, but neither of them said anything. What exactly did Brittany say to you, mate?" he asked, his eyes roving my face for answers.

My body heat rose. "I was in such a frantic out-of-body mode that I hardly remember, but I know she didn't deny it. She was shaking her head, saying no, but then she said something about just trying to embarrass Julia, not kill her." I turned to see a look of horror on Tabitha's face. "I want to talk to them."

Tabitha slowly bobbed her head. "Let's check on Julia, and then we'll head back to camp. Hopefully, they will talk to you."

I stood. "They're going to have to talk to the cops, so they might as well talk with me first." I looked her square in the eyes. "They could be charged with attempted murder."

TWENTY-EIGHT

Julia

Everyone, including the police, filtered back into the room and allowed my father his freak-out moment, his chance to shout and scream and rip the camp and the two girls who had harmed me to shreds. He was certainly due at least that.

Once he was through, the Slob spoke up for the first time, "Mr. Pearl, uh…Mrs. Pearl, and, Julia, we are every bit as angry and upset and mortified…stupefied even as to how this could have happened. We are taking every measure possible to understand not only how this happened but why." He paused.

My dad stood, facing him, his arms crossed, with a look of disgust on his face. Bob was sweating and messy, and he kept pushing his glasses up the bridge of his nose and rubbing the back of his neck with a handkerchief. If ever my father wanted to hurl daggers in the form of verbal abuse at someone, it was right then and there. I just knew it. But he showed an impressive amount of self-control and let Bob finish.

"While we were out in the hall," Bob said, "the doctor and I briefed the officers on what had happened, but they would like to talk to Julia themselves, if that's okay with you." He glanced quickly at my father, who was staring at him like a bull would with a matador. "I didn't have the details about what had happened until after we arrived here, and I spoke with the doctor, so in the meantime, I will head back to camp to talk with the girls, which we have not had a chance to do as Julia's health and safety was our first and only concern."

My dad spoke softly, shocking us all, "My daughter has asked me to restrain myself, and I have agreed to do that in her presence. However"—he lifted a hand—"once I am out of her presence, I'm going to call the state's attorney—who was my roommate in law school and who owes me a favor—and I intend to come down hard on the camp and on those two girls. I don't care how old they are, how rich they are, or how connected their idiot parents are because no one is older, richer, or more connected than I am." He paused for effect. "I would run back and let their parents know those girls have just signed up for prison camp."

I burst into tears again. All I wanted was to get back to camp and Jack and Emma and the bonfire and the mosquitoes and the damp, smelly bathhouse. If Brittany and Brianna got kicked out, then that would be icing on the cake, but I didn't want my father to destroy the entire camp in his wake.

Bob and Miss Alice scurried out of the room, all backward and frightened and stumbling over one another, like Dorothy and the Cowardly Lion after the Wizard had yelled at them from behind the curtain.

Officer McCaffery spoke, "We would like to talk with Julia and get a statement from her."

"Not now," Dad said. "You can come back in a few hours and check in with me first. I don't want anyone coming in here and questioning her without my permission and my presence. Are we perfectly clear on that?"

"Of course," the officer said. Then, he motioned for the other two to follow him out.

My father leaned in close to me once the room had cleared. "Why are you crying?"

I sniffed. "Please don't punish the camp. I just want to get out of here and get back to my friends. I'm happy there! None of us thought I would be, but I am. Please just handle this quietly and behind the scenes and let everything get back to normal. Can you *please* do that for me?"

My father and Sharlene exchanged looks, and he took a frustrated deep breath before continuing, "Those girls almost killed you tonight. Killed you, Julia. Not teased you, not bullied you, not short-sheeted your bunk or replaced your shampoo with Elmer's

Glue. They almost *killed* you, same as if they'd fired a gun at your chest." He was getting choked up, which only made me more upset. "I understand that you don't want to draw attention to yourself, but unfortunately, they've done it for you."

Sharlene handed me a tissue and helped me wipe my nose. Then, she spoke, "I think all she's asking is that we let the authorities handle this. She's just told us how much she has enjoyed her time there, as she said in her letters—had you bothered to read them—detailing the many *wonderful* people she's met and befriended. I think you and I both know that the camp is filled with caring, honest, kind folks, who are as appalled and horrified by what these two girls have done as we are."

I looked up at Sharlene, and she smiled at me before looking back at my dad. "So, let's focus on Julia, and let the police and the camp deal with the sisters."

Thank you, I mouthed to her. "That's all I'm asking, Dad. Please, for once, stay on the sidelines, and just step in when absolutely necessary."

He sighed. "How in the hell am I supposed to send you back to that place? You think I'm letting you go back to camp?"

He threw his arms up and looked to Sharlene for some backup support, but she said nothing. Either she wanted me dead and thought sending me back would be the best chance at sealing the deal, or she was doing everything she could to make sure I got what I wanted, not what I deserved for once. And hell if it wasn't a nice change.

"You know I'll be fine! You sent me in the first place when you knew I didn't want to go. Now that I actually do want to go, you're going to keep me from it?"

He started pacing. "After what just happened, you think you're going to waltz in there and go back to roasting marshmallows and singing 'Hallelujah' and everyone is going to treat you like you didn't almost just die? These girls have irrevocably altered your camp experience, not me." He let out a long breath and studied my face. "How many weeks are left?"

"Just two. Two weeks—that's it. And I promise you that I will not eat anything outside of the mess hall. I promise. I will even have all my meals—breakfast, lunch, and dinner—in Miss Alice's office if that will make you feel better."

Dad rubbed his forehead and looked at me like I was crazy. "You just said yourself that you weren't looking forward to spending the summer here. So, why on earth wouldn't you want to cut ties and come home early and be done? You were begging to come to Aspen with us, and we're leaving in two days. You can even bring a friend if you want."

"Please let me stay. I have my reasons, and I'm happy here."

Sharlene leaned in and kissed the top of my head. "What do you say, Mel?"

Before he could answer, someone poked his head between the curtains. It was Jack.

"May I come in?" he asked.

The three of us faced him, and the room went silent. The fluorescent lights of the emergency room accented his richly tanned skin and the two emeralds he carried in his eye sockets, causing us all to pause and soak him up like the sun. Well, I sure did anyway.

Then, Jack looked at me and smiled, as if nothing had happened. As if my face and mouth and arms weren't covered in hives. As if my cheeks and lips were not slowly shrinking. As if I hadn't puked on his flip-flops. As if he still wanted to kiss me.

"Ah, hell." Dad leaned over me and grumbled to Sharlene, "Something tells me her reason has just arrived."

Jack approached my father first. "You must be Mr. Pearl, Julia's father. I've heard a lot about you." He shook my dad's hand and then looked at the floor in shame.

I could have sworn he'd been crying.

"I'm Jack Dempsey, her Voyagers leader. I wish I knew what to say. I'm sorry just doesn't seem even remotely close to how regretful I am that this happened on my watch."

My dad shook his hand. "Jack Dempsey, huh? Like the boxer? You ever heard of him?"

"I have, sir. I get that a lot."

"For God's sake, don't call me sir. My name is Mel."

"Sorry, Mel."

"You can call me Mr. Pearl." My dad crossed his arms.

"Of course." Jack nodded.

Sharlene glanced at me and met my gaze. She was grinning like a schoolgirl, and she widened her eyes in that way older women do, as if to say, *He's a cutie!*

My dad looked him over. "Where are you from?"

"I'm originally from Chicago, but I've lived up here since I lost my parents when I was five."

"Ah, Jesus." Dad dropped his arms, all annoyed, in a way that said, *Why the hell do you have to make me feel sorry for you?* "You go to school?" Dad moved on. He never wanted to be bothered with anyone's sob story.

"I do. Just finished my freshman year at the University of Wisconsin in Madison, and I'll be there for a while. I'm planning on getting my master's in child psychology."

My dad looked over at me. "Let me guess, Jules. You want to go to the University of Wisconsin now, don't you?"

Sharlene interjected before I could strangle my father with my IV line, "Lovely to meet you, Jack." She shook his hand. "I'm Sharlene, Julia's stepmom."

Jack shook her hand and glanced at me with confusion since I'd, of course, painted Sharlene as some horrifying, wine-guzzling, aloof, narcissistic witch, and there she was, holding my hand and petting my hair, refusing to leave my side.

"Were you the boy who administered the EpiPen?" she asked.

That got my dad's attention.

"Yes, ma'am. I'd never even seen one before, but her friend Emma told me how to do it. Julia is one tough girl. I knew that before this happened, but now, I have proof. She gave us all a real scare. Thank God she's still with us."

My dad made his don't-bullshit-a-bullshitter face, faking a smile and blinking. "Yes, you and God were the people I was most interested in chatting with. In fact, I've ordered two gratuity plaques—"

"Mel, honey." Sharlene briskly walked around to the other side of the bed and wrapped her arm around my father's waist. "Why don't we let them talk alone and finish up our conversation with the doctor outside?"

I'd never cared for Sharlene more than I did in that moment.

Come to think of it, I've never cared for Sharlene.

Dad narrowed his eyes and glanced back at Jack before he walked out.

Jack took a seat on the stool next to the bed and held my hand. "Is this good-bye?"

"I hope not."

"Is he going to let you come back to camp?"

"He doesn't want to, but I think he will. For once in my life, Sharlene seems to be on board with everything, shocking as it seems."

"Maybe she loves you and cares about you." Jack glanced at the curtains.

"More like, maybe she's had a feng shui expert harmonize our house while I've been away and wants me the feng out of there for good. I'm sure she doesn't want me to come home yet. Well, maybe just to walk Bo, assuming she hasn't accidentally left the front door open."

"She's nothing like I pictured. Walking in here, no one would guess that there's any bad blood between the two of you. I'm guessing your issues with her are really just that—your issues. She seems genuinely concerned."

"You love to practice your psychology."

He thought for a second. "I really do."

"What do you know about teenage psycho killers?"

Jack furrowed his brows and let out a laboriously pained sigh. "I don't even know what to say. I'm so sorry this happened. You have no idea. Did you talk to the police?"

I shook my head and went to sit up, but the IV line was preventing me from getting too comfortable. "I think they will be back tonight for my statement. Have they been to the camp to talk to anyone?"

"I don't know. What are you going to say to them?"

He reached his hand to my face and brushed my hair out of my eyes. His touch was tender and warm and caught me off guard while his face was full of regret and devoid of a smile. Jack always had a light, an energy, a radiant positivity beaming from his pores at all times. I hated to see him so down like this on my account.

"I can only tell them what I know. Brittany handed me a cookie from a tray in the cooler, and I ate it. But once I was chewing, the two of them were looking at me funny, like they were waiting for my reaction...or basically waiting for me to—I don't know—die?" I slid under the thin white blanket covering me and wiped my eyes. "I was so scared."

He shook his head and dragged his hands through his hair. "I'm so sorry. I made you come to that dinner."

"No, don't say that. I wanted to be there, to be with you. I just mean, I've never felt so helpless and out of control in my life. It was beyond fear. It was like another level altogether. I was certain I was going to die, and at some point—I don't know exactly when—when I was lying on the ground, I found peace within the terror. Almost like free-falling and knowing there's no going back. That's how I knew I was dying. Thanks to you, I didn't die, but I *was* dying." I narrowed my eyes. "How weird is that?"

He let out a small laugh at the absurdity of it all, and so did I.

Then, he nodded and moved his eyes to my hand, leaving them suspended there for a moment. "I'd really like to hold your hand, but I can't," Jack said quietly.

I glanced at the curtain. "I know." I flashed him a wistful look. "Maybe one day?"

"Maybe." He touched my wrist and then pulled away.

TWENTY-NINE

JACK

My stomach growled as I walked out of Julia's room. I saw her father in the waiting area, and we made eye contact. He waved me over, and I placed my hand over my abdomen as I moved toward him.

"Sit down." He gestured to a seat next to him. "I want you to be straight with me, no bullshit."

"Yes, sir."

"How the fuck did this happen?" he asked with a scowl on his face.

Sharlene smiled at me and then got up and went to Julia.

I swallowed hard and straightened my spine. He wanted answers that I didn't have. Brittany and Brianna were flirtatious idiots but not killers. One time, Brianna had had me capture a dragonfly that was trapped in the boathouse, and she'd let him free because she felt sorry for it. Mr. Pearl was justified in his question, but I was empty-handed.

"I'm going to head back to camp and find out exactly why they did this."

"Is my daughter unpopular?"

I shook my head. "No, sir, she's not."

"Did she mistreat these girls in some way? Spit in their scrambled eggs, take a shit in their Cheerios?"

I shook my head again.

He stood. "No need to answer because it wouldn't matter, would it? *Nothing* could justify what happened here!"

He sat back down on the edge of the chair, pointing a finger at me, while a few people stared at us. But I refused to come undone.

His voice returned to a mild roar. "I know you and my daughter are close, and I know this was not your fault. In fact, I've been told that I might have very well been planning her funeral if it weren't for you. So, for that, I will be forever grateful." He paused. "But this isn't going to bode well for those girls or the camp, and I want you to promise me that I and the authorities will have your full cooperation, that you will have Julia's best interests in mind when dealing with the fallout."

I took a deep breath. "I care a lot about Julia. She and I have become close…friends, and I want you to know how hard this is for me to see her like this, to see her like she was—suffering and unable to breathe. I have never been so worried about anything before in my life. Those girls deserve everything that will come down on them, but the camp is devastated by this, too. No one there will take this lightly or take for granted the fact that Julia survived. Hollow Creek is a good place with really, really good people, and we will all be forever changed by this."

He scanned my face. "The director—that's your uncle?"

"Yes."

He let out a sigh filled with pity. "Shit."

"Mr. Pearl, I really don't know what else to say. The fact that Julia almost died is not lost on any of us. I can't imagine how you feel and how badly you want justice. I don't blame you. I think the best thing we can all do right now is focus on getting her back to feeling a hundred percent and moving past this."

"You let me worry about what's going to happen next, and I'll let you keep a close eye on her for the next few weeks since I'm not going to win the battle to bring her home."

"You have my word."

We both stood, and Mr. Pearl slapped my shoulder. "Go on. Get out of here."

The air outside the automatic doors was exactly as it should be—fresh, warm, and full of promise—and the moon was shining bright and void of any unrest. Will and Tabby were waiting for me on the bench.

Tabby jumped to her feet. "How is she?"

"She's good. Really good, I think."

"Thank God," she said.

Will got up. "You want us to hang around longer?"

I shook my head. "No. Let's head back to camp." My stomach growled again.

"You hungry, mate?"

"Just nerves I guess."

Tabitha wrapped her arm around my waist. "It's all going to be okay. You're such a sweetheart to worry so much."

"She almost died."

Tabitha cocked her head to the side. "I know, Jack, but she didn't. You saved her life."

"I wish everybody would stop saying that." I threw my head back. "Emma handed me the EpiPen, and I did what I was told. I didn't even think about it."

"If you had, Julia might not be here," Tabby said.

I started to walk. "Please, just get me back."

We rode back to camp in silence. It was dark and just after eleven p.m. as the car pulled off the main road and onto the dimly lit drive, passing the sign that said, *Welcome to Hollow Creek*. I could hear the familiar sound of gravel crunching beneath the tires until Will parked behind the main office.

But everything had changed.

There were three police cars and two unmarked black vehicles with flashing lights on their dashboard, and a small crowd of people was gathered by the front steps. There was a collective gasp when I emerged from behind the building.

"Jack!" Emma ran to me.

Liz followed.

"How is Julia?" Emma's eyes were red and eager. "Miss Alice said she survived and that she's doing good. Is that true?"

"Yes."

I hugged her, and she broke down. Liz rubbed Emma's back and met my eyes until I pulled back.

"She's going to be fine, and she's coming back here," I said.

"When?"

"I don't know, but she told her dad she wanted to come back."

Emma wiped her nose and nodded. "Okay. I can't wait to see her. Can you take me to the hospital?"

I shook my head. "She needs to rest, and I'm sure they don't want too many visitors." I placed my hand on Emma's shoulder. "She owes you her life, Emma." It felt good to say that to her because it'd felt wrong when people said it to me.

Emma just furrowed her brows and shook her head. She was about to say something when two men approached me. They were both in khaki pants and short-sleeved dress shirts. One had a notepad in his hand, and the other had a pager and a walkie-talkie clipped to his belt.

"Mr. Dempsey?" The one with the notepad introduced himself, but I didn't catch his name because Emma was still hurling questions at me.

I shook some hair out of my eyes. "Yeah."

"Can you come with us?"

"Of course."

I said good-bye to Emma and followed them to Bob's office where there were two officers and a woman behind the desk, typing into her laptop with great concentration. Squidward was guarding his bowl of kibble in the corner of the room, but he ran over to me as soon as I entered. I rustled the fur on his head, and he sat at my feet, tail wagging. The two men who had escorted me in there stood just outside the door.

"Please have a seat," the woman said without looking away from the screen. "And thank you for attracting the dog. I don't think he likes me very much."

"He's friendly. You're just sitting close to his food."

"Ah, I see." She finally made eye contact with me. She stood up halfway and extended her hand. "I'm Gina DiVito, Assistant State's Attorney here in Wisconsin. Can I ask you a few questions, Jack?"

I nodded.

She sat back and glanced at a few papers in front of her. "Would you mind telling me your account of what happened earlier tonight?"

I shifted my body in the chair and stretched out my legs. The stupid chair was so uncomfortable and too small for me. My eyes went to the floor as I recounted the story for her. She was an attractive woman, maybe in her late forties, with dark brown hair pulled back into a tight bun, and she kept her focus on me with her

198

arms folded on the desktop until I finished about fifteen minutes later.

Before she spoke, she took a sip of coffee from a chipped Hollow Creek mug that Bob probably hadn't rinsed out for years until tonight. "How long have you known these two girls, Brittany and Brianna Bingham?"

I shrugged. "A few summers maybe."

"Do you think they intended to kill Miss Pearl?"

I shrugged again. "Have you asked them?"

She nodded and flashed a grin. "We have."

"And what did they say?"

"I'm curious to hear your thoughts on it first."

"No." I sighed. "I don't think they tried to kill her." I lowered my head. "I think they were trying to embarrass her, watch her swell up or something. It's equally appalling, but I don't know if they even knew she could die from eating nuts."

Ms. DiVito placed her palms on the desk. "I don't either." Then, she stood and walked around to the front of the desk and leaned against it, her arms crossed. "Did you know how severe Julia's allergy was?"

I made eye contact with her. She was both disarming and intimidating, especially up close. She struck me as the type of woman who always got her way, even at the inconvenience of others. The type who would march to the front of a long line of people just to ask a question, and she'd get away with it.

Squidward lifted his head and stared at her, too.

"I knew she had a peanut allergy, but I honestly don't know much about that or what it entails, other than she can't eat peanuts."

She uncrossed her arms and placed her hands beside her on the desk. "Did the staff ever provide any sort of training for you and the other staff in regard to Miss Pearl and"—she lifted a piece of paper—"the four other campers who have food allergies?"

I waited before shaking my head. "I know the kitchen staff prepares special meals for them when necessary, and there's a section in the mess hall with safe foods that's only for them."

"Yes, we've talked with the kitchen staff, too." She smiled, her lips together. "Who prepared the dinner for your Voyagers picnic this evening?"

"The kitchen staff."

"Do you know that for a fact?" she asked.

I blinked and ran my hand across my forehead. "I picked it up from them right before dinner. They knew Julia and Emma were going to be eating it. There's no way they would have allowed those cookies to be in there. You're not trying to pin this on the kitchen, are you?"

"I'm just trying to get all the facts."

"It sounds like you're looking to blame the camp for not training us. Who could have been trained for a situation like what happened tonight? Two spoiled brats pulled a prank that no one could have prepared themselves for."

Ms. DiVito walked back to Bob's dinosaur of a desk chair and sat down. "So, you were aware of the allergies your campers had. Were you aware they carried EpiPens?"

"I'd never even heard of an EpiPen before tonight."

She gestured to me with her hand. "So, you were never trained on how to use one?"

"Like I said, I never knew such a thing existed."

"Well, you passed your crash course with flying colors, I hear."

"Thanks."

She smiled again. "Last question—are you and Miss Pearl involved in a romantic relationship?"

My mouth dropped open. "Why would you ask me that?"

"Just want to get all the facts." She glanced at her notes and squinted, running her finger down the page, looking for something. "Here. Yes, Julia's counselor, Liz, mentioned it to me."

I nearly fell off my chair, but instead, I locked eyes with Ms. DiVito. We were like two animals vying for the same piece of meat.

"Staff and campers are forbidden from getting 'romantic' with one another," I said, adding air quotes for the hell of it.

She nodded. "I'm not here to cause trouble, Jack. I'm only here to get all the information I need from everyone involved. We're not out to hurt the camp, but we do need to make sure that proper protocol was followed."

"Can I talk to the twins?" I asked.

"No, I'm sorry."

"Why not?"

She shook her head. "They've been taken to the station to be booked and charged, and they will have to spend the night in jail since it appears that their parents won't be able to get here tonight.

They'll go before the judge in the morning, they'll arrange for bond, and then they can be turned over to their parents once they post bail."

"Booked?"

"Yes, Jack. Brittany admitted to giving Miss Pearl the peanuts."

"Can you tell me what she said?"

She shook her head. "I can tell you, it was close to your assumption that they meant to harm Miss Pearl without intent to kill."

The words *intent to kill* floated between us.

"Can you tell me what will happen to them?" I asked.

She stood and scratched her head. "It will be up to the judge in the morning, but they won't be coming back here."

A man approached her, and they exchanged a few quiet words that I couldn't make out.

She looked at me. "That's all for now, but don't go too far, okay?"

I nodded and stood up to shake her hand. "I want to help in any way I can."

"We appreciate that. Thank you."

Once we were through, I turned, took a deep breath, and went looking for Liz.

Thirty

Julia

I woke up in the middle of the night and puked. I'd been ridiculously nauseous on account of the steroids they had been giving me. Combined with the green Jell-O and the IV needle tugging on my skin every time I moved, dizziness was becoming my norm.

Then, I saw my mom. I would have visions of her every once in a while, and I'd hallucinated before, so it didn't surprise me that she was appearing in my hospital room. In fact, I was more surprised she hadn't come to me when I was curled up on the dirt next to the picnic table with the remnants of the Killer Cookie.

One time, about a month after my mom had left, I had refused to eat for forty-eight hours until my dad would let me call her. On the forty-ninth hour, when he hadn't budged and I had seen leprechauns in my bathtub, I had broken down and ordered Jimmy John's. There was only one person who would suffer when you starved—yourself. Lesson learned. But before my turkey and provolone sub had arrived, I had seen my mom standing over me with her bullshit apologetic face filled with far more pity than guilt. It was the face I'd imagined a hundred times.

I'd seen her another time when I was sick with the flu, and my fever had spiked to one hundred and five degrees. I had been rolling around in my bed, one big sweaty mess, swatting away at Sharlene like a swarm of gnats, as she'd tried to get a washcloth on my forehead. But when our housekeeper, Mary, had tried, I'd hugged her and thanked her and called her mom, saying how much I had hoped she'd show up and take care of me. Also, she'd brought me Baskin-Robbins mint chocolate chip.

So, it made perfect sense that the Grim Reaper would deliver my mother to me at this time.

"Hi, Mom," I tried talking to her. *Why waste a good delusion on awkward silence?*

She bent down to hug me and didn't let go, and neither did I.

After what seemed like a lifetime, the sun started to come through the paper-thin shades, and a nurse walked in with some applesauce and a bagel. Mom had dissipated by then.

"Could you take this out?" I pointed to my IV because I couldn't look at it. "It's making me queasy, and I'm feeling much better."

She checked my vitals and then scribbled something on my chart. "Let's wait for Dr. Akbarnia to check on you. She's scheduled to be in by ten this morning."

"Okay. Thank you." I put my head back on the pillow.

There was a knock on the door, and it opened before I could say anything.

"Good morning," Sharlene said, carrying a bag from Starbucks for me and a hot venti something for herself. "Dad's just on a quick call. He'll be right in."

She handed me the bag, and I found a glazed doughnut and a cinnamon scone. I devoured the doughnut and saved the scone for the doctor.

"Where did you guys stay last night?"

Sharlene shook her hand in the direction of the window. "Oh, someplace up the road. DoubleTree, I think. You should have heard your father arguing with the front desk about why they didn't offer twenty-four-hour room service."

"Is he mad at me?"

She placed her coffee down on the shelflike table hanging near my feet. "Oh, honey, no. Of course not. He was worried sick. I've never seen him like that before."

I lowered my eyes. Despite everything I had gone through with my mom, I'd forget all too often that the same awful things had happened to my father, too. He hadn't been immune to the hurt and rejection brought on by my mom either. In fact, he'd had his own shitshow to deal with while I'd been wrapped up in avoiding bus fumes and therapists. He had been cheated on and humiliated by someone he loved and worshiped, someone everyone he knew thought was too good for him. Then, he'd been left to survive as a single parent with a sixteen-hours-a-day job and no clue where to purchase a training bra.

"I'm so sorry I scared him...and you."

She sat on the edge of the bed, and I shifted my legs to make room for her.

"All that matters is that you're okay. He had a long talk with the doctor last night, and she assured him that you will be perfectly perfect again, so he's going to let you go back to camp." She sat up straight. "We both are going to insist on strict monitoring by the nursing staff, but you will be back to normal otherwise."

That's all I want.

Sharlene tentatively leaned forward and planted a kiss on my forehead, and I was grateful that she had.

"Your dad is not an emotional man, but when he *feels*, he feels very deeply." She patted her heart. "Bottom line is, he wants you to be happy. He knows you haven't had an easy few years with everything that happened with your mom, and he also doesn't think he's handled everything in the best way possible, but he loves you so, so much. He just wants the very best for you."

It was weird, hearing these things from Sharlene. It was weird to hear them at all because my father would never admit to me that he'd mishandled anything. He abided by the I'm-always-right-and-do-what-I-say-not-as-I-do philosophy. It was nice to know he was human.

"Who's watching Liam and Lulu?" I asked about my stepsiblings.

"My mom picked them up from day camp yesterday and is staying with them at the house. They miss you."

"Sure they do."

"They do!" She slapped my leg. "They...we would all love to have you join us on our vacation, but I know you want to get back to camp, and I'm glad. This incident has been unfortunate, to put it mildly, but I'm so thrilled for you that you've enjoyed your experience overall." She smiled. "And I'm glad you're going back there. I think Jack Dempsey is, too."

"Thanks."

The door flew open.

"I spilled my coffee," Dad announced as he walked in, dabbing his shirt with a handful of small square napkins. "How's my girl?"

"I'm good."

He walked over and kissed my hair. "Just bumped into the doc. She'll be in here in a sec. Shar?" He turned to his wife with a helpless look.

"I'll get you a new coffee." Sharlene stood and took his stack of dirty napkins. Then, she dragged her hand over his shoulder and left.

My father cleared his throat. "You sleep okay?"

I shrugged. "I just want this IV out. It's driving me crazy."

"You just leave your care to the professionals."

There was a knock at the door, and it opened. Apparently, hospital protocol did not require waiting for the patient to say, *Come in!*

Dr. Akbarnia looked well rested.

She nodded to my father, who took a seat in the corner and started texting.

"How are you today?" she asked me.

Our eyes met.

"I feel good. Fine."

"Good or fine?" My dad couldn't resist commenting from the sidelines.

I grabbed on to one of the side rails and pulled myself up off the pillow. "I feel great," I said to the doctor. "A little tired and a lot sick of this IV, but I feel good, and I would love to get out of here. No offense."

"None taken, and I'm glad to hear it. I thought you would probably feel like yourself again." She lifted a clipboard from the end of the bed. "Some people are prone to delayed anaphylactic reactions, so we're going to watch you for one more day and then release you tomorrow morning with a five-day prescription for prednisone. I'll send all the instructions to the camp nurse."

"Thank you," I said. "Dad?" I looked over at him.

"What?"

"She's releasing me tomorrow morning."

Dad stood and shook the doctor's hand. "Thank you," he said. "I know I can be a little over-the-top sometimes, but I appreciate everything you've done for her. I realize that thank you doesn't really cover it. I owe you everything…yet I hope we never have to see you again."

The doctor laughed. "I don't blame you one bit." She turned to me. "I'll get someone in here immediately to remove the IV," she said before leaving.

Sharlene returned with a full Styrofoam cup and handed it to my father. He groaned as he stood, and he exchanged a strange look with Sharlene before sitting on the edge of my bed.

"What's going on?" I asked after she nodded to him.

"Your mother is here," he said through gritted teeth.

"What?"

He looked at me. "You heard me. Your mom is here. I called her as soon as I got the news from the camp, and she drove up from Indiana."

"Indiana? What? Why was she there?" My words quickly tumbled out. "Was she here last night? I thought I saw her."

"I don't think so, but she's here now."

I looked over at Sharlene whose arms were wrapped around her abdomen and then back at my father. "I can't believe she's here." My chest went warm. "I can't believe you called her."

My dad began to pace. "We had a deal." He tossed his hand in the air. "If you were ever severely injured or in danger of losing your life, I agreed to contact her, and she would then be allowed to present herself."

Sharlene rolled her eyes. "Spoken like a true attorney." She came over to me and reached for my hand. "Your mother deserved to know what happened because she loves you…and she's your mother," she said matter-of-factly, as though she were telling me what she'd had for lunch.

I whipped the blanket off and swung my feet over the edge of the bed. My head was light, and my palms were sweaty.

"Hold on." Dad put his hand on my shoulder. "Just relax. She's not outside the door with a brass band. Don't get all crazy on me."

I lay back down on the bed and curled into the fetal position. It was too much to handle. My mother was in the building, possibly grabbing coffee from the cafeteria or a bag of Doritos from a vending machine. Or maybe she was in the ladies' room, applying her lipstick like she used to when I was little. She'd put powder on her lips first and then her favorite MAC color, followed by liner.

"Always line your lips after the lipstick," she'd say.

Then, she'd apply a thick layer of goopy shiny gloss that would always stick to my hair when I kissed her good-bye.

"Where is she then?" I asked.

My dad sat on the boxy pleather chair next to my heart rate monitor. "I don't want her to make a scene. She's outside, I think. I don't know. I will find her in a minute. She has a friend with her."

She has friends, so that must be a good sign, I thought to myself as the initial shock and nerves turned to excitement.

A smile spread across my face, and I could hardly believe it. In that moment, nothing else mattered. My mom had come back. She cared about me after all, and it didn't bother me one bit that it had taken me being on the brink of death for her to finally resurface. In fact, I reveled in it.

"Please go find her then," I said.

My dad threw out a bunch of jumbled words, "This might be hard for you. I don't think you're prepared for this. I wish she hadn't come."

"Dad, please go get her for me. I'm fine." But I really wasn't. I felt like someone had planned a huge surprise party for me. But I'd found out about it, and I was now anticipating the big reveal, but I had to keep my emotions in check, not letting on that I knew.

My dad walked out, and I stared at the door as it closed.

Sharlene spoke, startling me, "He's just worried about you. We both are. We never wanted to spring her on you like this, but given the circumstances, we simply had to contact her, and I—*we* knew she would come." She folded her hands. "Your father really wishes she hadn't."

I didn't care why my mother had come or what my father wished for. He'd wished her away for long enough as far as I was concerned.

"Well, I'm so excited." I almost laughed. "Do I look okay?" I leaped out of bed and walked to the bathroom. My hair was a tangled mess. "Bring me a brush or a comb, please. Do you have one?" I shouted over my shoulder.

"You look great, honey."

"Shar, please. A comb, lip gloss, anything?"

Sharlene came into the bathroom with her purse, and her lips pushed together into a forced smile. She handed me a fold-up brush and some ChapStick with aloe. I brushed my hair and applied the lip balm, trying to force a shine out of it but to no avail.

Then, I waited.

Dad came back first. "She'll be here in a minute. She wanted to get you some flowers from the gift shop, but of course, she had no money on her." He looked at Sharlene. "Maybe I can have someone check my blood pressure while we're here?"

Sharlene tipped her head to the side.

Then, the door opened, and my mom walked through it. Her entrance was just as I remembered—strong and fast and bold as always. We both burst into tears as she wrapped me in her arms so fast that I barely had a second to look at her face, and Dad and Sharlene snuck out.

I held my mom for as long as it took to make up for five years of lost time.

THIRTY-ONE

JACK

After my meeting with Ms. DiVito, I sprinted down the lit long path, back to the senior village. I was pissed. It was close to midnight, and the air was warm, so I'd built up a mild sweat by the time I reached Liz and Maggie's cabin. I announced myself as I pounded on the flimsy door. Male staff members were not permitted to enter unless it was an emergency.

One of the campers opened the screen door, and most of the heads inside turned to face me.

"Is Liz here?"

The girl rubbed her eyes and held the door with her foot. "Liz!"

"She's at the bathhouse, Jack," Maggie said from her room. "Everything okay? Is it Julia?"

"She's fine. Everything's fine. Thanks." I turned and walked toward the bathhouse where I stopped and leaned against a tree, out of creeper distance from the front door, until Liz finally emerged.

"Liz! Over here." I stayed by the tree and waved.

She looked pleased to see me. "Well, if it isn't our resident hero. Have you heard anything? How's Julia doing?"

"She's going to be fine."

"It's been a long night. We all saw the cops taking the twins away. It was so sad. I know they did a horrible thing, but they were an absolute wreck. Poor Brianna was terrified. I think she was in shock. She wouldn't say anything or look anyone in the eyes—"

"Did you tell anyone that something was going on between Julia and me?"

Liz pulled her head back. "No."

"Didn't you talk with the police or that DiVito lady?"

"Of course. She talked with both Maggie and me since we're Julia's counselors. Why are you asking me? And wipe that scowl off your face."

"Because that lady said you mentioned something to that effect, and she would have had absolutely no reason to ask me if I was romantically involved with a camper unless someone—you—had planted the idea in her head."

She shrugged. "I don't remember talking about you."

My temples were pulsating with rage. I grabbed Liz by the tops of her arms. "Did you make up some story about me?" I released her with a gentle shove.

"Ow, Jack. What the fuck?"

"You tell me. Have you been telling people that I'm involved with Julia? Because you know I will get in trouble for that, so I can't fathom what would have made you do such a thing, except that you're jealous."

Liz's nostrils flared at the accusation. "Well, are you?" she yelled.

"It's none of your business if I am or if I'm not."

"Oh, hell yes, it is. I'm her counselor, and I'm the one in charge of her well-being on a daily basis. If some sleazebag waterfront director has been forcing himself on her, it's *my obligation to report even my slightest concerns*," she mockingly said the last few words. "And you and I both know you're all too willing to hook up with whoever is giving you the attention you're so desperate for in any given moment!"

I took a deep breath. Her hysterics would only make things worse.

"I saved your ass when you were naked and puking in my room."

"You saved your own ass. You'd have been in just as much trouble, probably more, as me."

"They're onto you, Liz. Bob and Sally already know you're trying to cause trouble, so do everyone a favor and stay the fuck out of everyone's shit." I turned my back to her and began to walk away.

"What happened on the overnight, Jack?"

I stopped but didn't face her.

"I heard you two were up to no good," she added.

"No, you didn't," I said over my shoulder.

Liz walked over and stood in front of me. Her head was just about level with my chest as she looked up at my face, but I refused to glance at her.

"I know what went on between the two of you. Julia told me everything."

I kept my gaze over her head. "Oh, yeah? What did she tell you?"

"That you hit on her."

I couldn't contain my laughter. "Okay. Good night, Liz."

"I'm right, aren't I? You kissed her on the Voyagers overnight. You took advantage of a camper and the situation, not to mention your position of authority," she said the last part in a deeper tone.

"I know you're full of shit because Julia would never confide in you."

"So, something did happen then?"

I stepped around her.

"But she'd confide in Emma, now wouldn't she?" Liz said. "And that is what happened. When I got wind of it, I confronted Julia and made her tell me the truth."

I turned around to try to read her expression. "You're lying," I said.

She smiled, which did not put me at ease. "You're the one who's lying, and I can tell by the look on your face that you have something going on with that girl. I've heard them whispering about you, and your face confirms all of it." She crossed her arms. "You've worked here long enough to know that I have to report this."

I met her eyes. She was loving every second of this exchange. If she couldn't be with me, then she would make sure no one else could.

"You know what will happen if you blow this up. I'll get kicked out and lose my credits, and you will embarrass Julia to no end. And for what? Don't you think she's been through enough in the past twenty-four hours? Or did someone die and make you resident bitch? Oh, no. They didn't die. They just went to jail." I paused. "Sorry things didn't work out between us, Liz."

Liz pulled a rubber band off her wrist and twisted her hair into a ponytail. "I know you and your ego think this is because you rejected me—"

"I didn't reject you. We had some fun, and that was it. Seriously, Liz, grow up."

She crossed her arms. "Seriously?"

I sighed. "Please don't go reporting what you don't fucking know. I covered for you, and I expect the same courtesy back whether I deserve it or not. I thought we were friends."

"You thought wrong." She patted my cheek and ran back to her cabin.

Thirty-Two

Julia

I only let go of my mom because it was time. She pulled away, wiping streams of tears from her nose and face while gently laughing and sniffling simultaneously.

She placed her hands on my cheeks for a second and shook her head. "I've missed you terribly. You have no idea."

"I do. I've missed you, too. I love you so much, Mom."

"I love you, too, honey." She stood up and took a step back.

Her hair was shorter, reaching her shoulders, and she looked like I remembered her looking every morning when she'd wake up—tired and makeup-free yet still beautiful.

"Can you get me a chair?"

"Um, sure." I quickly swung my legs over the side of the bed before noticing that we weren't alone. "Oh."

A woman who looked like she should be sitting in a rocking chair, knitting or reading fairy tales to preschoolers, slowly dragged a seat next to the bed for my mother to sit. "Hello, Julia. I'm Linda James, your mother's sponsor."

They both smiled at me as if that nugget of information would clear everything up.

"Her what?" I asked.

"Linda is my recovery sponsor."

I looked at the woman, and she pushed her glasses up on her nose before returning to her seat near the door. She never said another word to me.

My heart sank. "You're still doing drugs?"

Mom sat down with one hand on her lap and one hand holding mine. "It's been a tough battle for me." She dabbed her eyes with a tissue. "But I'm going on five months of sobriety this time." She smiled. "I haven't been allowed to see you because I haven't been able to stay clean for longer than six months, honey, but this time, things will be different. I'm back in the Midwest now, and I've found someone wonderful. His name is Gerard, and he owns an adult game center in Indianapolis—you know, like a Dave and Buster's type place. Have you heard of Dave and Buster's?"

I nodded.

"Good, because it's just like that, only better because Gerard is in charge!" She clapped her hands. "I can't wait for you to meet him."

She glanced back at Mother Goose and then focused on me. "Oh, honey, look at you." She shook her head. "You are the most beautiful girl I've ever seen. You always were, and you still are." She choked up again and began to sob.

"Don't cry, Mom."

"I've failed you so badly. I never meant for any of this to happen, but your father was right to keep me away. He was trying to protect both of us, and I was not in a good place. He did what he had to do, so don't blame him, okay? He's a good man, and he did what he thought was right," she said, obviously trying to convince herself as well.

"So, you live in Indianapolis?"

"Yes!" she squealed.

Then, she went on for about an hour, telling me about the townhouse she lived in, the boutique where she worked, the clientele who shopped there and how they loved her and took all her fashion advice because she was a former model. And how none of it would have been possible without my dad.

"He bought you a house?"

"Rented. He's taken care of me since the day I left. I would probably be dead if it wasn't for him."

I swallowed.

She continued, "I know this can't be easy, seeing me swoop in here after what you went through at camp." She shook her head. "But I couldn't stay away. The first call I got...well, they didn't know if you were dead or alive." She brought her hand to her mouth and looked up at the ceiling, wide-eyed.

"It's okay, Mom. I'm fine now."

"How could those kids have done this to you? How could they?"

"I don't know. I think they're stupid."

She laughed. "Your father is going to go after them pretty hard."

I nodded.

A nurse came in and fiddled around with some buttons and shit, and then she left. Mom lay with me in the hospital bed for a while as I flipped channels and told her about camp. If I could spend the next year in that bed with her, it wouldn't be long enough. She smelled like happiness to me, reminiscent of a time when I'd felt safe and carefree every minute of every day. Even though she hadn't been home a lot, she had been a presence and a comfort to me that I had never known since—except maybe for Jack.

I thought for a moment and pondered whom I'd rather lay in that bed with for twelve months, and I couldn't decide.

After a while, Linda said it was getting late and that they should let me rest.

"Can you come back later or tomorrow? Can you come to my camp? They're discharging me in the morning, and I would love for you to meet some of my friends," I pleaded.

"You betcha!" she said without hesitation. "I will be back here first thing in the morning with glazed doughnuts. Your favorite, right?"

I nodded. They had been five years ago.

"All righty then, doughnuts and camp it is!" She slapped her hands together. "This is going to be fun." She paused and leaned forward to touch my hair. "I'm so happy to see you. Things are going to be so great between us from now on."

She stared at me for a moment, and I realized that I didn't know her at all.

She was the one person in my life who I'd put all my energy into, all my longing, with years of unfulfilled wishes, days of hopes and prayers…and for what? I hardly knew her. She was an erratic drug user claiming to be sober and looking for my approval of some dude named Gerard who owned a fancy Pop-a-Shot joint.

Even seeing her sitting there...I still missed my mom.

"I love you, honey," she said.

"I love you, too." I stood up out of bed and hugged her. "I can't wait for my doughnuts."

Linda slid a long, thin purse strap over her shoulder and held the door open. My mom kissed me on the cheek and left.

Once the door closed, I just stood there, numb, for maybe four minutes until my father walked back in. He and Sharlene had been waiting downstairs for hours.

"You okay?" he asked me.

I nodded.

"Why are you standing there?"

I shrugged. "Just stretching my legs." I wrapped my arms around his waist.

My dad kissed the top of my head. There was nothing he could say. He hated talking about my mother—he always had—but that hadn't stopped him from doing the right thing, from taking care of her and keeping her safe and alive. He might have hated discussing her...but he didn't hate her.

"You know I'm not good at this stuff, kid." He pulled away.

"I know."

He winked at me.

"Mom said she's going to come by the hospital with doughnuts in the morning and then drop me off at camp with you guys. Is that okay? I really want you all to meet my friends."

Dad shook his head. "That's not a good idea—"

Sharlene tugged on his shoulder and interrupted him, "It sounds perfect."

I sat back down on the bed and crossed my legs. "Dad?"

"Shar's right. It's fine. Let's just get you out of here and settled back at camp as soon as possible." My father looked tired, but not the I-haven't-slept-in-days tired. It was more like the enough-already tired.

It consumed me with guilt, even worse now that I knew my father was supporting two wives, two stepkids, and a teenage daughter with enough baggage at the ripe age of sixteen to fill a jumbo jet. I wanted happiness for this man.

"Thanks, Dad. Love you so much."

"Love you, too, kid."

The next morning, after hours of watching game shows and soap operas, I was finally allowed to leave the hospital just before noon, but there was no sign of my mom.

"Can I just call her? Please."

"I tried her cell and the woman, Linda, who was with her and left a voice mail for each one of them," Dad said.

I held out my hand. "I would like to try myself."

Dad dialed and handed me the phone, which went straight to voice mail.

It was my mother's voice. "You know the drill! Leave a message after the tone, and make it interesting!"

Beep.

"Hi, Mom. It's me. We're ready to leave, so if you can…bring the doughnuts to the camp, okay? Dad said he left the address with Linda. Can't wait to see you there. Love you." I flipped the phone shut and handed it back to my dad. "I know she's coming. She promised she would."

"Okay," he said. "We'll meet her there then."

Dad and Sharlene drove me back to camp, and we were quickly ushered into the main office where we were greeted by Bob, Sally, Liz, and Maggie. I wanted to be anywhere else.

Bob gave me an uncomfortable hug. "We're so glad to have you back in one piece."

Liz and Maggie rushed to me for a much more sincere embrace.

"We're *so* sorry about this, Julia," Liz said. "And Brittany and Brianna are gone. They're in jail, and—"

Sally pulled them off me. "I think we should give Julia a chance to relax and breathe first before we overwhelm her with everything."

My stomach tightened. Hearing that the twins were in jail made my head spin. It made everything real.

I took a step back, and my dad gave me a look that said, *You're sure you want to be here?*

I nodded at him.

"I would like to have a moment with my daughter before we head out, if that can be arranged?"

"Of course. Yes," Bob said.

"And forget the no-phone-call rule where she's concerned. That's done. I will be checking in on her these next couple of weeks, and if she wants to call me, then so be it."

"Of course. Yes," Bob repeated.

Then, he pulled Liz's and Maggie's elbows toward the door. For the first time all summer, they blew me kisses.

Bob was just about to say something when I interrupted and addressed him and Sally, "Thank you for all your help. I just really want to get back to my routine here. No special attention, please."

"Of course," Sally said. "We completely understand, and we just want you to know how happy we are that you're healthy and back with us."

They left, and I hugged Sharlene and then my father.

"I've got nothing left to say, Jules. I just knew you didn't want all the commotion." He tousled my hair.

"Thanks, Dad. Love you," I said.

We stared at each other, thinking the same thing about the absence of my mother, but he wasn't going to say it. I turned my head and looked at Sharlene, who had tears in her eyes, so I walked over and embraced her. She wrapped her arms tightly around me and stroked my hair. It was hard not to cry.

"She's not coming, is she?" I mumbled into Sharlene's chest.

"No, sweetie, she's not."

"How do you know for sure?"

"Seeing your beautiful self yesterday was too much for her to handle apparently. Your mother just couldn't bear it. Linda left us a message very early this morning, saying they were heading back to Indianapolis." Sharlene pulled away before I did. "Come with me," she said.

I looked at my dad, and he nodded.

Sharlene took my hand, and Dad followed us to the car. She popped the trunk, pulled out two-dozen Krispy Kreme doughnuts, and handed me the boxes. It was hard not to cry then, too.

"We didn't want you to be disappointed twice in one morning," she said with a wink.

Everyone had come to terms with who my mother was a long time ago, and now, it was my turn.

"Thank you." I leaned forward and gave Sharlene a kiss. "You, too, Dad."

"Wasn't my idea," he mumbled. "In fact, these are for your friends only. The store manager said they don't use nuts but wouldn't guarantee there was no cross contamination."

I shrugged and smiled at him.

"But you're welcome," he continued. "Just stay away from the crazies from now on, and leave them to me. Can your ole man get out of this mosquito net and go enjoy his vacation?"

I nodded and waved to them with one arm as I clutched the boxes, and they pulled away. My heart was racing. I was back at camp, and I couldn't wait to see Jack.

Then, I heard a scream, a piercing loud scream, and there was only one person with the lung capacity to produce it. I turned to find Emma and Amber running toward me like bears were chasing them.

Thirty-Three

JACK

I was in the mess hall when I heard Emma screaming. Tabitha had told me that Julia was back at camp and that her parents were with her in Bob's office. I'd thought her parents might ask to speak with me or say good-bye, but they hadn't.

Once Emma and some of the other girls had descended on Julia, I figured I'd wait until later to welcome her back, so I headed down to the docks with Will.

"Tabby said you had words with Liz last night. What's up with that?"

There was nothing sacred at camp, and I should have known better than to pick a public place to have a pissing match. "She's nuts."

Will laughed. "She sure is, brother."

"But this time, she might actually cause some real trouble."

"Like puking in *my* bed next? 'Cause I can tell you that will get her in some real trouble!"

I pulled a bunch of orange life vests off the wall and tossed them into a pile on the dock. Then, I grabbed a hose to rinse them off. "I did something I probably shouldn't have done."

"Those are always the best things to do, aren't they, mate?" Will plopped down into a plastic deck chair. "Give it up."

I squeezed the spray nozzle and watched about ten spiders scurry. "I kissed Julia on the Voyagers overnight." I released the handle and looked at him.

Neither of us could hold back a smirk.

"Dude, how did that happen?"

I began spraying again and shook my head. "It was my doing—obviously. Honestly, I didn't even think about it. I wanted to hook up with her, so I did."

"You got the hots for this one?"

I nodded.

"Anyone know?"

I finished up with the life vests and dropped the hose. "Liz says she does, but I think she's lying to try to get me to admit to something because I tossed her drunken ass out of my room, and it pissed her off." I took the chair next to him and leaned back on the back legs.

Will pulled a toothpick out of his pocket and stuck it in his mouth. "That, and she's got the hots for you, Jackie Boy."

"Whatever. That was a mistake."

"So, you like the peanut girl. She feel the same about you?"

"I think so," I added with a nod. But it was stupid really. There were only a couple of weeks left of camp, and now, I was going to start a secret relationship with a camper who had almost lost her life on my watch.

Will rolled his neck in a stretch. "Liz won't say anything about it. It's hearsay and BS as far as she knows."

Will and I sat in silence, working on our tans, while the rest of the camp prepped for lunch.

After a while, Theo came pounding down the planks.

"Hey, guys," he said.

"What up, Big T?" Will raised his hand.

"You two lose your walkies?"

Will and I both sat up and looked around.

"Shit. Sorry. We tossed our backpacks in the boathouse. What's up?" I said.

"Bob's looking for you, Jack."

I looked over at Will and then back at Theo.

"And he's too lazy to drag his ass down here, so he sent you?" Will asked.

"You got that straight."

"Thanks, man," I said. "I'll be up there in a sec."

"I'll take your seat then."

I smiled at him and stood. "Fair enough. You two finish working on your tans, and I'll swear that I saw you both knee-deep in time-consuming manual labor."

I stepped over the hose and walked up the hill, passing the mess hall. I entered the main office building where Bob, Sally, and Tabitha were waiting for me. Tabitha had been crying.

Thirty-Four

Julia

D ad was right. Transitioning back to camp wasn't as easy as I'd hoped, but there was nowhere else I wanted to be.

People did their best to be discreet, but you didn't have to point and whisper in order for someone to know you were gossiping about them. Shifty eyes, halted chatter, lowering of one's chin—all signs that something was being said in secrecy. Only, people were so bad at doing it.

My dad always said, "If you have nothing nice to say about someone, wait until the person is gone, and then call your friends and bitch about that person behind their back."

But I didn't care. I'd come back to camp for one reason and one reason alone—to be near Jack. Only, I hadn't seen him more than twice. During dinner my first night back, he'd walked through the mess hall, grabbed a roll, winked at me, and disappeared into the kitchen. Then, later that evening, we'd made eye contact at the bonfire, but I hadn't had a chance to talk to him afterward because Liz was all over me.

My second night back, Emma, Amber, and some of my cabinmates threw an impromptu welcome-back, yay-for-not-dying party. Emma had themed it by drawing pictures of peanuts and Brittany's face, both circled with a slash through them. Maggie promptly took them down, but we had a good laugh. My yay-for-not-dying party was meant to be down by the beach, but there was heavy rain in the forecast, so Liz and Maggie let us have it in our cabin. They even let us use their DVD player to watch movies.

Sure enough, it rained really hard that night, and the roof of our cabin sounded like a tap dancer invasion. We all felt trapped in there but in a good way. We were huddled together under sleeping bags and blankets with no reason to leave and nowhere to go. Emma slept on the floor next to my bunk because it was pouring so hard that she didn't even want to walk the few yards back to her cabin.

I was so happy to be there, but I was desperate to talk to Jack.

The next morning, I went down to the docks before breakfast because I knew Jack would be there, rinsing and drying the boats after the storm. Poor guy was dripping with sweat, and it was only seven thirty.

"Hey you," I said with a wave of my hand.

He stopped what he was doing and stood tall.

"Thought you might need some help."

He raised a brow. "Well, you're two hours too late. I've been out here since the butt crack of dawn, pulling twigs and branches out of every crevice of these boats, because Will forgot to tarp them last night."

Jack was wearing the gray hoodie he'd lent me during the opening ceremony with no shirt underneath, navy board shorts, and sunglasses. I walked closer to him, and he took a sip from his water bottle.

"Ah." He let out a long breath. "It's great to see you up and about. Sorry I haven't had a chance to check on you because I really wanted to. What's on your agenda today?" he asked.

"Drama, then archery, and then tennis."

"Sounds like a nice mildly active day." He put his water bottle down, placed his hands in the front pockets of his sweatshirt, and smiled.

"I wanted to talk to you," I said.

Jack lowered his chin and waited while I looked down at the dock and let the seconds tick by.

"Are you feeling okay?" he asked tenderly.

"Yes, I'm fine. I wanted to thank you." I looked behind me to make sure no one was coming. "And I wanted to be honest with you."

He took a breath as we stood there, silently trying to read each other's thoughts. He inhaled again and gazed up at the sky. He seemed uncomfortable. He wasn't rude or off-putting—he would never be that—but something in his demeanor told me he was worried.

"Don't worry. I'm not going to get mushy or anything," I assured him.

He smiled and relaxed a little, pushing his shoulders forward.

"Can we sit for a second, so I don't have to crane my neck?"

"Sure thing, Pearl."

Jack sat with his legs dangling over the water and leaned back on his hands while I sat cross-legged next to him. A moment passed as I assembled my thoughts.

"I wanted to thank you for what you did for me—really, what you've done for me."

He met my eyes. "You don't have to—"

"Let me finish." I lifted my hand off my knee. "You saved my life, and at the very least, that deserves a pat on the back. But I was lying in bed last night, listening to branches snapping and thunder cracking and waiting for the impossibly thin roof on our cabin to collapse, and I realized something. You saved my life even before the peanut debacle."

He tilted his head to one side and squinted his eyes, confused.

"I did not want to be here. I did everything in my power to convince my dad to let me stay home, but he wouldn't let me, and I assumed it was because my stepmom wanted me gone, that she just wanted the house to herself and her kids and to have time alone with my dad."

"Is that such a bad thing?" he asked.

"No. See? There you go. It's not a bad thing, but six weeks ago, my answer would have been much different. Without even realizing it, you've taught me so much about my family and myself. You've taught me to believe in the good in people and to be kind first and bitchy second—only if absolutely necessary."

He laughed, flashing a grin that made me melt.

"When Sharlene came to the hospital, it was the first time in four years that I actually believed she cared about whether I lived or died. Maybe it's because I did almost die, but I think it was my own bitterness and stubbornness that was clouding everything for me before."

He lifted his legs, bent his knees, and placed his feet on the dock. "Julia, I'm glad you think this was all my doing, but I think you've just grown up a little. And, hey, a near-death experience can do a lot as far as putting one's life in perspective."

I shook my head. He deserved credit, and I wanted him to have it. More importantly, I wanted him to know how I felt about him, and I didn't care if it was against the rules or not.

How could there be restrictions on how people felt about one another?

I knew he cared about me. I'd seen it in his eyes and his smile and his posture on more than one occasion.

"Also, I…" I paused to catch my breath. My heart was pounding, and I knew that I could potentially alienate him from here on out by creating a wall of words. It might turn into a barrier of awkward tension once I barfed my heart out. "My mom came to the hospital." I'd meant to say something else.

His eyes went wide as he turned to face me. "You're kidding."

"I'm not. She was there with her sponsor or whatever. I guess she and my dad had some mystery agreement that if I was about to bite it, he had to let her know. So, she showed."

"What was that like?"

The sun was officially awake by then, and I could feel it radiating on my skin. I had to pause for a moment and squint as I looked to the sky, trying to find the words that would describe what it had been like to see her after all this time.

Truthfully, it was like being surprised with a pair of front row tickets to see your favorite band in concert. You'd freak out, squeal, pace, and pull your hair out. Then, you'd pick out the cutest outfit—because, surely, the lead singer would fall in love with you when you made eye contact with him, and you'd bear his children and live in a mansion with a pool table in the foyer—before renting a limo to drive you to the arena where they'd slip a VIP lanyard over your head, and a special usher would show you and your best friend to your seats.

Then, an hour after you'd arrived, the show would be canceled, and not only had you not gotten to make eye contact with the lead singer, but he also wouldn't bring you doughnuts the next morning, like he'd promised either.

"It was stressful and weird and sad," I said.

"This is huge, Pearl. What did she say? Was it good to catch up? You gonna make me beg for information here?"

"She said she missed me, and I believed her, but she seemed preoccupied with other things—her job, her boyfriend, trying to stay sober. I mean, I get it. I haven't been on her radar for some time, but I felt more distance than I had expected. Maybe because it was all a big mess? My dad sort of sprang the news on me, and I didn't have time to prepare myself. I don't know. She seems happy I guess."

Jack just stared at me.

"She was supposed to come see me the next day and drop me back at camp with my dad and stepmom, but she didn't show up. Sharlene said she freaked out and couldn't handle it." I shrugged.

He touched my hand, and I inhaled.

"I'm sorry about that," he said.

"It's okay, you know…it's really okay. She's still my mom but just not one I remember. In a weird way, it kind of makes missing her much easier."

"That makes sense." He pulled back his hand.

I stared down at the water. It was like glass this morning, gracefully moving under the dock, not yet disturbed by boats and ducks and splashing campers.

For a second, I was distracted by the thought of Brittany. I'd become used to her lurking around and trying to sabotage my friendship with Jack at every turn, but now, she was headed off to jail or court or juvie, and there was no need to look over my shoulder.

"I really like you, Jack."

His lips parted, but no words came out.

I lifted a hand to keep him quiet for a minute. "I know I said I wouldn't get mushy, so just take it for what it is. I like you—a lot." I paused to read his expression. "And not just as a friend. And not just because you stuck a needle in my thigh. I just really like you, and I thought you should know." I laughed a little at the end of my confession.

Jack closed his eyes for a moment. "I like you, too, Julia—a lot. But I don't know how to be close to you without it feeling wrong.

We're in a situation that prevents me from being with you the way I want to be with you."

I was desperate for him to elaborate when his eyes widened, and he jumped to his feet.

"Morning, Bob." He waved over me.

I turned around and saw Bob approaching the docks.

"Morning, Jack, Julia." He pressed his lips together and fidgeted with his walkie-talkie. "Jack, can I have a word?"

"Sure thing. I was just finishing up down here and about to grab some grub."

I stood slowly. "Me, too. I'll see you guys later."

I walked past Bob and left them both standing behind me. Once I was a few feet away, I ran up the hill and went to the mess hall where I met Emma and waited for Jack to walk through the door.

But he never did.

THIRTY-FIVE

Julia

The next morning, Amber and Emma nearly tackled me on the way out of the shower.

"Have you heard what happened?" Amber asked.

I shook my head. "With what?"

They exchanged looks with each other before Emma spoke, "With Jack. He's leaving camp today. He was let go."

My heart sank to my heels, and my shower caddy fell out of my grasp. "What? Why? Who told you? How do you know?"

"Amber overheard Liz telling someone about it, but the entire camp knows about it, except no one has any details. You picked the wrong day to sleep in."

I struggled to think clearly. If this were on account of me, I would never forgive myself. "We have to find him. Will you help me?"

"Shit yeah, we will. How hard could it be? He's probably in his room, packing," Emma said.

I ran to my cabin and threw on the nearest clothes I could find, which were the denim shorts and black tank I'd had on the day before. Then, Emma and I walked over to the staff village while Amber went to see if she could get any more info from our counselors.

Emma gently tugged my elbow before we arrived. "I heard a rumor," she said, "about you and Jack."

I looked away and gazed at a group of girls walking by, carrying tennis rackets. "What did you hear?"

"That you hooked up with him on the overnight, but of course, I knew that to be false because if that had happened, you would have told me about it."

I stared at her.

"Holy crap. Seriously?" she gasped. "You and Jack did it in the dirt?"

I grabbed her arm and pulled her to the side of the building. "We did hook up, but we didn't do it. I'm sorry I didn't tell you."

"You should be. I mean, it's not like I don't enjoy hearing about how many lanyards you made or how you really should send your sheets to the laundry or how much ranch dressing you put on your salad. No, no, I mean, why would I want to hear about you getting down and dirty with the J.D.?"

I smiled at her. "I'm sorry. I was so afraid it was going to get out, and it looks like I was right."

"Well, it wasn't me!" She pointed to her mouth. "I did, however, tell everyone you're growing mushrooms in those stank-ass sheets of yours."

"I'll fill you in later, okay? I promise."

"You'd better."

The staff village looked like most of the other villages, except they had electricity and indoor plumbing in each building. They also had a rec room with a TV and a telephone. Campers had no real reason to enter the staff housing, but there were occasions where campers would be sent there to retrieve someone or something. There were no locked gates or doors, and it wasn't guarded by rabid coyotes, so Emma and I had little resistance when we entered Jack's building.

We found him in his room almost immediately.

"Hey you two," he greeted us like nothing had happened. "What's up?"

We both stared at the half-full duffel on his bed.

"You tell us," I said.

His face was as still and relaxed as always when he looked at me and gently shrugged. Emma took that as a cue to leave.

"I'll be out front," she whispered before walking away.

Jack tossed a folded T-shirt on his bed and ran his hand through his hair.

"This is my fault, isn't it?" I said on the verge of tears.

"No, Pearl. It's all mine." He smiled, defeated.

"Can I come in?"

"It's probably not the best idea," he said.

"Can you please tell me what happened?" I paused. "I will leave as soon as you do."

He sat on the edge of the desk and took a long breath.

The room was small but comfortable. It looked more like a college dorm room than a cabin in the woods.

Jack had a picture of a young couple on his windowsill, which I guessed was him as a child with his parents. There was a striped throw rug on the floor between the two twin beds. I wondered how someone so tall could sleep on such a small mattress.

"I need your word that you will keep this to yourself," he said.

"You have it."

He looked away, past me, out into the hall. "Brittany reported me before she poisoned you. I guess she told Bob and Sally that you and I had an inappropriate relationship." He met my troubled eyes. "She obviously made it up based on suspicion, and they didn't believe her at first, nor did they confront me about it, but they started keeping tabs."

I crossed my arms tightly around my stomach. "Tabs on what?"

"On me. On you. On us." He shrugged and shook his head. "Then, a couple of nights ago, Liz and I got into an argument. She told me that you'd told her that I kissed you on the overnight."

I gasped. "I never said that! I told no one!"

He nodded. "I figured, but she was hell-bent on believing there was something between us...and...and she is jealous."

I turned my face to the window and said nothing. He and I hadn't even done anything. It wasn't like we'd snuck around camp, holding hands and swapping spit all over the place. We'd just become close. *Were two jealous, lying bitches all it took to bring someone down?*

"There's one more thing," Jack continued. "I guess in the hospital, after your father met me and saw the two of us together, he asked Bob if anything was going on with us."

I choked and brought my hand to my mouth. "No."

"Julia"—he stood—"your dad didn't mean anything by it. In fact, according to Bob, your dad was simply being conversational,

dina silver

supportive even. Look…he didn't know anything, and he certainly wasn't trying to get me in trouble, but because of Brittany's claims and Liz's insistence, too…they had to act on it."

I felt light-headed and leaned against the doorframe, so I wouldn't tumble forward. "Jack, you'll lose your college credits. Bob must know you've done nothing wrong. You are everyone's favorite person here. He *must* know that, and if he doesn't, Sally does! And they know Brittany is a troublemaker. She's a criminal, for God's sake!" My hands were balled up into fists at my sides.

"Bob is an asshole, who's always been looking for a reason to get rid of me, and with everything that happened with you…I guess he finally got one."

I placed my hand on my forehead, trying to think. "This isn't right," I whispered.

"Please don't get upset. I'll be fine. You know I will."

He walked toward me, but I ran away, heading down two hallways and into the rec room. I picked up the phone and dialed my father's cell.

"Mel Pearl," he answered.

"Dad!"

"Holy hell, please tell me you haven't severed a limb on the zip line."

"Jack is getting fired because of you," I whisper-shouted into the receiver.

"Who's what?"

"Jack Dempsey, the boy who gave me the EpiPen and who you met in the emergency room, is getting fired and losing his college credits because you couldn't keep your mouth shut for once."

"Watch yourself, Julia, and slow down. My big mouth is the reason you can afford to while away the summer at camp and why your sassy self is still there. So, take a deep breath and explain what is going on—like an adult, please, not some hysterical teenager."

I took a deep breath and looked around the room and outside. No one was around, except for Emma. She was sitting on the stairs, burying her gym shoes in dirt.

"Apparently, at the hospital, you said something to the camp director, Bob, about Jack—again, the boy who saved my life—that made Bob think that there was an inappropriate relationship between Jack and me, and that is strictly forbidden."

236

"I'm forbidden to ask about the staff?"

I wound the cord around my fingers. "Can you please be serious for one second? A camper-staff relationship is forbidden."

"Then, you shouldn't be having one."

"I never said I was."

He cleared his throat. "I didn't mean anything by it, honey. I was just making conversation with the guy...Bob. He looked like a wreck."

"He always looks like a wreck! People here literally call him the Slob," I said.

"So, what do you want me to do? Are you in some sort of relationship with this kid or not?"

I took a moment to carefully choose my response. "No. I like him, but he's been respectful and careful and a pure gentleman. And he doesn't deserve to be let go and have his reputation ruined and his credits taken from him, especially on account of me and some stupid rumors." I paused and leaned my head on the wall. "I'm sorry, Dad. If it's anyone's fault, it's probably mine. There must be something you can do."

If ever in my sixteen years there was a time when I wanted my dad to use his authority and his influence and his loud and obnoxious roar, it was then.

He sighed. "Look, I can put a call in and see if it'll do any good, but I can't make any promises. Once these decisions are made, there's usually no going back."

"Thanks, Dad. I love you." I hung up with him and turned around to find Jack walking up behind me.

"Why did you run off?"

"I needed to make a phone call."

"Come with me." He took my hand and led me back to his room. Once we were inside, he closed the door. "I think you're beautiful, Julia, not just pretty." He placed a hand on my heart. "And I couldn't be happier that this thing is still beating." He lowered his chin and met my eyes. "Can I kiss you again?"

I nodded, and before I knew it, his hands were in my hair, and his lips were on mine, moving gently but with great concentration. I tilted my head back, and he moved one hand to my lower back. He guided me to the bed where our bodies folded onto the mattress, his hovering over mine. I melted beneath him, and my chest heaved as we kissed. I knew if I was going to get anyone to allow him to stay, this was the wrong way to go about it, but I didn't care.

"Hold on," I whispered when he moved his mouth to my neck. "What if someone walks in?"

He shrugged. "You're the first person to ever make me want to break the rules, and hell, I'm leaving anyway."

"I can't help but feel like this is all my fault."

"I have no regrets," he whispered.

I lifted myself to him, and we broke the rules for about ten minutes until there was a knock on the door.

Jack kissed my cheek and sat up.

"It's Emma," she said from behind the door. "Tabitha and Sally are walking toward here."

"You'd better go," he said to me.

Our entwined fingers slipped out of each other's grasp.

I jumped up and opened the door to find Emma craning her neck for a better view of Jack and his room.

"Please come find me before you leave," I said to him.

I memorized his face before Emma and I hightailed it out of there down a back hallway.

Thirty-Six

JACK

"Come in," I said after the knock on the doorframe.

Julia had left the door open, so it didn't really matter. Tabby closed it behind her.

"I thought you were with Sally?"

She looked surprised. "Why did you think that?"

I shrugged. "No reason."

Tabitha took a seat on Will's bed and removed two Pop-Tarts from the silver packaging she was holding. "Want one?"

I shook my head and threw my iPod and some books into my backpack.

"This is bullshit," she said, mid-chew.

I crumpled up two T-shirts and tossed them in with the books. "It's fine."

"I'm not even talking to Dad. I yelled at him for thirty minutes this morning."

I zipped my bag and sat on my bed. "It is what it is, and your dad couldn't be happier to have me out of his hair."

"You are a fixture here! The campers adore you. I adore you. What kind of place will this be without you, Jack?"

I leaned forward with my elbows on my knees. "A place where our boy, Will, sings a cappella, I guess?"

I smiled at her, and she started to cry.

"Ah, hell, please don't get upset." I took a seat next to her and kissed her head.

"Where will you go?"

"I'm going to head up to Madison and find an apartment on campus, which I was planning on doing in two weeks anyway. I've got plenty of people to stay with up there. Don't worry about me." I grabbed a tissue and handed it to her.

"You don't deserve this. You've always deserved better. I'm so sorry he's doing this to you."

"Tabitha, I'll be fine."

"What about your credits? Dad's so spooked by Julia's father and the police that he refuses to bend the rules."

I shrugged. That was a huge bummer. "If I have to make them up, I'll make them up."

She wiped her cheeks and turned to face me. "I can't believe what these girls did and how this has all blown up. Have you heard what's happened to them?"

I shook my head and raised my brows.

"Mom told me last night that the state's attorney called her and said the girls had been charged with attempted murder. They've been released to their parents on two-hundred-thousand-dollars bond—each! And they can't leave the state. They're waiting in some hotel until the judge gives them permission to go back home."

"Holy shit."

"I guess the bond was higher, but their attorney argued to lower it and is trying to get a lesser charge, like aggravated battery or something. Miss Alice's nephew is an attorney and said since they are minors—and if they have a great lawyer, which you know they will—they might not have to serve any jail time."

I lowered my head into my hands. "I don't think they should go to prison. Do you?" I looked over at her.

"I don't know. You kind of have to think about, if Julia had died, what then?"

I was tired of thinking about that. "Thankfully, she didn't."

I touched Tabitha's back, and she leaned over for a hug.

"I'm going to miss you. Everyone is." She pulled back. "And Liz…Liz is on my shit list."

"Not a good place for anyone to be." I stood, tossed my backpack over my shoulder, and grabbed my duffel. "I guess I should go say some good-byes, but first, I need to do one thing."

I grabbed an empty plastic bottle and walked into the men's showers. On the wall, there was a shampoo dispenser filled with the same shampoo that had been in those showers for decades. I filled my empty bottle, took a whiff, and grinned. The smell of that shampoo would bring me back to camp, no matter where in the world I was. I tucked the bottle in my bag and met Tabby outside.

Bob was with her. "I see you have your things." He was no good at formalities. Hell, he was no good at anything.

"Yep."

"Can I have a word with you in my office before you go?"

"Sure. I'm in no hurry."

He grunted, and I followed him to his office where I placed my bags.

"I assume you won't mind if I leave these here while I say good-bye to people?"

He shook his head and sat at his desk. The chair hinges hollered in agony.

Bob placed his forearms on the armrests and leaned back. "I have some good news."

I gave him a skeptical look.

"I just got off the phone with Julia Pearl's father, and he's assured me he's not going to press charges against the camp."

I raised a brow. "Great news, Bob."

He sat up and folded his hands on the desk. "Also, he wants to make sure you don't lose your college credits after all, and he's asked that I do everything in my power to make sure that doesn't happen."

I stared at him, unflinching, as he waited for my excitement and gratitude, but they never came.

I had only contempt for him. I always had. Maybe I should have been more grateful to him for taking me in as a child, for allowing me the last scoop of mashed potatoes or whatever leftover milk was there for my cereal bowl after Tabby had filled hers.

"It's better than foster care."

How many times had I heard that statement in one lifetime?

Perhaps I should have been more appreciative for the summer work he'd given me over the years—and for not paying me as much as everyone else because I was family. But family was expected to work twice as hard and deal with twice as much BS.

But that was what family did for each other. Family supported each other. At least that was what I was told anytime I'd questioned the situation.

My voice was low. "You should've made sure that wouldn't happen anyway, all on your own."

He threw back his head. "I couldn't do that without knowing whether Julia's family was going to press charges against the camp."

"Yes, you could have."

He shook his head. "How was I supposed to know—"

"It doesn't matter. You should have fought for me and defended me from day one. I saved a girl's life on camp property. Your property!" I tilted my head to the side. "Do you know how many times that state's attorney asked me about proper training and what knowledge I have—as a staff member—of the kids with the allergies and what to do with them in case of a reaction?" I stood and let that simmer. "Forget about Julia's father. It's me who could sink this place if I wanted to, and you should have *supported* me, not thrown me under the bus on account of some bullshit gossip. You never even asked me for my side of the story." I shook my head and turned to leave.

"Well, I'm sorry you feel that way," he muttered.

I paused with my hand on the doorknob and my back to him. "What happened to my mother's ring?"

Bob let out an exasperated sigh. "Not this again."

I kept my hand on the knob but turned back around. "It was meant for me, and I deserve to know. Did it pay for a new stove? Busted pipes? New carburetor? What?"

"I honestly don't recall, but I'm sure you benefited from it, whatever it was. Money was tight back then. Still is."

I met his gaze. "I'll never forgive you for that."

Bob threw his flabby arms up and rolled his eyes, as if that was one more thing he needed to worry about.

Thirty-Seven

Julia

Emma and I were down by the lake where I was catching her up on Jack and me when Amber found us with our feet in the water. The heat and humidity were at an all-time frizzy-hair, pit-dripping high that day.

"A bunch of people are in the mess hall, saying good-bye to Jack. You guys want to come up?" Amber asked.

We both stood and brushed the sand off our shorts.

"We'll be right there," Emma said.

Amber scampered off.

"I was hoping he'd come find me before he left." I grabbed my water bottle/fan/body-mister thing out of my bag.

Emma pulled a Tootsie Pop out of her back pocket. "Spray me, too." She closed her eyes. "He's probably mobbed with people. I'm sure he would have if he could."

"Yeah."

"So, are you going to be all miserable and lovesick for the next couple of weeks while he's gone?"

"Yeah."

Emma rolled her eyes. "Great. Well, let's get this over with then."

We were silent on the walk up to the mess hall.

I'd begged my father to let me return to camp, and the main reason for that pleading was now leaving.

Emma pushed through the doors first, and a group of maybe twelve people were near the kitchen, saying their good-byes. There was no doubt that the rumors that Emma had first heard about Jack and me had spread through the entire camp faster than pinkeye by then. A couple of uncomfortable stares from people confirmed it.

I shoved my hands in my pockets and moved to the side. Once the group began to dissipate, Emma and I approached Jack and a few stragglers—Tabitha, Will, and Theo.

Emma hugged Jack. "Sorry to see you go, dude," she said.

"You, too, Em. Great work this summer. You should be really proud of yourself."

"I bet you say that to all the pretty girls."

She stepped back, and I moved forward for a hug, too.

Jack hugged me. "Walk me to my car?" he said to me in front of the group.

I was afraid to look around. "Sure."

"Great. Wait here for me while I say good-bye to James in the back."

Tabitha and Will smiled at me and then left. Theo let Emma jump on his back, and he gave her a lift to the Franteen.

I took a seat at one of the tables and lifted a knife from the silverware tray to try to check my reflection. *Hair—down. Teeth—free of food. Lips—mildly chapped.*

Jack appeared in my peripheral vision as I was lowering the mirrored utensil.

"You look great," he said.

I stood quickly, and the knife fell onto the table. "Just, you know…that was embarrassing."

His eyes held mine for a moment. "Come on, Pearl. Let's get this over with."

Jack waved to a few people as we passed, and I followed him to the staff parking lot about twenty yards behind the back of the main lodge, far enough away from any snoops…or so I'd thought.

Jack popped the rear hatch on a beat-up red Chevy Blazer and tossed his bags in the back of the car. His mood was a mixture of upbeat and nostalgic.

"Wouldn't you rather have Tabitha and Will here with you?"

"Nah. I'll see them in a few days." He slammed the door shut and then leaned against it.

I stood with my arms hanging awkwardly at my sides until he reached for one of my hands and pulled me closer to him.

"What a summer, huh?" he said.

I nodded, sensing a pit forming in my stomach. "I wish you didn't have to go. You're the reason I came back."

He lifted my chin with his other hand and wiped a tear from my cheek with his thumb. "Don't be upset."

"I'm not. It's the heat." I wiped my face with a sniff.

He twisted his mouth into half a smile, his white teeth bright against his tan skin. "Good to know," he said. He pulled a crumpled sheet of paper out of his front pocket. "Here. It's my email and cell number. When you get home, I want you to call me."

I took the paper. "I will as soon as I get back. Thanks for everything, Jack."

"You don't have to be so formal. This won't be the last time I see you. I promise."

He was being sweet and kind with that statement because that was who he was. But he was also about to be a college sophomore with way more things to worry about than a lovesick, moody teenage allergy freak. *Who would want to pack that baggage when going away to college? I knew I wouldn't.*

"How can you promise that?"

He answered quickly with somewhat of a laugh, "Because I want to be with you again." He acted as if I should have assumed all my schoolgirl fantasies were completely sane and bound to come true.

My cheeks went flush but not on account of the heat. "I would love that, but I don't want you to feel like you have—"

Jack reached for my other hand and pulled my body and lips to his. Then, I wrapped my arms around his neck and kissed him as if his promise would never come true.

After Jack pulled out of the parking lot, I sat on the sidewalk for a few minutes, preferring to be alone. When I eventually stood and shuffled around to the front of the building, Emma was waiting for me.

She smiled at me. "You okay?"

I nodded.

"I have something for you."

"Fun Dip?"

She shook her head. "Nope."

"You didn't have to get me anything."

"I didn't. Follow me."

Emma and I walked back to her cabin, and I followed her inside to her bunk. Under her pillow was Jack's gray hoodie.

"It's for you." She handed it to me.

"How on earth did you manage to steal this from him?"

She let out a mock gasp and drew her head back. "I did no such thing. He gave it to me to give to you, and there's a note inside the front pocket, which you are going to read out loud to me this instant, or else I will secretly use your toothbrush to comb Bob Hanson's armpit hair."

We both laughed as I ripped the sweatshirt from her hands.

"And I don't care what the envelope says," Emma mentioned as I slid the note from the pocket.

The front of the envelope read, *This is for Julia—not you, Emma. Put it back in the pocket and give it to her when I'm gone, please.*

My lips curled into a smile. "He doesn't want you to read it."

"Well he's not here anymore, is he?"

I pleaded with my eyes for her to leave me alone, and she did, sort of.

"I will sit on this bunk over here while you read it. But just know that I'll be staring at your face the entire time." Emma hopped off her bed and sat across from me.

I folded my legs up on the mattress and opened the letter.

Dear Julia,

Before you got to camp, it was business as usual. I've greeted campers arriving on those busses for as long as I can remember, yet no one has ever made an impression on me like you have. I'm not very good at expressing my feelings, but I wanted you to know how much I care about you and how much you mean to me. I thought maybe if you had it in writing, it would be permanent. I can never take back these words, nor would I want to. They are yours to read and hold on to now that I've left.

Being at Hollow Creek every summer has never been easy for me, but every time I saw you, my troubles would disappear. Bob and I have a terrible relationship, yet I've stayed true to my commitment to Sally and Tabitha to be here for them and the good of the camp. But never again. I will not be coming back there.

I guess it took a tragedy to show me what a waste of time that place has been for me. It hasn't always been that way. I've learned so much and met some amazing people, but I deserve better, and I intend on finding it—hopefully, with you.

These past six weeks have been some of the best of my life—with the exception of your date with the Grim Reaper. Way to shake things up, Pearl. Thankfully, we can laugh about it now, but I'm mostly thankful for meeting you. Maybe I'm not great at expressing my feelings because it's scary when you care about someone…and even scarier when you can't be together.

Just know that you are very special to me, and I'll be coming for you one day soon.

—Jack

"That's the cheesiest grin I've ever seen, so I'm guessing he didn't dump you," Emma said, breaking the silence, but she couldn't crack the love-letter induced haze I was floating in. "So? What did it say?"

I took a deep breath through my nose. "It was awesome."

She rolled her eyes and came over to me. "What the hell does that mean? Did he say he loves you?"

I shook my head, but my smile remained intact. I felt electric. It was as if my body were overcome with currents of energy and ecstasy, and if I didn't ground myself, I might combust from too much joy.

Emma nudged my shoulder. "Can I read it?"

I handed her the letter, and she crossed her legs and hunched over the piece of paper.

Once she was done, she handed it back to me and wrapped her arm around my shoulders. "From what I just read, he definitely loves you," she said.

The last day of camp was a distant yet searing memory.

Emma's older brother, Tom, had driven up from Indiana to pick her up. She and I exchanged phone numbers, emails, photographs, T-shirts, and anything else we could think of so that we'd have a piece of each other to hold on to and connect us until the end of time. We also filled out applications to be CITs at Hollow Creek the following summer.

I remembered waiting in line to board the bus home when Tabitha had approached me.

"I hope you had a great summer, Julia. We couldn't have dreamed up a worse situation than what happened to you." She placed a hand on my shoulder.

"Thank you. I had an amazing summer."

Her hand went back to her side. "I know Jack wishes he were here to see everyone off."

Our eyes met.

"I wish he were here, too."

"I also know he's really glad you two have become close."

I blushed. "Me, too."

With that, Tabitha leaned in for a hug and my summer at Hollow Creek came to an end.

Julia
Five Months Later

There were four things that had made an indelible impression on my soul and shaped me into the person I became that winter, a seventeen-year-old high school junior with a new lease on life.

The first was when I'd lost my mother. I would never criticize my father's choices because I loved him, but I would always question whether he had been given the best advice from a slew of overzealous child psychologists and whether he had made the best decision as far as forbidding me to contact her. With little explanation, my mom had been taken from me, and I had been left to question all of it. I'd spent my formative years wondering how I would survive and how anyone would ever truly love me if my own mother couldn't.

When I'd turned seventeen, two months after camp had ended, I'd received a gift from her for the first time in years. It was a dress from the shop where she worked and ten dollars in game tokens, redeemable at her boyfriend's joint. Maybe one day, I'd get down to Indy and cash them in.

The second was my experience at summer camp—the friends, bonfires, ticks, bonds I'd made with Emma and Amber, time away on my own to sort things out, and nearly losing my life to the Killer Cookie. Saying good-bye to Emma had been torture. We'd hugged and cried and hugged some more and laughed and then cried again. I could say she'd become like a sister to me, but an appendage seemed more accurate.

The third thing was that someone, peers of mine, had attempted to kill me. My second to last day at camp, I'd received a letter from Brittany and Brianna.

Dear Julia,

We are so sorry for what we put you through. I know you might not want to accept our apology, but we wanted you to know that we never meant to hurt you so badly, and we definitely never meant to kill you. We were stupid and had no idea you would get so sick! We cannot express how

*ashamed we are that we even went through with such a
horrendous act. We will forever be haunted by that day. We
hope you are healthy and happy and that nothing bad
happens to you ever again!*

—*Brittany and Brianna*

Emma had tossed the letter in the bonfire for me. But the fact
that they had been punished didn't make me feel like any less of a
target, and I hadn't believed for a second that apologizing to me
was their own idea. In a way, I felt sorry for them. The same day
I'd received their letter, the state's attorney had come to see me at
camp.

"How are you feeling?" Ms. DiVito asked soon after introducing
herself.

I sat at the edge of my chair in Bob's office. The air
conditioner unit in his window was churning out more noise than
cool air.

Ms. DiVito took a sip of ice water before walking out from
behind the desk and taking a seat next to me. "This must've been
terrifying for you."

"For all of us!" My father was on speakerphone, his voice
filling the room and vibrating the desk.

"I feel good. Thank you."

She proceeded to ask me my account of that day, which was a
little fuzzy, and whether I thought the twins had meant to hurt me
or not, and then she asked me something that startled me.

"What's your idea of justice for these two girls?"

I sat and pondered as my father had a mini tirade and shared
his idea of justice, much like witches being burned at the stake. But
I didn't share his hatred for them. I thought of Brianna and how
she was undoubtedly a pawn in Brittany's personal battle against
her own insecurity demons.

"Dad, please, can I have a minute to talk with her?" I said with
my eyes on the phone. Then, I turned back to Ms. DiVito.

She smiled at me. "These are our options," she started. "They are currently charged with aggravated battery, a felony. The charge will require a trial in which you will have to testify against them, and we will have to prove that they caused great bodily harm. Otherwise, we can try to get them to plead to battery, which is a misdemeanor, and they will likely get community service and probation."

The thought of Brittany picking up McDonald's ketchup packets and used cigarette butts on the side of the road in a bright orange jumpsuit was almost better than sending her to the slammer.

"You know how I feel about this," my father said. "I want aggravated battery."

I placed my hands on my lap and played with the lanyard bracelet on my right wrist. "I don't want a trial. I just want it to go away."

My comment incited unhappy ramblings from my father.

Ms. DiVito placed a hand on my knee. "I understand," she whispered.

We'd eventually learned that the twins had pleaded guilty to the battery charges and had been sentenced to six months in juvenile detention. However, after just forty-eight hours in a facility in Southern Illinois, they'd been released due to overcrowding and given three years probation and ten months of community service. I prayed they would be scrubbing toilets somewhere nasty.

The fourth thing that had impacted my life was the amazing, sweet, caring, kind, handsome, messy-haired Jack Dempsey and his killer smile. They made a great pair—Jack and his teeth. He and I had been in constant contact since the summer—calling, texting, emailing—but we hadn't had a chance to see each other.

Until Saturday, December 15.

This was the night. The night I'd thought about, cried about, talked about, and dreamed about for months. My stepsiblings were sleeping at their grandma's, and Sharlene and my dad were at his firm's Christmas party in the city.

"You can invite Jack to spend the night, but I'd better find him alone, on the couch in the basement, when I get home from my stupid office party, or there will be no child psychologist on the planet who can relieve you of the mental torture I will inflict," Dad had warned.

Jack was due to arrive at seven p.m. on account of a late exam and a nasty snowstorm.

So, at five p.m., I checked the fridge three times to make sure we had enough soda. I fluffed the pillows on the couch in the TV room, like Sharlene had taught me, and I fanned out her copies of *People* magazine on the coffee table. I checked myself in the mirror no less than once every five minutes. I spritzed the back of my neck—also like Sharlene had taught me—with a new bottle of Lovely by Sarah Jessica Parker. I made sure that Bo was clean and dry, and I gave her a bone, one of her favorites, so she wouldn't maul Jack's crotch when he arrived. Then, I went about microwaving myself some popcorn, so my stomach wouldn't growl during our reunion.

Sharlene had also left me her credit card and told me to order us a pizza. "I'm certain he'll be famished after the long drive in this weather. Be sure and get the cinnamon sticks, too," she'd insisted with a wink.

A few hours later, I awoke to a knock at the door and began fumbling for my phone. It was close to nine thirty, and I couldn't believe I had fallen asleep on the couch. I stood and walked to the front door when I heard a second knock.

"Who is it?" I shouted. "Jack?" I said, but there was no answer.

I should've just torn the door off its hinges, but the eight-year-old in me could still hear my father's voice.

"Don't you dare open that door unless you know who it is!"

I repeated Jack's name, and as I was doing so, a piece of paper slid out from under the door.

WHISPER IF YOU NEED ME.

I slapped my hand over my delirious grin, and a second piece of paper appeared behind it immediately.

OPEN THE DOOR. IT'S FUCKING COLD OUT HERE.

I laughed out loud and swiftly opened the door.

Jack was standing there, grinning and gorgeous, wearing blue jeans torn at the knees, a down jacket, a knit Wisconsin Badgers hat, and hiking boots. He was also carrying a brown shopping bag in one hand. A gust of bitter cold wind blew past me and took with it every insecurity I'd held on to for the past few months.

Jack Dempsey was at my house and looked pretty darn glad to see me.

I leaped forward with my bare feet on the front step, and he wrapped me in his damp cold arms.

"Come in. It's freezing!" I scampered back inside.

"Thought you'd never ask," he mumbled. Jack entered the foyer and removed his hat, snow falling off his shoulders. "Nice digs, Pearl." His gaze went from the dining room to the top of the stairwell and landed on the formal living room.

"I'm not allowed in there," I commented.

"Why not?"

"No one is. It's too fancy. My dad calls it the most expensive storage unit on the North Shore."

Jack kicked his boots off onto the area rug and handed me the bag. "I brought you a couple of things."

"You didn't have to do that."

He lifted both brows in mock surprise. "I didn't? Well, shit. I totally thought it was customary to bring a gift to someone's home if you were an invited guest, especially around the holidays." He shrugged. "No sweat. I'll take them back."

I rolled my eyes and smiled. "You didn't have to do that, but I'm glad you did. Thank you. Why don't we go sit in the den?"

Jack followed me down the hall. "I'm sorry I'm so late. The roads were really bad."

"I actually fell asleep—next to my phone, of course, in case of an emergency."

"Of course. I'll remember never to make you an emergency contact."

We walked past the kitchen and into the den where we both sat on the couch.

"Should I open it now?" I placed the bag on my lap.

He flashed a crooked smile. "Sure, but before you get any grand illusions about cards and ribbons and Rudolph-themed wrapping paper, let it be known that the bag is the gift wrap."

"Got it." I stuck my hand inside. My cheeks rose with delight as I slid a hardcover edition of *Charlie and the Chocolate Factory* out of the bag. I blinked and then held it to my chest. "I love it so much. Thank you. Best gift ever."

I leaned over to hug him, and he pressed his mouth to my ear, sending chills straight through me, as if the front door had blown open. After a moment, we slowly inched apart.

"Want me to read it to you?" I asked.

His head tilted back a bit. "I would love that," he said quietly with his eyes on mine.

We both sat back and folded into each other. Jack placed his arm around my shoulders, and I wrapped my legs over his.

I took a deep breath. "Chapter one—'Here Comes Charlie.' *These two very old people are the father and mother of Mr. Bucket. Their names are Grandpa Joe and Grandma Josephine.*"

I paused to look up at him, and he was staring at me.

I continued to read, "*And these two very old people are the father and mother of Mrs. Bucket.*" I took in a quick breath and cleared my throat as Jack's hand moved closer toward my waist. "Uh…*their names are Grandpa George and Grandma Georgina.*"

Just as I finished the sentence, Jack moved his arm from my shoulder and began to gently run his hand through the ends of my hair, the tips of his fingers grazing the skin on the back of my neck.

Good thing I spritzed back there.

"*This is Mr. Bucket.*" I quickly wiped my forehead and stretched my head ever so slightly to meet Jack's touch. The heat must've been cranked in the house because I was getting uncomfortably warm.

"*This is Mrs. Bucket,*" I tried to continue.

Jack lowered his head and kissed me just below my earlobe. I swallowed but didn't look at him. My breathing intensified.

"*Mr. and Mrs. Bucket have a small boy whose…whose name is Charlie Bucket.*"

He stroked my hair and kissed me again while my shoulders elevated—right along with my body temperature. Without realizing it, I tilted my head away from Jack, exposing more of my ear and neck to him in case he wanted it. He did.

"*This is Charlie. How d'you do? And how d'you do? And how d'you do again? He is pleased to meet you.*"

Jack finally took the book from my hands and tossed it on the coffee table. "Charlie would be pleased if we continued story time later," he said. "Is that okay with you?"

I nodded, unable to speak, move, breathe, think.

He leaned in, fastened his arms around me, and kissed me with enthusiasm, equal to our first time alone in the woods. We lay our bodies down on the cushions, and I never wanted the night to end. Kissing Jack felt as natural as anything I'd ever done, as if the two of us were meant to fit together in this way. His breathing increased, and his hands moved to my hair as he pulled his mouth away and placed it on my neck.

I wrapped my arms around him and shivered as he whispered in my ear, "I can't tell you how long I've wanted to do this." He scanned my face.

I pulled him back to me and clung to him, kissing his lips and neck and shoulders, until he pushed the coffee table aside, and we moved to the floor.

Bo attempted to separate us at least three times.

Our bodies moved together, rolling, reaching, and relishing every inch of each other. I sensed Jack's eagerness to take things further and faster.

Just when I'd convinced myself to go along with it, he reeled himself in, slowing his pace from a ravenous hunger to a healthy appetite.

After what seemed like thirty seconds but was actually closer to two hours, Jack sat up, and so did I.

"Are you okay?" I asked.

He nodded. "I know it's getting late, and I just don't want this to get out of hand before your dad walks in."

Both our shirts were off, and we were glowing as if we'd just run a 5K. If my dad had walked in at any point, it would have been considered out of hand already. I reached for my sweater, wishing it were three hours earlier and I were three years older.

"We can order pizza if you want," I offered.

"I want! I'm starving. Haven't eaten a thing since breakfast."

Jack leaned his bare back against the couch and stretched his legs out in front of him in the space where the coffee table was while I called Domino's.

"It should be here in about forty minutes." I tossed him his shirt. "I guess you should put this on," I said regretfully.

Jack stood up, his jeans hanging low on his hips, and slid his T-shirt over his head. I just stared at him as he moved through the space of my family room like a mountain lion. He retrieved his phone from between the couch cushions, pulled the coffee table back into position, and reached for the brown bag he'd brought with him before taking a seat.

"Sit." He tapped the couch. "There's one more thing."

I threw myself next to him. "I feel terrible. Can the cinnamon sticks be my gift to you?"

"Absolutely," he said. "I got you something else." Jack reached into the bag, pulled out a manila envelope, and handed it to me. "Open it."

I slid my fingernail under the back flap and reached inside, revealing an application to the University of Wisconsin with a handwritten note on a Post-it attached to the front page.

WHISPER IF YOU LOVE ME.

He smiled at me and shrugged. "Cheesy?"

I shook my head, wanting to cry.

"I know you have a year before you need to think about where you might want to go, but I thought—"

I leaned forward and kissed him, astounded that my heart could handle the weight of emotions I was feeling in that moment. He held the back of my head and pressed into me, and we kissed until I pulled away.

"I love you, Jack," I whispered. "So much."

"I love you, too," he said, reaching out to tuck my hair behind my ear. "I don't know what will happen between us, but I'm willing to stay committed to you for as long as you'll put up with me."

Jack lay back on the couch, and I placed my ear against his chest, listening to his heartbeat and thinking about life and, more specifically, death.

The thing about *almost* dying was that it didn't garner you the notoriety that *actually* dying would. And why should it? So, by almost dying, I had been given the golden ticket in life—the chance to see everyday things in my world in a new way, with brighter colors and bigger smiles, and the chance to taste and feel and experience the things around me as if I'd never seen them before. By escaping death, I had spared my friends and family an insufferable loss. I'd been given another chance to live my life and appreciate the things I'd taken for granted—like a stepmother and stepsiblings, a snarky father who forced me into situations he knew I'd hate yet ultimately thrive from. And I'd fallen in love.

Almost dying had allowed me to be comfortable with living.

I lifted my head and moved up so that my cheek was next to Jack's, and then I closed my eyes. I would forever treasure the lessons I'd learned, and I promised myself to focus on the things that made me feel happy and safe.

Starting with Jack Dempsey...

The End

Acknowledgments

When my son, Ryan—my only child, my TV-watching partner, my comic relief, and my best bud—decided he wanted to go to overnight camp for FOUR weeks during the summer of 2014, I was crushed. He was only eleven—it's young!—and I had no desire to send him. But, as usual, he got his way, and off he went, loving every last second of it—so much so that he now goes every year, and I've come to terms with the fact that his father and I will have to spend Fourth of July without him until he outgrows camp.

In his absence that first summer, I became inspired by overnight camp and the relationships forged there. This book is a result of too much time without my little buddy.

This book is also my first young adult novel. Writing for and about teenagers was an absolute thrill, and I hope to do it again soon.

The best part about writing this particular story was that I was given the opportunity to work directly with seven real-live teenagers during the process! As part of a writing project with Ms. Solis's English class at Highland Park High School in Highland Park, Illinois, I worked for two months with a select group of her students who read chapters of the book each week. Every Monday, I would sit with them during their English period, and they would give me feedback on the book—what they liked, what they loved, what they didn't like, and what they thought a teenager would never say. As a writer, it was an unbelievable experience for me...and as a wannabe teenager, it was tons of fun. I would like to thank Ari Cole, Noa Cole, Zach Auerbach, Bryan Rodriguez,

Michael Gallo, Maddie Jaffe-Richter, and Becky Melamed for their honesty, their eagerness, their insight, their passion for books, and their love for this story. I could not have done it without you!

As with any of my novels, there is always so much research to do. And since I loathe research, I like to compile a team of experts who can quickly answer questions and are (reluctantly) at my beck and call. Joanie Metzner Henson, I have known you since you were five years old, and you are still as fun to talk to as you were then! Thank God you spent as many years as you did attending and working at overnight camps. The fact that you met your hubby there didn't hurt either. Thank you for spending so much time with me and for expertly describing the anatomy of a tick.

To Halleh Akbarnia, thank you for being an ER doctor. In my mind, writing books is right up there with saving lives…

Anyway, for someone who works crazy, stressful, life-altering hours, you never failed to get back to me when I peppered you with ridiculous questions. Your knowledge is invaluable. Thank you also for that one time when my son sliced his leg open, and you let me text pictures of it to you because I thought it was infected. You rock.

To Gina DiVito, assistant state's attorney, princess, and all-around cool chick with killer stories—and I do mean, *killer*—thank you for the emails, phone calls, for texting me pictures from law journals, and for saying that I can come hang with you at work one day. You have such an amazing job with access to the wackiest people out there, and I'm a little jealous. I love me some wack jobs, and I mean that in the best possible way. I also love that you let me invent crimes and then fervently helped me come up with the appropriate legal punishments. Much appreciated!

To my fellow authors, Claire Contreras and Tiffany King, thank you so much for your enthusiasm for this book and for taking time away from your own writing to spend it with mine.

Last but never least are my beta readers—Julie Lyon Wisel, Wendy Wilken, Chloe Costigan, Meg Costigan, Beth Suit, and my mom. You guys are the best! After writing for months and months, there's nothing better than handing the book off to trusted friends and family and then biting my nails, waiting for their feedback. Thank you so much for your candor. Your opinions mean the world to me.

Super-duper last…I would like to personally thank whoever read this page of acknowledgments. If you got this far, I commend you. Visit my website at dinasilver.com. Send me a message saying, "I acknowledge you!" and I'll send you a little gift for your effort. Cheers!

About the Author

Dina Silver is an author, a wine lover, and an excellent parallel parker. She lives with her husband, son, and twenty-pound tabby cat in suburban Chicago. She'd prefer to live somewhere where it's warm year-round, but then she'd never stay home and write anything. She is the author of four other novels, including *One Pink Line*, *Kat Fight*, *Finding Bliss*, and *The Unimaginable*. To find out more about Dina and her books, visit dinasilver.com.

Made in the USA
Las Vegas, NV
25 March 2022